SPIRIT HORSE

also by

MANUELA SCHNEIDER

Arma del Diablo: The Colt of Destiny

Jealousy: A Restless Souls Western

The Memoirs of Madame Moustache. Growing Up to Be a Gambler

The Unknown Enemy: A Restless Souls Western

The Silence Of Echoes

A Prospector's Dream

The Unforgiving Daughter

Texas Blood Oath: Book 1 by H.M. Taylor

The Doc Hatcher Mountain Man Series

with Jeff Crawford

Hope Carries A Flintlock

In German:

Die Tochter des Sheriffs

Der Traum des Silbers

Das Tor Zur Vergangenheit: Geheimnisse Des Bird Cage Theaters

Die Waffe Des Teufels

Lovecraft Schriften des Grauens: Unbekannter Feind

Geronimo Der Apachen Krieger Band 1: Frei Wie Der Wind

Geronimo Der Apachen Krieger Band 2: Tage Der Rache

SPIRIT HORSE

MANUELA SCHNEIDER

WILL ROGERS MEDALLION-WINNING AUTHOR

HAT CREEK

HAT CREEK

An Imprint of Roan & Weatherford Publishing Associates, LLC
Bentonville, Arkansas
www.roanweatherford.com

Library of Congress Cataloging-in-Publication Data
Names: Schneider, Manuela, author
Title: Spirit Horse
Description: First Edition. | Bentonville: Hat Creek, 2024.
Identifiers: LCCN: 2024946262 | ISBN: 978-1-63373-992-5 (trade paperback) |
ISBN: 978-1-63373-993-2 (eBook)
Subjects: | BISAC: FICTION/Westerns | FICTION/Romance/Western |
FICTION/Romance/Sports
LC record available at: https://lccn.loc.gov/2024946262

Hat Creek trade paperback edition November, 2024

Cover Design by Casey W. Cowan
Interior Design by Staci Troilo
Editing by Dennis Doty & Lisa Lindsey

This book is a work of historical fiction. Apart from the well-known actual people, events, and locales that figure in the narrative, all names, characters, places, and incidents are the product of the author's imagination or are used fictitiously. Any resemblance to current events or locales, or to living persons, is entirely coincidental.

*This book is dedicated to all the men and women
who dare to face the challenges of rodeo
and the unique bond between Cowboys and Cowgirls
and their wonderful four-legged companions.*

ONE
Stranded

CODY AWOKE MOANING. His bed covers lay rumpled at his feet, and cold sweat covered his muscular chest. He shielded his eyes with his lower arm to block the rays of the rising sun as if they were attacking enemies.

His eyelids fluttered beneath his elbow, and dropping his arm to his side, he gazed into the semidarkness of the room's windowless wall. He turned his head toward the orange glow of the sunrise peeking cheekily through the old blinds. Dust danced in the dim light.

He was alone. Another day without hope. Again, the same horrible nightmare had awoken him from sleep. He rolled to his side, and his right hand moved toward the long scar on his chest. He wouldn't have been surprised if warm, sticky blood appeared on his fingertips. He remembered the feel of it. But that lay in the past.

Filling his lungs deeply and slowly, he felt relief that he was able to breathe evenly. He knew the terrifying sensation of not being able to breathe. His left hand slid over the mattress toward the nightstand. He fumbled for the glass bottle in the weak light of the early morning hours. But there was none, and with God's help, there would never again be a bottle next to his bed.

However, he still felt the craving for booze. It had been so much easier to drown the memories instead of facing them day by day. During his drinking days, he slept better, and life in general had been easier as long as he drenched his sorrow in whiskey. His problems hadn't mattered so much in a drunken state. But since he'd been sober, worries about his future had caught up with him.

"Oh, man, when will I stop looking for a drink first thing in the morning?" he whispered. His doctors were sure he'd overcome his alcohol addiction, but he knew better. So far, he'd only left the physical aspect behind. The psychological picture was a different one. He chuckled into the empty room.

"As if booze was my only problem," he growled. He could still taste the last sip of Jack Daniels on his tongue even though it had been two years ago. The drinking and the bitter poison of betrayal had thrown him off track from a promising career.

Like most mornings after a restless night, he was in a grouchy mood. Cody swung his legs out of bed and rose. Naked as he was, he walked to the blinds and parted them with two fingers to peek into the parking lot. It promised to be a beautiful day. Cody remembered the time at his father's ranch, and a grin raised the corners of his lips. However, the smile never reached his sad eyes.

Oh, how he had loved sunrises in the past! He always looked forward to the new day. As a matter of fact, Cody had been a person full of plans and ambition in his younger years, but no longer. As quickly as his smile appeared, the painful memories wiped it off his handsome face.

He didn't want to think about the past, and before the familiar frustration lifted its ugly head, he rubbed the sleep from his eyes and walked toward the adjoining bathroom. A cold shower would fulfill its purpose and chase the depressing thoughts away.

As he gazed at his reflection in the mirror, his thoughts spun. Would he ever be the same man again? Exhausted from poor sleep, he rasped his hands across the stubble of a beard.

Reluctantly, he glanced at his torso in the grimy glass of the old mirror. The familiar white scars crisscrossed the right side of his tanned chest like pale tracks. They always caught his attention when he looked into the mirror. Every time he saw this part of his body, the memories of the most horrifying hours in his life popped up in his mind's eye. Externally, his injuries were healed. Inside—well, that was a different story. He longed to escape the memories of pain.

Cody stepped under the shower head and turned on the cold faucet full blast before leaning into the water jet. He gasped and reached for the soap with a loud, "Brrrrrr."

"Jesus in heaven, I'm definitely awake now," he whispered with chattering teeth. The frigid water beating down in the shower rinsed the soapy foam from his firm abdominal muscles. Cody turned off the water and reached for the towel.

Twenty minutes later, he sat at the kitchen table and gobbled scrambled eggs and a slice of crunchy bacon. A cup of steaming Arbuckle coffee stood next to his plate.

"The coffee that conquered the West," he quoted the famous commercial like he did almost daily. He thought of his late father who used to preach the slogan every morning. Thinking sadly of his family, Cody did the same while taking a sip of the hot beverage. He drank his coffee black but with two spoons of sugar. It was strong enough for his Colt to float in. That was real cowboy coffee!

Cody remembered the days well when he and his dad camped during a cattle drive in the mountains not far from the ranch. Their camp was located right next to their herd of Black Angus cattle. His father had prepared breakfast in the Dutch oven on the embers of their campfire every morning. Cody closed his eyes and imagined he smelled the delicious aroma of baking cornbread. The first morning of their cattle drive together, he drank his first mug of Arbuckle coffee. Cody recalled thinking life couldn't get any better than it was on that particular day. It had been a wonderful time until ambition took control of his life and ruined it all.

Cody looked around the trailer. This place was nothing special. A former rodeo pal helped him out by letting him use this place. The fellow had moved in with his new rodeo sweetheart, and Cody needed a place to stay after leaving his hometown for good. He avoided thinking about what might have caused the ugly stains on the carpet in the bedroom. The countertops and the faucet in the kitchen were badly scratched, and the sink in the bathroom was cracked.

He rented these accommodations from month to month but pre-paid two months ahead. Cody assumed that after a couple of months he would have a better idea of what he wanted to do next in his life. *If only I knew where I should go from here.*

He couldn't go back home because the ranch his father built with his own hands and the sweat of hard work didn't belong to him anymore.

God, I want my old life back! He pushed his plate aside and covered his face with his hands. *Come on, don't be a fool. You are lying to yourself. What you really want is a new life—a happier life and leave the old mess behind once and for all.* "God, give me strength to start over again. I know I have to start from scratch," he whispered into the empty kitchen.

Try to look at it positively. You're not starting from square one because you have all this experience behind you.

He could have done without some of the lessons he'd had to endure in the past. Cody wasn't scared of having to start all over, but he feared failure and that he might disappoint the people who were important to him, but then he recalled there was nobody left he could disappoint. He was alone, and it was an ugly feeling.

Cody had frequently battled fate, and he was exhausted. The mischievous sparkle in his eyes was gone, and his mouth showed a downward curve these days. He barely laughed and appeared thoughtful most of the time. Dark circles under his eyes gave his face a haggard appearance. Without being aware of it, he often let his broad shoulders hang like an old man would. There wasn't much left of the once so-proud rodeo hero.

Angry with himself, he shook his head. *Pull yourself together and look ahead.* He pushed back his chair, got up, and carried his dishes to the sink. It was time to look for a job because, like everybody else, he had to earn money to pay his way in life. Today he planned to drive to the sawmill and ask the boss if he would hire him. Cody was accustomed to hard physical work and didn't shy away from it.

Determined, he grabbed his keys from the countertop and left the trailer. His old pickup awaited him like a faithful friend. Cody headed into town and hoped for the best.

He had been living in Ruidoso for a little over four weeks. Despite being without a job and friends, Cody liked the area. There were mountains and forests, and the scenery provided him with something resembling inner peace. But it wasn't the real peace he sought.

He passed the city limits sign and saw the buildings of the sawmill to the right. Cody turned off Main Street and drove straight toward the log cabin they used for the office. He parked in front of it and studied the billboard that promised customers the best construction timber in the county.

He climbed the steps to the front door three at a time with his long, muscular legs. When he opened the door, an old-fashioned bell above its frame announced his arrival.

A woman in her late forties looked up with a curious expression on her face. Immediately, she came toward the polished wooden counter.

Cody removed his hat, smiled, and greeted the lady cordially. "Good morning, ma'am. My name is Cody Ferguson, and I wanted to ask if it's possible to talk to the owner of this sawmill. I'm looking for a job and wondered if he is hiring at present."

Cody noticed the woman tried her best to look younger than she was. Her hair was bleached blonde with rather unspectacular brown roots shot through the carefully styled waves. Her nose was a bit too prominent, but her face had a pleasant appearance, except she wore more makeup than suited Cody's taste. She was dressed in tight jeans and a checked blouse, which failed to hide her impressive breasts. She seemed friendly—although the lady eyeballed Cody with obvious interest.

Her cheeks turned a charming rose shade when she picked up the phone and dialed a number. She spoke softly with someone on the other end of the line, then replaced the receiver. She returned her attention to the visitor in front of the counter, sporting her best smile. "Mister Miller will be with you in a moment. Please take a seat over there." She pointed toward two plastic chairs, the kind you would find in the waiting room of a public health office.

Cody was aware that the woman's glance followed him, but he didn't think anything of it. He knew most women considered him quite attractive. It didn't matter to Cody because his interest in women had declined thanks to his ex-wife.

It didn't take long before a man in his mid-fifties with a receding hairline entered the building through the back door. His enormous abdomen suggested he had a taste for good food and a beer or two on a regular basis. His belly swallowed the waistband and belt of his khaki pants. He marched forward and shook his visitor's hand. The strength of the man's grip astonished Cody.

"Gladys told me you're looking for a job." This man was not the kind who beat around the bush, and his voice was as loud as his physique was large.

"Yes, sir. My name is Cody Ferguson, and I moved here from northern Arizona a couple of weeks ago. I'm used to hard work and wondered if you need a former rancher."

"Well, I want to be honest with you. I would love to give you a chance, but at present our orders don't look very promising. In fact, I'll consider myself lucky if I don't have to fire anybody in the next few weeks. Those dang construction companies would rather import their timber at a cheaper rate from God-knows-where instead of supporting our local businesses. I tell you, son, this government will ruin us all in no time."

"I understand you well, sir, but maybe your secretary here can write down my name and phone number just in case you change your mind. I would be grateful if you called me when the situation improves, Mister Miller."

"Definitely, Mister Ferguson."

The two men bid their farewells, and Cody noticed how disappointed Gladys looked.

She handed him a notepad and her pen. "I'll make sure that he remembers you as soon as orders increase," she promised and winked at him cheekily.

Cody smiled at her, put his battered black Stetson on his thick curls, and tipped it. "Have a great day, ma'am."

He opened the door, stepped outside, and pulled the door shut. He heard the soft ting-a-ling of the doorbell but missed Gladys's enthusiastic, "What a picture of a man."

Cody pushed his hand into the pocket of his faded jeans, pulled his car keys out, and got behind the wheel. For a moment, he sat there, not moving, lost in thought. After a moment, he put the key into the ignition and started the engine. It rumbled to life, growling like an angry, old cougar whose prey had escaped.

What now, Cowboy? Maybe you should try the gas station. Cody didn't want to be discouraged, but he knew the current state of the economy wouldn't make it easy to find a decent job. Sighing as he contemplated his situation, he turned on the radio.

"Amarillo by Morning" was playing. He sang along with a few lines. A boyish smile lit his face. Good old George Strait. Cody had always loved his music, and this song was one of his absolute favorites. It reminded him of good times at the ranch and his first few successes at the rodeo. A trigger for happier times that never failed to make him smile.

Cody shifted gears, drove through the parking lot of the sawmill, and turned back onto Main Street. He sang along loudly, stubbornly chasing away gloomy thoughts about being without a job. If his mobile phone hadn't vibrated in the pocket of his denim jacket, he wouldn't have heard it. He pulled his phone out but wasn't at all in the mood to take the call. Most likely it was some fellow from the bank again.

Now what in God's name could they want from me? The auction date is set already.

"Might as well leave me alone," he growled, but answered, his voice grouchy as it could be. "Ferguson!"

TWO
Old Gary Bradshaw

"**H**OW ARE YOU *doing, son?*" a deep, raspy voice said. It sounded familiar, but Cody couldn't place it.

He remained silent.

The low chuckle at the other end confused him. *"I'll be darned. Don't you tell me that you don't recognize the voice of your old mentor, Gary Bradshaw?"*

He almost dropped the phone. Immediately pictures of old Gary appeared in his mind's eye. Once, the man had been the livestock boss at his father's ranch, and moreover, he had indeed been Cody's mentor.

Cody gasped. "Now butter my butt and call me a biscuit. What a surprise! Oh, man, I'm thrilled to hear from you, Gary! It must have been ages since we last spoke."

"Well, it's a lucky thing that you're not the kind of guy who changes his phone number as often as some change their britches."

Cody guffawed. He couldn't even recall when he last laughed so hard. He flipped his phone to the other ear and shifted gears.

"Where do you live now, son? I was looking for you in Payson, but folks over there told me that you moved and left the area."

He sighed. "It's a long story, Gary. But yes, it's true, I left Payson for good. I just couldn't stand to live there anymore."

So, Gary had been in his former hometown, and for sure, he met old friends. Immediately Cody felt the familiar feeling of guilt, and bile rose in his throat. He didn't have to ask Gary if he had heard the news about the auction. He was certain Gary knew about it, and of all the people that Cody once called friend, he felt the most embarrassed about his failure with Gary Bradshaw.

Cody chewed his lower lip like a small boy who had been caught stealing. He just couldn't bring himself to admit he'd lost everything, including his father's legacy—not on the phone anyway. He swallowed because he was close to tears. The only thing that made it a bit easier for him was knowing his father hadn't seen the day his ranch had gone into foreclosure and would be auctioned off, away from the family's ownership. It seemed like a mercy he died of a heart attack a few months ago. Unfortunately, that happened two days after a terrible fight, and Cody still blamed himself for his father's death. So, what might be a mercy for his father would be a thorn in his heart for the rest of his days.

Gary remained silent on the other end of the line. Cody wondered if the call had been dropped. He listened to the crackling sound through the phone's speaker.

Gary's husky voice came on again. *"Do you have a job?"*

"No, sir!" Cody again felt like the teenager who once paid the highest respect to the most important man at the ranch besides his own father. He sat straighter behind the wheel, paying more attention to his posture.

Gary taught him some of life's most important lessons, using his infallible instinct for human beings as well as for livestock. Sloppy posture was unacceptable for Bradshaw, a man who followed traditions.

Cody cleared his throat before saying more. "I'm looking for a job. I just left a sawmill where I applied for work. Unfortunately, they're not hiring at present because the economy looks as crappy in New Mexico as everywhere else. I guess you could say that things don't look too rosy right now."

"*Sawmill, hmm? How are you doing health wise? Have you recovered from your injuries? Can you work such heavy physical labor?*"

Cody bit his tongue to avoid asking his old friend which injuries he meant. He shook his head to clear it and tried to concentrate. *Come on, pull yourself together. Gary doesn't deserve your sarcasm. He's always been a good friend and advisor.*

"I'm doing okay, but some days really suck, especially when the weather changes. Doctors told me I recovered well, considering the circumstances, but things will remain a bit touchy where they had to screw the bones back together. But you know I had a real good teacher who always told me to cowboy up. Whining is not an option, right?" said Cody while grinning from ear to ear.

Gary laughed at the top of his lungs, and Cody swallowed hard. *God how much I missed this sound.* His friend's laughter was the melody of years gone by when his world had been in good order.

"*Do you have obligations in New Mexico?*"

"What do you mean by obligations?" asked Cody, frowning.

"Well, you know, like your wife or maybe a house you bought over there... whatever."

Cody scoffed. "No. Nothing like that. I don't have a house, and as for my wife, she's gone."

"I see. Listen, youngster, I could use some help. I'm getting too old for repairing fences or taming crazy mustangs. I built up a nice little ranch here in Montana, and lately I've been wondering if you would like to come up here and help me out a bit. I could use a good man like you."

He was certain he misunderstood Gary. Why would a successful rancher invite a broken-down old rodeo hand to come a thousand miles to work for him?

"Wait a minute, are you offering me a job? Gary, you know that I'm a failure when it comes to being a rancher. For Christ's sake, I wasn't even able to save my father's ranch. I don't believe that any rancher with common sense should hire a fellow like me, apart from the fact that I'm a rodeo cripple."

"Cody Ferguson, the only thing I would call crippled at present is your self-confidence. So, get a grip on yourself and come home, boy! You earned your place at my campfire a long time ago, way before that dang ride in Cheyenne. I'm not like the flag in the wind that changes direction as soon as the breeze blows a bit harder around one's nose. I know you have been in the middle of a storm since your accident, and I want to stand by your side until it calms down. So, pack your bags, grab your saddle, get in your pickup, and drag those healed bones of yours up here to Montana." Gary remained silent for a moment, giving Cody a chance to think about his words. After a moment, he spoke again. *"Winter might be a bit harsh for you because Jack Frost can be quite tough in our area, but nevertheless, I'm convinced that you'll find some inner peace if you work for me. Think about it, son. My offer will stand."*

There was another brief pause, and Cody didn't know what to say.

"I can't pay as much as the rodeo circuit would, but nine hundred and fifty dollars per week plus housing and meals would be a mighty good start, don't you think? Besides, you can train as much as you want. I have more than enough horses waiting for you here."

Cody felt tears in his eyes. "Gary, I don't train for the rodeo anymore."

"Never say never. You need time and some distance from all the hardship you faced, and I need help. One doesn't have to be a genius in mathematics to understand that this could be a win-win situation for both of us. I live close to the small town of Dillon. Bozeman and Helena aren't far away, and there's a lot to do there. There are more than enough saloons where a cowboy could find some amusement, and the steakhouses serve great food. Hell, you can even two-step with a nice cowgirl from time to time."

Cody laughed out loud. "Okay, okay, I'll think about your offer and let you know tomorrow. However, you won't be able to tempt me with saloons. I had to leave those behind. Since you were in Payson, I'm sure you heard that it's better for me to avoid all sorts of bars and liquor stores," he added softly.

Gary scoffed. *"All I know is that you gave up drinking, and I'm dang proud of you for doing so. I know that ain't easy, Cody, but you did it. I have seen others who failed at getting off the booze."*

"Thank you, Gary. Coming from you, that means a lot to me. But I must admit that I battle the urge to drink every single day. But with God's help, I'll stay away from the bottle."

"Amen," Gary answered sincerely.

After Cody promised to let him know his decision within the next twenty-four hours, Gary said goodbye. Cody put his phone back into his jacket and unwrapped a piece of chewing gum. For a moment, he hardly saw the street in front of him because tears flowed freely. Gary's offer out of the blue when his need was so great seemed like a miracle. Just to hear from his mentor after three years seemed like a message from God. What a welcome surprise.

"You couldn't have chosen a better moment, my old friend," Cody mumbled and stuck the chewing gum into his mouth. He stopped at the gas station and walked into the convenience store.

While waiting in line to pay for his gas, he knew what he had to do. He would follow his gut feeling. Cody turned and walked along the aisles, picking up items that would come in handy on the long drive ahead. He carried everything with his left arm and opened the doors to the cooler, where he grabbed a six pack of Diet Coke. After settling the bill, he walked to his pickup truck and placed the items on the passenger seat. Then, he pumped gas into the tank.

As he stood next to his vehicle, Cody looked down at his well-worn cowboy boots and noticed a puddle of diesel on the pavement. The sun reflected in the spill. The iridescent colors reminded him of a rainbow, and the song "Somewhere over the Rainbow" came to mind and made him smile.

Maybe there is such a place where the skies are blue once the storm is over. If I don't give it a try, I'll never know. After all, what do I have to lose? I'll be starting from scratch no matter where I am.

The loud clicking of the gas pump brought Cody back to reality. In the car next to his was a teenage girl with pink hair. She stared at him, her mouth open, her head tilted awkwardly to one side. He laughed at her and winked. Immediately, her acne-spotted cheeks turned the same color as her hair, and she quickly swiveled her head to gaze through the opposite window toward the other side of the gas station.

Cody was still laughing when he got behind the wheel and drove off. He felt better than he had for many weeks and drove straight to his trailer, where he packed his belongings. He hadn't brought much to New Mexico, and it took him a little over an hour to stuff everything into his scratched leather luggage.

He sat at the kitchen table and dialed the number of the last call he had accepted on his mobile phone. Behind him, the coffee maker gurgled and hissed, and the strong aroma of his favorite coffee wafted through the kitchen. Nervously, he drummed his fingers in the same impatient rhythm his father had always used.

He was about to hang up when Gary's gruff voice answered. *"Bradshaw."*

Cody swallowed. *What if Gary hadn't meant his offer seriously? What if he changed his mind?* Angry with himself, Cody shook his head, but he couldn't stop his hands from trembling.

My God, what has gotten into me? I was never afraid of anything. Take a plunge into this next stage of your life.

He took a deep breath and spoke into the phone. "Howdy, Gary. This is Cody. I thought about that job, and if your offer still stands, I would like to give it a try on your ranch."

"Praise the Lord and Hallelujah! Now if this isn't good news, then I don't know what is," said Gary. Cody thought he heard him chuckle. *"Well, in that case, let me send you the exact address. I'm sure you'll need to spend a night in a motel somewhere on the way because it'll take you almost two days to get to Dillon."*

"I've packed my stuff already and will hit the road in about an hour. I'm pretty sure I can drive five or six hours before I need to stop at a motel to get some rest. But before that, I have to talk to my rodeo pal to let him know I am moving out and return the keys to this trailer. He was kind enough to let me use his old place after he moved in with his new sweetheart. He was mighty generous to me since I came to New Mexico. Didn't ask for much rent either knowing that I am more or less broke."

"Do you think he'll give you a hard time for leaving right away?"

"I don't think so. I'll suggest that he can keep the prepaid two months' rent. I don't pay much anyway. As I said, he helped me out when I needed a new place to stay. Didn't hesitate. He knew it would be a temporary solution until I found a job and I reckon I just found one. I guess he will sell the place as soon as I move out. He and his fiancé want to tie the knot pretty soon, you know. He could use the money to remodel their new home."

"All right, in that case everything is clear. Don't forget, it's not only a job waiting for you but a home as well. All you need to do is to accept it."

"Thanks, Gary. I don't even know what to say."

"Nothing, of course. Squeeze your cowboy butt behind the wheel and hit the road, son. Safe travels and see you soon."

"Yes, sir!" said Cody with a chuckle. He rose, made himself a cup of coffee, and poured the rest of it into his old thermos flask. He added a few spoons of sugar and shook the flask. Then, he picked up his phone and called the fellow who owned the trailer. Just as he had assumed, his old pal had no problem with him moving out the same day. He didn't even want to keep the two months pre-paid rent but Cody insisted on it. "Listen, you helped me when nobody else in my old hometown would have moved a finger for me. I am grateful that I had a place to stay for a few weeks. I wish you and your lady the very best. Try to be a better example of a marriage than I have been.

For the last time, Cody walked through the trailer and checked every cabinet and drawer. After making sure he hadn't left behind any of his few personal belongings, he grabbed the coffee pot, walked out, and locked the door. He loaded his luggage onto the back seat of his pickup and his saddle on the floor of the passenger seat. It was his most precious belonging, and he did not want to expose it to the weather in the bed of his truck. Cody won the saddle along with the rodeo championship back in the days when he had been the well-known saddle bronc champion, Cody Ferguson. The saddle stood for his past and the better days of his life when he had plenty of reasons to smile.

THREE
A New Beginning

O N HIS WAY out of town, he stopped at his friend's place and dropped the key through the door slot. Cody didn't look back. He always knew this town was only a temporary stop until he knew where he wanted to go and what he wanted to do with the rest of his life. Therefore, he hadn't developed any emotional ties to this place. A hometown was something different. Cody didn't know any people here, but he sure knew what a true home was. And he knew how it felt to lose a real home.

Many hours of driving lay ahead of him. Cody grabbed a can of Diet Coke from his heavily scratched blue cooler on the passenger seat. He had filled it with ice cubes from the gas station, and it would keep his drinks cool for quite some time.

He wiped his wet hands on his faded jeans. For a brief moment, he steered the vehicle with his knee while holding the can between his legs to open the lid. He took a swig and tasted the slight cinnamon aroma of the beverage. For some reason, he felt much more alive today compared to the past weeks. Maybe because he finally had a goal and a place to go to. *Kind of like the good old days, saddle in the trunk and on the way to the next city, the next ranch, or the next rodeo,* he thought while he watched the city limits sign disappear from view in the mirror.

Mile after mile, the scenery of New Mexico rolled by. So far, red rocks dominated the landscape of the area, but the more distance he covered, the closer the impressive silhouette of the Grand Tetons and the Rocky Mountains loomed on the horizon. The beauty of the valleys he passed took Cody's breath away, and he couldn't get enough of the dark forests with all different kinds of pine trees. He wondered if they smelled as aromatic as he recalled them. *Why not find out?* He pushed the small control button on the driver's door to lower the side window.

Cool wind blew into the cabin of the pickup and ruffled through his thick, dark curls. He sniffed the breeze like a puppy leaning his head out the window and wasn't disappointed by the spicy scent of the trees. It reminded him of the lush forests in northern Arizona, where his father's ranch stood empty, waiting for a new owner. He tried not to think too often about his home back in Payson. The pain of losing the property stung like a fresh wound.

Cody turned on the radio and searched for a country station. He thought about Gary's job offer and wondered what kind of working arrangement he should expect. He was too realistic to think he would have a special status among the crew members just because he had known Gary for many years. He had to wait and see how things developed and earn his position among the ranch hands. That was the way it went for a newcomer on a team. He trusted Gary and knew if he worked hard enough and behaved honorably, he would likely have a stable job for years to come.

Gary Bradshaw always had an open ear and patience for the ambitious rodeo rider. He taught Cody a lot and had forgiven him for more than one lapse in the past.

"You remind me of myself when I was your age. I had all kinds of nonsense and crazy ideas in my head, and it was hard for me to obey my parents," Gary told him over a glass of whiskey at the campfire one evening.

While Cody drove on, he thought about the years Gary Bradshaw had worked for Cody's father. He couldn't recall there ever having been any disagreements with Gary. His friendship with his father's head wrangler had always been based on trust and respect.

A memory arose that contradicted that line of thought. Cody remembered their friendship turned frosty a few weeks after he brought Lynn Karshley home. She was his fiancée at the time. There had been no reason for the friendship to change. They hadn't fought at all and had exchanged no unpleasant words. Cody had been too busy being in love with and trying to impress his future wife to notice how much his friendship with Gary changed in a short period of time. Besides Lynn, all he really cared about in those days was becoming a rodeo champion.

Thinking about it, he realized Gary had avoided Lynn's company as long as he still worked at the ranch. Cody took another sip of Coke and placed the can into the cup holder. He combed his right hand through his tousled hair.

"I must ask him why he didn't want to be around my ex," Cody mumbled. Gary had been much smarter on that account than Cody himself.

Usually, he tried not to think about his marriage. The disappointment and pain Lynn caused him had left a scar and still hurt bad from time to time. It was a dull pain now but still too strong to be ignored. However, he couldn't prevent the image of his ex-wife from popping up in his thoughts occasionally. Oh, yes, she was a looker with her long blonde hair and curvy figure. Her bust size was quite impressive and could have easily played a major role in most men's dreams. She wore too much makeup for his taste, but he reckoned that to be normal for the cheerleader type she represented.

He remembered when he met her for the first time at the rodeo in Prescott as if it was yesterday. She entered the barrel race, and most cowboys who watched her from behind the fences were fascinated by her appealing backside in those tight jeans. Cody was no exception. After all, he was only a man. He grimaced, recalling how the other guys whistled through their fingers when she rode by. Some called some rather racy offers after her.

Lynn achieved third place in the barrel race competition that weekend. When some of the rodeo participants met for barbecue later in the evening, she crossed his path. Whether she was looking for his company or they met accidentally, he didn't know. After they got together, she claimed that she had been searching for him on purpose. Whether that was the truth or just another of her countless lies, he couldn't say.

They talked for a while and clicked immediately. It didn't take long before they left the group and sat down on an old blanket that Cody spread over the bed of his truck. Their conversation about riding, ranch life, and horse breeding lasted for hours. They drank beer from the bottle while leaning against a bale of hay. Cody enjoyed her company, but he couldn't shake the feeling that Lynn was more concerned about her looks than the next good position in the ranking of the barrel racing championship. She constantly played with her curly, blonde hair, and the way she winked at him seemed like a well-rehearsed gesture. Nevertheless, he couldn't resist the fascination and desire he felt, and she drew him to her like a moth to a candle flame.

The first few kisses on the tailgate of his pickup were passionate, and need flashed through his young body like a blazing fire. He was unable to control his desire, and they ended up in the narrow bunk bed of his trailer that very first night. Cody recalled that he wondered how in the world a hardworking rodeo participant could have such long, perfectly polished fingernails, but as the storm of passion took hold of him, he gave it no further thought.

Sex with her was fiery. Lynn was a very tempestuous lover who knew exactly what to do to drive her partner crazy with desire. He was pretty sure many of the other guys envied him for spending the night with her. Cody knew hardly any of the rodeo cowboys would have pushed her off their bunk. But today he was wiser and knew better. After being married to Lynn, he'd learned that she had never worked hard in her entire life. Cody was aware that more than a perfect figure and alluring makeup were necessary to make a satisfying relationship.

Good sex was enjoyable but not enough of a firm base to spend an entire life together or raise kids. There were many little hints which should have warned him Lynn wasn't the right woman for him—he simply didn't want to pay attention to them. Disgruntled, Cody threw the empty Coke can behind the seat. She wasn't worth the real estate he allowed her to occupy in his thoughts. She had caused worse wounds than that dang sunfisher which bucked him off, sending him into the dirt of the arena in Cheyenne.

FOUR

G.B. Ranch, Dillon, Montana

IN THE LATE afternoon, his growling stomach reminded him that he
hadn't eaten since breakfast. He was on the highway headed in the
direction of Denver, Colorado, when he saw a billboard announcing
a Cracker Barrel restaurant five miles away.

*Oh, a Cracker Barrel, I haven't eaten at one of those for a long time. Yep,
I'll pamper myself with a nice dinner there.* Ten minutes later, he pulled into
the parking lot of the restaurant. It wasn't crowded since it was late
afternoon but not yet dinnertime. He asked the hostess for a table next
to the window from which he could see his car. Everything he owned
was in that vehicle, and he wanted to keep an eye on it.

A pretty waitress walked toward him, a broad smile on her face. She
wore a red and white checked blouse, black jeans, and the typical brown

apron with its embroidered yellow stars on it. It was wrapped around her slim waist and secured with a double knot.

The girl greeted Cody cordially. "Hi, I'm Clarissa. Here's your menu. Have you already decided what you want to drink?" She gazed into his face, holding her pad in her left hand, her pencil ready to jot down his order.

Cody preferred the traditional style of being served. He didn't like the new electronic devises waitresses pointed at a guest like a loaded six shooter nowadays. He was glad that Cracker Barrel stuck to some traditions at least. He often wondered if he had been born in the wrong century. He despised the way technology replaced the good old ways.

"I'd like some iced tea, but not too sweet if possible."

"Certainly. I'll bring you unsweet tea and you can sweeten it to your liking with the sugar on the table." She walked back to the counter. Her long brunette hair was bound into a ponytail, which swung from one side to the other with each step she took.

Pulling his gaze away from her, he concentrated on the menu in front of him. He didn't have to think twice when he saw that today's special was the very meal his mom used to cook for him all the time. His beloved mother had been stricken with Alzheimer's disease and didn't even remember who she was. It tore out his heart that she hadn't recognized her own son in months.

Clarissa returned to his table, carrying his cutlery and iced tea in hand instead of on a tray. She placed the items in front of him. "Ready to order, Cowboy?" she said with a flirtatious wink. She was way too young for him.

"I'll take the meatloaf with mashed potatoes and the small side salad with ranch dressing, please. Oh, and a cup of coffee and a portion of your tasty, fried cinnamon apples. I know it's a side dish, but I'll eat it for dessert. Got to watch my figure."

"Oh, someone knows our menu well," she remarked with a perky laugh.

"Yes, ma'am, true that." He smiled back at her, and her cheeks blushed a deep rose.

Cody often witnessed that kind of reaction, but he didn't brag about it. He wasn't the kind of guy who used his good looks to take advantage of women and didn't like to play with their emotions. As a matter of fact, he was relieved when he was left alone because he had learned the bitter lesson that love was more than a game. "Once burned, twice shy," they said, and it applied to Cody. Besides, this girl was barely out of high school, or maybe she wasn't.

His waitress quickly returned with a tray. She arranged his plate with the salad and the apples on the table and placed a cup of steaming coffee next to the bowl with the apples. But instead of leaving the table, she remained standing in front of him for a moment longer than necessary, hesitating. He knew she was looking for small talk with him. Cody didn't want to appear unfriendly, but he wasn't interested in any further conversation with the girl.

He looked up from his plate and said firmly, "Thanks, that's all for the moment."

Her face changed into a mask of disappointment, her eyebrows raising in the center and the corners of her mouth dropping. She turned and walked briskly to a table close by to clear the dirty dishes, producing more clattering than necessary.

Although the meatloaf tasted good, it was far from the mouthwatering experience his mother used to serve in their cozy ranch kitchen back home. Like he used to when he was a child, Cody formed a gravy lake in the middle of his mashed potatoes. He studied his food sculpture and chuckled at himself. *Some things never change.*

He scraped his plate and scooped the last bite into his mouth, followed by a sip of the now lukewarm coffee. Then, he left a tip for Clarissa under the white coffee mug, picked up his check, and walked toward the cashier. On his way, he grabbed two glass jars containing fried apples from the merchandise area. He held them with his left arm while he pulled his wallet from his hip pocket. Cody remembered that Gary was as crazy for that sweet treat as he was. In Cody's opinion, there was hardly any better eating than cinnamon and honey flavored fried golden delicious apples. Well, apart from peach cobbler, of course. And not to forget, his mother's famous Black Forest cake with the extra layer of Schnapps-soaked cherries between the folds of whipped cream.

While crossing the parking lot of Cracker Barrel, Cody inhaled the cool, fresh evening air. Although the restaurant wasn't packed, it had been too full for his taste. As a real cowboy, he preferred quiet and tranquil places. Of course, he enjoyed the company of people and never said no to a good conversation, but timing as well as the folks he talked to had to be a good fit. He was selective when it came to who he wanted to spend his free time with, especially since he'd been burned a couple of times.

He packed the two jars of apples into his travel bag and climbed behind the wheel. Thanks to the GPS on his smartphone, he knew the drive to Gary's ranch would take around eighteen hours altogether, and he planned to cover at least another two hours before looking for a motel where he could get some rest. Cody wanted to leave the crowded big city streets of Denver and its constantly growing suburbs behind before he called it a day.

It was after 9:00 p.m. when he became too fatigued to concentrate on traffic. His eyes burned and teared, and he stifled a yawn every few minutes. When he saw the blue sign announcing a Best Western motel, he decided to call it a day.

No one else was at the front desk, and after just a few minutes, Cody walked back to his car, key card in his hand. After parking his pickup in front of Room 118, he took his bag from the back seat and unlocked the door. He dropped his luggage on the floor in front of his bed. Then, he returned to his pickup and carried all his other belongings into the room. There was no way he would leave anything in the car, although the area looked safe. The last thing he brought into the room before closing the door was his gear bag with his saddle.

The wonderful, handcrafted piece was the only positive reminder of his successful time as saddle bronc champion. A well-known saddle maker from Texas made it. The saddle was beautifully adorned with silver conchos and exquisite floral ornaments punched into the leather.

Cody took good care of the precious piece and polished it with saddle soap and saddle butter regularly. Even during the darkest hours when he didn't know how he would pay for his next meal, he'd never considered selling the saddle. God only knew how hard he worked and how much sweat, tears, and pain he went through to finally win the title along with this fine piece of craftsmanship.

The familiar smell of beeswax, one of the ingredients he used to tend to the leather, tickled his nose as he touched the leather lovingly. There were a few scratches here and there, but it didn't matter. After all, it was a working saddle, not an exhibition piece like one might see in some rich dude's office. In Cody's book, a saddle needed the touch of a horse and wasn't a piece of decoration. He had seen too many wannabes who thought all it took to make them a cowboy was to buy a pair of boots and a cowboy hat.

He remembered the day he'd achieved his first title. Some folks called him a greenhorn even though he'd won. Like most fellow Americans, he would never forget that year—nobody could forget September 2001. It was the very year when this nation lost a great deal of its self-confidence due to the terror attacks that destroyed the twin towers of the World Trade Center in New York City. The very year when Cody's self-confidence had been skyrocketing, and he had felt like a real rodeo hero with the sky as his limit. *Long ago days of a happier life.*

He walked to the door and locked it. On the way to the bathroom, he pulled his T-shirt over his head and dropped it onto the bed. He undressed completely and stepped under the shower, allowing himself the luxury of warm water.

A few minutes later, he sat on the bed and opened a bag of his favorite jalapeno-flavored chips. He took a sip of Diet Coke and placed the can next to the made-in-China motel alarm clock. *At least that's one of the advantages of being single. I can crackle around with this bag and eat unhealthy stuff in bed without having anybody nagging me for it.* He chuckled at that thought and switched from one TV channel to the next, a habit that annoyed Lynn constantly when they were together.

"OK, Cowboy, it's better if you get some sleep," he mumbled and turned off the TV. The lights from the parking lot sneaked through the small slit between the two curtains into his room, so it wasn't completely dark. Cody could make out the furniture around him.

He tried to unwind from the day's journey. He'd completed more than one third of the drive and assumed he would arrive at his final destination in Montana by four o'clock in the afternoon the following day. With his hands behind his head and the air conditioning blowing a cool breeze across his naked torso, he lay there thinking about the new job.

Jesus, what if I fail and disappoint Gary? He covered his face with his hands, feeling the old anxiety rising. The thought that he might not be able to keep up with the expectations his only real friend had for him scared the wits out of him. The familiar panic lifted its ugly head and caused his heart rate to quicken. Cody quickly folded his hands and whispered a prayer,

The Apostles' Creed.

"I believe in God, the Father almighty,

Creator of heaven and earth.

I believe in Jesus Christ, his only Son, our Lord.

He was conceived by the power of the Holy Spirit

and born of the Virgin Mary.

He suffered under Pontius Pilate,

was crucified, died, and was buried.

He descended to the dead.

On the third day, he rose again.

He ascended into Heaven,

and is seated at the right hand of the Father.

He will come again to judge the living and the dead.

I believe in the Holy Spirit,

the holy Catholic Church,

the communion of saints,

the forgiveness of sins,

the resurrection of the body,

and the life everlasting.

Amen."

Cody had always been a faithful Christian, but during his rodeo times, he hadn't prayed regularly. The difficult circumstances in his life brought him back to it. Praying helped keep his fears at bay and the urge to drink under control.

As he said "amen," he felt his muscles relax and his breathing slow. Calm washed over him, and he let go of the anxiety. Taking another deep breath, he closed his eyes and drifted to sleep.

Despite his calming preparation for sleep, he couldn't avoid the frightening images that harassed him. His legs moved restlessly, and he rolled over again and again under the covers, searching for comfort. The most horrible moments of his life replayed in countless nightmares throughout the long dark hours.

Cody awoke before daylight and dragged himself to the bathroom. "Jesus, will I ever sleep peacefully again?" he moaned, throwing some cold water on his face.

He leaned on the edges of the single sink with both hands and heaved a sigh. A glance at the gaunt face reflected back at him showed the dark stubble of his beard and swollen eyelids.

Oh, my, I look like a skid-row drunk. Better get cleaned up and respectable. At least I'm up early enough to hit the road.

Half an hour later, he started the engine and took a sip of the lukewarm coffee from the Styrofoam cup he got in the lobby of the motel. Grimacing at the dishwater taste of the beverage, he thought of pouring it out, but he needed caffeine to stay awake on the road. It would have to do until the next stop at the gas station.

The route his GPS calculated led him through towns such as Colorado Springs and Fort Collins. Like most cowboys, he was a true fan of westerns and knew those places for their pioneer history.

Unfortunately, he didn't have the time to stop for a visit because he wanted to get to Gary's place as soon as possible. He hadn't worked for quite some time and was impatient to begin. Maybe he would have a chance to visit one of these towns later after he settled at the ranch. Cody loved historical towns that breathed pioneer history and intended to add them to his bucket list.

His route took him through valleys filled with aspens and along gurgling rivers. It was late summer, and some of the trees already started to change the color of their leaves in this part of the country. Cody smiled at seeing such natural beauty all around him.

Mom would love this scenery, he thought. She often crossed his mind. Cody loved his mother dearly, and it pained him that she didn't recognize him anymore. She wasn't the mother he had grown up with. Alzheimer's was one of the cruelest diseases because it destroyed the memories of the loved one and left the family with a person who was still alive but hardly had a life.

Cody left Colorado behind and entered the state of Wyoming. Valleys of fertile soil and blue rivers created peaceful scenery. This was true cowboy country, and the views warmed his heart. Off in the distance to the west, the majestic peaks of the Grand Tetons reached so high into the sky it seemed they wanted to greet God Himself.

How can people doubt God's existence when His wonders are laid before them on a daily basis? he wondered as he unwrapped the sandwich purchased at his last stop for gas.

When he reached the city of Idaho Falls, he walked around a bit to exercise his legs, but despite the beauty of the place, he didn't spend much time there. He was eager to drive the last three hours and reach Gary's place.

Finally, in the early afternoon, he drove his pickup through the ranch gate bearing the black smithed initials "G.B." Cody remembered Gary to be a down-to-earth yet hardworking rancher, and therefore, he expected a small ranch operation with a plain ranch house and likely a bunkhouse for Gary's ranch hands. He wasn't at all prepared for the palatial home that was more like a mansion than a log cabin. It was an impressive building, its wood walls painted in a warm, honey-colored shade and the big glass windows offering panoramic views into the lush scenery. Cody whistled through his teeth approvingly.

The tin roof sported the same rich green color as the ponderosa pines next to the building. The dormer windows on the upper floor added to the charm of the house. To the left, Cody noticed numerous corrals and a compact building, which he assumed to be the tack room. A few horses dozed behind the fences, enjoying the warm afternoon sun. They were well-kept animals and in good shape, from what he could see. Everything around Cody looked tidy and well organized.

A wide wrap-around porch surrounded the house, and an inviting swing hung near the front door. Plump pillows were covered with a fabric of floral design. Cody loved traditional ranch porches. In his opinion, they had a special atmosphere and were one of the best spots to have a decent conversation with family or friends.

To the right, three smaller log cabins stood a short distance away, surrounded by a cluster of trees. Each of the cabins had a covered porch with cedar wood posts supporting the roof.

"Holy cow. This property is a long way from what I expected it to be," Cody whispered.

FIVE
Meeting an Old Mentor

C ODY CLOSED THE door of his vehicle but left the key in the ignition. Just as he was about to jump the four steps to the front door, it opened a crack. The weathered skin and prominent nose of his friend's face, a heritage of Gary's Cherokee grandmother, greeted him as the door swung open.

Cody looked at the toes of his boots, his chest burning with shame at losing his father's ranch. Gary had contributed as much to developing the property as Mr. Ferguson, Sr. had. Where Cody had failed to make the ranch a success because of his drinking, Gary had contributed to the prosperity of his parents' ranch. Cody considered himself a failure for losing it to the bank. He was sure Gary thought the same.

But there was no awkward silence. Gary looked him straight in the face and smiled broadly. Then, he opened his arms and said, "Welcome home, son."

Cody didn't know what to say, but he walked up those steps toward the tall, sturdy Gary Bradshaw and embraced the older man warmly. Although his wrinkles had deepened, Gary hadn't changed much. He resembled the same father figure Cody always saw in him, just like those days when he was a teenager. It seemed that Gary would help him move forward in his life once again, like he did during Cody's first inexperienced days at the rodeo.

"Come on in and join me for a cup of Arbuckle coffee. For this special occasion, my friend Ruth made a pecan pie that no bakery could beat. I told her that's your favorite pie. I hope it hasn't changed, has it?"

"No, sir. It's still my absolute favorite pie." Cody smiled and followed his friend into the house. As he walked behind him, he realized that Gary had lost at least an inch of his once six-foot and one-half inch height from his impressive tall and muscular figure. But he still wore his starched white western shirts, well-cut Wrangler denims, and fancy cowboy boots with pride.

Cody immediately recognized the buckle that Gary won as a bull rider during one of the bigger Oklahoma rodeos many years ago. He pointed to it and laughed. "Do you remember how often I bugged you to tell me the story about you winning this buckle? And how I begged you again and again to teach me everything that you knew about the rodeo so that I could become as successful a bull or bronc rider as you were in those days?"

Gary laid his strong hands around the imposing piece and nodded. A warm smile lit his weathered face. "How could I forget? Every time I told the tale, your face shone like a little boy's Christmas morning."

Cody studied Gary's hands. A life of hard work had covered the old cowboy's hands with calluses. Countless dark age spots dotted the backs of his friend's hands.

"I tell you, son. Those were good times. These days, I have to consider myself blessed if a bull doesn't kick me in my behind. A man does crazy things when he is young and careless and doesn't think twice about consequences. But I wouldn't want to have missed those crazy days for nothing."

"Talking about doing crazy things, who is Ruth?" Cody asked with a sly grin.

"I would say she's a real good friend and runs my household perfectly. Probably keeps me in good shape, too, but after two costly divorces, you would have to hold a loaded Winchester to my head to convince me to step into a third marriage."

Cody roared with laughter. *Oh, man, how good it feels to laugh out loud. I'm here less than half an hour and already feel much better.*

The entry area of the house seemed even bigger inside than it appeared from the outside. To the right and left of the hallway, doors led to different rooms, but Gary walked straight ahead to a beautifully carved double door made of polished oak.

Cody stood flabbergasted in the doorway and stared into the huge room, a tastefully decorated combination dining and living room. An imposing open fireplace on the opposite wall dominated the space. To his left, a round dining table constructed from the polished cross-section of an ancient tree trunk with hand-smithed metal legs invited guests to sit. He caressed the smooth surface of the table. He had always loved massive wood furniture that spoke of old carpentry craftsmanship.

Ten sturdy wooden chairs of Mexican design with polished brass fittings and carved geometric patterns added to the comfortable dining arrangement. A massive three-level chandelier fashioned from deer antlers hung above the table. The interior of the room appeared costly and elegant but nevertheless cozy. *Looks like Gary made good money since he left Dad's ranch*, Cody thought.

Bookshelves covered the right wall, and two rocking chairs stood in front of the fireplace with a low table between them.

"I see you still love to read a good book once in a while," Cody said, pointing to the bookshelves. It was an extensive private library. Cody shared Gary's passion for reading. He remembered many conversations when they'd discussed books they had enjoyed and suggested books to each other.

"Son, you know me. I have always preferred a good book to watching one of them senseless TV programs. By the way, my entire staff enjoys their meals together in this room, and my library is open to all my employees. You can borrow a book anytime you like. This ranch carries the family spirit, you know."

"Speaking of the crew, how many men work for you, Gary?"

"At present, we are nine people. Three of the boys take care of the livestock here on the ranch. Another three are on a cattle drive at present. I expect them to be back with all the cattle in about a week. Then, there is Takoda, an elder Lakota Indian. He is responsible for all the ranch vehicles, saddles, and bits, and does smaller repair jobs around the property. I call him my indispensable Jack of all trades. He's a quiet fellow, but I really like him. Sometimes we sit together at a campfire, and he tells me the old legends of his tribe, and many of them provide considerable food for thought. He is quite a storyteller and sleeps in a traditional teepee on my property. I can understand why he prefers it to the old shabby trailer on the reservation. The folks there face a truckload full of hardship."

Gary walked to the table and pulled back a chair for Cody, who removed his hat and sat. Gary took the coffeepot, filled one of the mugs standing next to it, and handed it to his young friend.

"And then there is Ruth, my housekeeper. She is a wonderful cook, the best you can imagine, and she spoils us rotten, but don't you dare step into the house wearing dirty cowboy boots right after she's cleaned it. Then she turns into one of those fierce Texas tornadoes," Gary added with a chuckle, but his sparkling eyes sent a clear message that he cared very much for the lady, likely more than he would ever admit to anybody, including himself.

Cody took a sip of coffee and set down the mug with a thump. "Okay, I admit I didn't expect your property and your crew to be so big. But it looks like you have enough help, and I'm wondering why you need me here?"

Gary passed the brown sugar to his guest, and Cody smiled. "You haven't forgotten anything, have you? If you truly care for your friends, you should know what they like. That includes the way they prefer to drink their coffee or their favorite meal." The old cowboy answered humbly and cut a piece of the pie, the filling bulging under the knife. He placed it on a plate and pushed it over to Cody.

The former rodeo champion took a sip of the strong coffee and shoved a piece of the pecan pie into his mouth. His eyes sparkled, and he smiled as he chewed.

Gary laughed out loud. "I told you Ruth is a fantastic cook."

As both men enjoyed the sweet treat, the only sound in the room was the clattering of the forks on their plates. Finally, Gary pushed his empty dish away and held the coffee mug between his hands. He watched his friend for a few moments without saying a word.

Cody knew he couldn't avoid answering Gary's questions. He wanted to talk about everything that had gone wrong since they parted ways three years ago. Until now, he had bottled all his sorrow inside of him and often had the feeling that he was close to choking to death on the bitterness and trouble he endured without sharing them with anyone. It was a heavy burden to bear.

"Do you want to talk about it?" Gary asked.

"I think so, but I must admit it won't be easy for me to open up. I simply don't know where to start. So much has happened. So much went wrong."

Gary nodded and refilled their coffee in silence. He sat and waited, giving Cody time to think about his words.

Cody stared into his coffee mug, the corners of his mouth turned down, and his cheeks blushed with the rising shame he felt. After several minutes, the younger man spilled what bothered him the most. His feelings poured out of him. "I lost Father's ranch, Gary. The bank had their boot on my neck after all the countless hospital bills for my injury. I wasn't able to work for months, and I couldn't pay the bills. I felt as if I was paralyzed, and my entire life crumpled like a house made of poker cards. What was worse, I used my injuries as an excuse for my downfall, but now I know that there were many signs that my life had started to take a wrong turn long before I got out of the hospital. I was too ignorant and too stubborn to listen to people and to read those signs. I should have known better, Gary. Things got out of control long before that one deadly ride." He took a sip of the coffee and cleared his throat.

Gary granted Cody all the time he needed to gather his thoughts. The man had always been a good listener.

"And then one day, Pa and I got into a terrible fight over the mess my life turned into. He called me a failure. That hurt me terribly, and I lashed out at him like I had never done before. I yelled at him, 'Who the heck do you think you are?' I asked him what he achieved except for that little bitty ranch that hardly kept us fed. I left home that evening, and four days later, I got a call from a nurse at the hospital saying that my father had a serious heart attack and that he was in a coma. I rushed to the hospital immediately, but I barely reached the intensive care unit before he died. I never knew he had a serious health condition, and for Christ's sake, I didn't expect him to die. I mean, Dad was always strong like an oak, right? We never had the chance to talk things over. Mom said he never regained consciousness after he dropped to the floor in the living room. When she found him, he held a picture of me at the Prescott rodeo in his hand. The first one I won, remember?"

Gary nodded and patted his friend's hand.

Cody shook his head and rubbed his hands over his face. "I still feel guilty for not being able to apologize to him. Likely my yelling at him even killed him. We separated after that nasty fight without exchanging another word, Gary. Father would turn in his grave if he knew that I lost the property to a bank foreclosure."

Cody's former mentor shook his head slowly. "I know the days when everything seems dark and hopeless only too well. Unfortunately, us humans tend to forget the beautiful moments as soon as we face difficulties in life. But those beautiful moments give us hope and strength to march forward."

Cody scoffed. "What beautiful moments?"

"See, that's exactly what I mean. Well, as an example, the fact that you survived to leave the hospital. That honker almost threw you six feet under. That beast tried to stomp you right into your grave, my friend, but you're alive, and you're not in a wheelchair. Sometimes we have to hit rock bottom to realize how good it feels to get up again on your feet." Gary turned his mug between his hands as if he had to think carefully about which words to use next. "It's sure tragic to lose the property, but there's so much more to life than material things. Have you ever thought about the fact that certain things had to happen the way they did to give you the chance to find your true purpose in life? You may not have realized it yet, but God might have a completely different plan for you."

Confused, Cody stared at Gary. "What are you trying to say?"

"If you had stayed at your parents' place, those surroundings would have reminded you every single day that nothing would ever be the same as it was the day before that rodeo in Cheyenne. You would have likely blamed yourself for your father's death for the rest of your life, and not only that, but you would also have remained depressed about the failure of your marriage. You wouldn't have a chance to heal if you remained there, that's for sure."

Cody opened his eyes wide in surprise.

"Oh, yes, my friend," said Gary. "I heard the rumors that she left you. I don't have the right to judge your marriage or whose fault the divorce was. It doesn't matter who is to blame for it because it needs two people to make a relationship work, and it takes two people to make it fail. Sadly, I can speak from firsthand experience. The most important fact is that you've been given the chance to start over, and this time you're not going to start from square one because you have experience. You're stronger than ever before, even if you don't believe it yet."

Cody swallowed hard, and tears misted his eyes. He had never seen it from this point of view. If Gary was right, he would have a chance to create a new and hopefully better life. "You never liked Lynn, did you?"

Gary shrugged his shoulders. "I would rather say I never trusted her. There was something in her eyes that worried me from the start. My gut feeling told me to remain skeptical about her. To be honest with you, I don't think she's a decent human being. I've known women like her. Her kind has ruined more than one of my close friends."

"I understand. You're probably right."

"It seems you have wounds that haven't healed yet. I advise you to take your time. You just arrived here. Get used to the ranch and our people first, and as soon as you feel like you want to talk about what happened in Cheyenne, I'll be here for you. Talking about these things helps to let them go, and one must be prepared to do so. By the way, nobody here knows how successful you once were as a saddle bronc rider. I'll leave it up to you who you tell about it or when. This way you're not under pressure, and you don't have to prove yourself to anybody."

SIX
Lightning the Stallion

A FTER ANOTHER CUP of coffee, Gary stood, and Cody followed his example.

"Come on, boy, I'll show you this place and your accommodations."

As they left the house through the back door, Cody surveyed the property. Countless corrals stretched toward the nearby hills behind the main house. He saw numerous horses grazing and colts kicking up their heels.

An Appaloosa gelding bobbed his head as he saw Gary and walked toward the fence. The rancher laughed and scratched him behind the ears. Two chestnut mares in a nearby corner snorted and trotted toward the two men. They turned their heads as they eyed Cody.

"May I introduce you to Hank, our Appaloosa, and these two curious ladies are Maya and Honeybee."

Cody reached out his hand. "Honeybee?"

"Yes because she is always looking for treats. If you have an apple, a carrot, or heaven help you, a cookie in your pocket, you won't be able to escape her."

As if the mare understood every word the man spoke, Honeybee nibbled at Cody's denim jacket, searching for food. Both men laughed.

"You still haven't told me why you need my help," remarked Cody.

Gary pointed to a pasture in the distance. There, a chocolate-colored stallion enjoyed the late afternoon sun, sniffing the colorful wildflowers around him. No other horses shared his pasture. He lifted his head and pointed his ears toward the two men as if listening to their conversation. The magnificent animal seemed to be aware that Gary was talking about him.

The stallion trotted closer to the nearest fence, making it easier for Cody to see him. Muscles rippled beneath the shiny coat of his chest. His thick mane bristled between his ears and fell in long waves over his finely arched neck. His dark tail almost touched the ground.

"I'll be darned. Now who is that beautiful feller back there?" Cody wanted to know.

Gary watched the stallion but remained silent. They walked toward the pasture together. He spoke softly when he answered Cody's question. "This, my dear friend, is a wounded soul just like you. He's one of the two reasons why I invited you to come here."

Puzzled, Cody waited for an explanation. As Gary took measured steps toward the fence, the horse watched him from a distance. Unlike the other three horses, which had been curious and trusting, the stallion remained where he was, keeping a distance between himself and the two men.

When the friends were only a few steps from the fence that separated them from the stallion, the beautiful animal scraped the ground with his right front hoof. He tossed his head, seeming nervous about Gary and Cody approaching his territory.

"He isn't very welcoming to visitors, is he?" Cody remarked. His experience as a horseman told him of the stallion's distrust.

Gary nodded. "Unfortunately, he has no reason to trust human beings because they've treated him badly. This magnificent boy's name used to be Fury Bullet Jack. I changed his name to Lightning because he can run as fast as lightning. I bought him off a rancher who treated him very poorly. I caught him beating the poor thing at one of the rodeos. The only thing that poor creature did wrong was to resist the torture he faced on a daily basis. People call me a sentimental fool because so far this stallion has cost me more money than any other animal on this ranch. But I gotta tell you, there's something in his eyes that makes me believe Lightning can do so much more than anybody thinks." His voice trailed off. "Anyway, no human being has the right to mistreat such a beautiful creature."

Cody watched the gorgeous animal but didn't answer.

Gary put his hand on the top of the split rail fence. "Unfortunately, he hasn't allowed any man to come close, let alone permit a rider on his back."

Lightning turned his gaze toward Cody. He snorted and raised his head, showing the white of his eye. Then, he pivoted and trotted away from the two intruders. As he turned his right flank toward the two ranchers, Cody had a clear view of it and gasped, shocked by what he saw. A pattern of countless scars across ribs and croup told a story of prolonged cruelty.

Gary shrugged his shoulders in a helpless gesture. Cody understood immediately why Gary rescued the animal from his former owner. He knew Gary had a soft spot for suffering horses. He rescued more than one in his long career as cowboy. He believed in treating them right and that they returned a lot to their owners if only the owner treated them with kindness and respect.

"The man who owned Lightning before carries the nickname Bullwhip Bill for good reason. This monster beat more than one horse to death, and he has the worst reputation in this state's horse breeding business. He is a giant of a man with Scandinavian roots. His real name is William Johansson. People fear him as much as his animals do. There are frequent rumors that he beats his wife even worse than his horses. He is a brutal jerk." Gary kicked the fence pole. "Lightning was a promising rodeo horse, but when he failed to achieve full points a couple of times in a row, Bullwhip tortured him more and more. I bet it was the fault of the wannabe cowboy on his back. One day the poor animal was loaded streaming with blood into the livestock transport."

Gary pushed his hands into his pockets and watched the stallion. "I walked up to that brutal idiot and offered him five hundred dollars for the horse. He laughed at me wondering what I wanted with a useless stallion. Then he tried to raise the price, but it takes much more to pull a trick on me, as you know. Story short, I ended up loading Lightning into my trailer at the end of the day. I knew this horse didn't deserve that kind of treatment and had the feeling that Lightning could be a successful roping champion if the right owner and rider got hold of him."

Lightning stood at the other side of the pasture, seeming to listen. His huge dark eyes blinked as he glanced from one man to the other. The stallion's eyes reminded Cody of deep, dark lakes. The fear and pain in them saddened him deeply. He swallowed hard and shook his head. With his arms resting on the fence pole, Cody watched the animal closely.

"If one person can gain his trust, it's you. I believe that you two can help each other. It will take a lot of patience, just like in your life, my friend. Patience is what you both need. Trust is the one thing which you both have to learn all over again." He patted Cody encouragingly on his broad shoulder. "The second reason I invited you here is to give you a chance to heal and return to the rodeo circuit if your body can take it. I have rarely seen such a talent as you, and I advise you not to give up on it too early."

Cody shook his head. "Listen Gary, I...."

But Gary held up his hand. "I know it'll take time, and maybe you'll never ride in an arena again. Maybe you should keep an open mind on the matter. It has been your big dream your whole life."

Cody gazed at his boots, his face pale.

Gary touched his shoulder. "Cody, all I'm saying is to listen to your inner self. Maybe the dream has really died, and you need to move on to the next thing. But maybe that old flame is still alive somewhere deep inside of you. If that is the case, you shouldn't betray your dream, or you'll regret it one day. Believe an old cowboy who's been down that road."

Cody nodded. "I'll think about it but not right now."

"Come on, let me show you where you'll be staying. I'm sure you're tired from the long drive."

They left the corrals and pastures behind. Gary walked toward the three log cabins between the towering ponderosa pines. Cody had seen

the cabins nestling in the woods upon his arrival, but his friend walked
past them toward a smaller cabin which Cody hadn't noticed before.

SEVEN
A New Temporary Home

THE PICTURESQUE CABIN hid behind the larger longhouses. Its smaller footprint suggested a compact living space. A sturdy rock chimney dominated the rear of the log structure. A craftsman-style rocking chair stood on the porch. The sun had bleached the logs of the cabin to a silvery shade, emphasizing the grains in the wood. White curtains with a crocheted trim fluttered in the open windows. The charming log cabin resembled a movie set from *The Little House on the Prairie* television series.

Gary unlocked the door and motioned him to step in. To Cody's surprise, the cabin appeared roomier inside than he expected. To his left, he found a kitchenette with a sink, coffee maker, and microwave. The refrigerator had been integrated into the corner so cleverly that Cody didn't notice it at first.

The highly polished oak floor was the same color as honey. The hand-laid planks formed a pleasing chevron design from the kitchenette into the main room. The wood creaked slightly when Cody walked from one side to the other. It was a cozy sound, as if the cabin welcomed him home.

Two rugs with Native American patterns in warm shades of red lay before the river-stone fireplace. A comfortable-looking leather armchair invited him to sit. A pile of firewood waited beside the hearth. Next to the fireplace, a rough-hewn door offered a view into a bathroom. It contained an old-fashioned copper sink, a toilet, and a glass shower enclosure with a rain shower head. Cody stood in awe. He hadn't expected to have his own bathroom, let alone a rain shower head.

His gaze followed a narrow staircase, which led from the kitchenette up to a loft under the roof of the cabin. There he discovered a bed constructed with cedar wood poles. The loft and platform for the mattress had been crafted from sturdy cedar beams.

Gary's head appeared at the top of the stairs. "I hope this staircase doesn't cause you any difficulty. We had to build it steeper than usual, or the stairs would have ended in the middle of the cabin. Although this place is smaller than the other bunkhouses, it offers privacy. I thought you might feel more comfortable keeping to yourself, at least until you get used to the crew. This little log cabin is older than the other ones, so it has no TV hook-up, but you have your own bathroom and a fireplace. This place is quieter than the other bunks as well. The guys can get rowdy from time to time—like all ranch hands. But I'm sure you know that as a former rodeo champion."

Cody stood under the peaked roof of the cabin and turned in a circle. "This place is very cozy. I love it. It's definitely big enough for me, and I don't need a TV anyway. You know I prefer a good book to the nonsense produced by Hollywood these days. I guess we still have that in common. I'm totally thrilled about the fireplace, and I even have a little kitchen to myself. That is way more than I expected. I don't know how to thank you."

Gary waved away Cody's protests. "You know how hard ranch work is. You're not getting anything for free. Now get your luggage and settle in. I placed a few things in your fridge. If you need anything else, let me know. We eat dinner at seven o'clock, which means you have another hour and a half. We meet in the same room where we had coffee."

Both men left the cabin. While Gary strode to the main house, Cody walked back to his pickup and drove it around the main building toward his new accommodation. He carried his luggage and the saddle inside and unpacked his few belongings. He could hardly believe he was here, and that he had a job. The acceptance Gary showed him melted his heart.

At seven o'clock sharp, Cody entered the dining room in the main house. The three other ranch hands who took care of the livestock waited at the table with Gary. They greeted him in a friendly manner and welcomed him warmly. Cody didn't tell them that he once was a successful and famous rodeo champion. His successes were all behind him, and he would look like a fool bragging about days gone by.

Each young man shared a little of his life story and how he had come to work at the G.B. Ranch. Cody explained that he had known Gary back in Arizona when he was a kid on his father's ranch.

Cody turned to Gary. "I was hoping to meet Ruth and Takoda this evening."

Gary accepted a half-empty serving bowl of mashed potatoes and spooned some onto his plate. "Tuesday is Ruth's day for Girl's Night Out.

She went to Dillon to... well, I don't really know what she does with her girlfriends. The tribe called Takoda away to preside over a traditional ceremony. You'll meet both of them tomorrow."

After a hearty dinner, the others withdrew early. All of them seemed tired from the daily chores. Cody suppressed a yawn. The long drive had exhausted him, and he was looking forward to resting and being alone. The bed crafted from cedar had looked very tempting before he came for dinner. Cody wished Gary a good night.

After a hot shower, he crawled into the bed in the attic of his cabin. He covered his body to the waist with the handmade quilt. To his right, the moon shone through the round window under the gable. The silvery rays of pale moonlight emphasized Cody's abs. Lying on his back, he fell asleep.

EIGHT
The Nightmares

THE DEAFENING NOISE of the people on the upper seats in the rodeo arena made it difficult for the announcer to make himself understood despite his microphone and the modern sound system. Cody's best friend, Tanner, just finished an eighty-four-point ride, and the audience was going wild. This weekend's competition was super important—whoever won his or her category in this rodeo would increase the chances for a ticket to the finals in Las Vegas.

Tanner was a crazy fellow, and he became better and better with each passing rodeo. However, Cody never saw him as a competitor. Indeed, he was proud of Tanner. The daredevil was like a brother to Cody, and they supported each other whenever necessary.

The two guys grew up together because Tanner's and Cody's parents had been neighbors. Both boys used every free minute to play and practice together, so it came as no surprise that they joined the rodeo circuit in the same month. They taught each other a lot and helped each other at every competition. They even traveled in the same trailer for a time to save costs, but that changed when Lynn walked into Cody's life.

The announcer was about to call his name, and it was Cody's turn to prove his skill to the judges and the crowd. He had already climbed over the gate and sat on the horse's back. The chestnut mare pushed against the chute, trying to pin his leg to prevent him from getting his spurs into position. This one obviously knew the game well and challenged Cody even before the gate of the chute opened.

Cody chuckled softly, which the mare answered by pulling back her ears. "You won't make it easy for me, I can sure as hell feel that."

As if to answer, she leaned heavier to the side of the chute, and for a moment it felt as if she wanted to squeeze his leg through the metal. Two of the rodeo crew members pushed her back to the middle and helped him to free his leg. The mare twitched her ears back and rolled her eyes, trying to look behind her to see the daring interloper. She snorted repeatedly, showed her teeth, and tried to snap at him. Try as she might, she couldn't turn her head far enough to reach his legs. If she could have, she would have taken a chunk out of him. As if frustrated, she bucked slightly, but fortunately space in the chute was limited.

Cody quickly reset his hold. He was ready for the challenge. "Well, girl, let's see who has the more determined spirit."

The speaker announced his name, and the audience applauded.

Cody didn't pay attention to it. He concentrated on the horse below him and clasped his hand around the rope. "Let's go, Jumping Jack Flash." Then, he pushed his boots into the stirrups.

The air smelled of sweat and dust, and the constant roar of the crowd filled the arena. Heat and glare from flood lights shone down on him from all directions. Cody felt the vibrations of the horse's snorting on his inner thigh and an increasing heat. If it came from the mare's body or himself getting sweaty, he couldn't tell. Cody looked for the horsehair he had used to mark the ideal length of the reins. If he kept the reins too short, she would simply jerk him over her head, sending him flying into the arena's soil. Nevertheless, he had to keep the reins short enough to pull back on them to grant him some balance. The exact length of the rein was crucial if one wanted to stay on the bucking horse long enough to make points. Once he got a firm grip, his attention closed in, and everything that was happening around him ceased to exist. The next few seconds were only about him and the mare.

Cody took a few deep, slow breaths. When he was ready, he gave the signal to open the gate. The mare shot out of the chute like a bullet from a gun, bucking and kicking. She jumped so high off the ground, she appeared to have springs under her hooves. Cody's task was to stay on the bronc for eight seconds. Hardly anyone in the audience could imagine how long those few seconds became with an enraged half-ton of horsemeat under them.

Cody's teeth rattled, and he felt shaken like he'd been in an earthquake. Relief washed through him when he heard the signal, and another rider galloped toward him to pull him off the bucking horse. Jumping Jack Flash had performed in a manner suitable for her name.

Cody landed firmly in the dirt of the arena floor, laughing, and waving with his hat to the audience. He knew it was a good ride and probably got him a high score. He looked around, searching for his wife Lynn. He wanted to see if she was as proud as he was, but she was nowhere around. Disappointed, he turned toward the exit.

The announcer read off his score—ninety-two points. He raised his fist and shook it in the air triumphantly. Then, he left the arena to look for his wife.

Cody opened his eyes. Another dream. He was relieved he woke up before the dream became unpleasant this time, before the same painful pictures of the past replayed themselves over and over. He turned his head to gaze out the round window. At first, he was confused about where he was. Seeing the first gleam of daylight through the window told him the sun was about to come up. He noticed the warm, colorful quilt and remembered he was at his friend's ranch. His first day as a ranch hand for Gary Bradshaw awaited him.

He swung his legs over the frame of the bed, stretched, and turned on the bronze light on the nightstand. He pulled on his faded jeans, slowly descended the steep stairs, and stepped into the bathroom. After refreshing himself, he walked over to the coffeemaker and scooped three soup spoons of the ground beans into the filter, added water, and flicked the switch. The gurgling sound of the brewing beverage drowned out the slapping sound of his bare feet on the wood floor.

He checked his watch—5:20 a.m. He grabbed his warm lumberjack shirt. Carrying the steaming coffee pot and a mug, he walked outside on the porch and sat in the rocking chair. Cody studied the thin orange line of first daylight atop the nearby hills. The sky grew more golden as a magnificent sunrise approached.

He sipped his coffee while marveling at the rich aroma and watched the natural wonder. It was the first time in months that he enjoyed the sunrise. *Maybe it was the right decision to come here*, he thought. Yet it was too early to judge if it was better for him to be here in Montana, or if he should have stayed in New Mexico. In any case, Cody felt a spark of hope after almost two years of darkness in his life.

It was close to six o'clock when he walked to the main building and stepped into the dining room. Gary and his crew members sat together, enjoying their breakfast. The mouthwatering smell of scrambled eggs and bacon filled the air, and Cody's stomach growled.

A woman in her early sixties stepped out of the kitchen. A fancy pair of jeans with a monogram stitched on the back pocket emphasized her trim figure. She put a plate in front of Cody, shook his hand, and said, "Good morning, Cowboy. I'm Ruth. Give me five minutes, and I'll bring you a pot of fresh coffee. Knowing my boys here, I'm pretty sure that the other one is already empty."

"Thank you so much, ma'am. That's very kind of you."

"Forget about the ma'am. We don't care much about formalities here at G.B. Ranch."

Cody smiled at her and nodded. He liked her right away. Ruth seemed to have an outgoing personality and appeared to be straightforward. Her easy-going ways created a welcoming atmosphere. It was plain to see why Gary seemed to have a crush on her.

While he gobbled down his eggs, Gary turned toward Cody. "I hope you slept well. Is anything missing in your cabin?"

"No, I have everything I need, and yes, I slept well, thank you."

Gary watched his friend for a moment without speaking. Despite his friend's words, the dark shadows under his eyes told a different story.

Gary had noticed them the previous day, and his friend didn't look any better today, but Gary was too discreet to dig for an answer in front of the other staff members.

"Cody, I would like to team you up with Takoda today. It's about time to check over and inventory the riding gear in the tack room. Some saddles and bridles suffered during the cattle drives this spring and summer. I'm pretty sure that some of the gear needs repairing or needs to be replaced. I'll give you a notepad and some pens so you can jot down how many new saddles, bridles, and bits we have to buy. I'm afraid that some stuff can't be fixed anymore, and we will likely have to invest a chunk of cash. Since you know best about riding gear, I'd be grateful if you could do an inventory for me."

"Where will I find Takoda?"

"He's waiting in front of the tack room. He's an early bird and welcomes each new day with traditional Lakota prayers right at sunrise."

"In that case, I better hurry up." Cody swallowed the rest of his coffee.

Ruth came around the corner, notepad and pen in her hand.

Gary smiled at her warmly. "As always, you have foreseen what we need, my precious pearl."

Her cheeky grin gave her a youthful look.

NINE
Takoda

CODY WALKED OVER to the shed next to the corrals where an older Native American man waited for him. He wore his long, gray hair in two braids which hung over his shoulders. His faded jeans were torn above the right knee. His red and yellow plaid shirt had seen better days, too. The countless wrinkles in his deeply tanned face told a story of a turbulent life, yet he still had the aura of his proud ancestors about him.

"Good morning. You must be Cody." He spoke softly with a trace of an accent, but his voice sounded warm and pleasant.

"That's right. Are you Mister Takoda?"

"That is correct, but leave out the *Mister*. The members of my tribe call me Grandfather, but I prefer Takoda. I feel the many summers of my life in every bone of my body and don't need to be reminded of my age by being called Grandfather," he said with a chuckle.

Cody laughed softly. He liked the Lakota man immediately.

"Come on, let's get started. I'll show you our treasures waiting in the building behind us. Some saddles look as if they were ridden before the Battle of the Greasy Grass."

At first, his remark puzzled Cody, and he didn't know how to answer. After studying the face of the old Lakota man, he noticed the corners of Takoda's lips twitching as he struggled to keep from laughing. Cody noticed a mischievous sparkle in the elder's dark eyes. Clearly, Takoda had a dark sense of humor.

The two men busied themselves with cleaning saddles, polishing dry leather with saddle butter, and sorting damaged bridles and bits. Cody listened carefully to what Takoda said about life on the reservation. He was cautious about his remarks because he knew the past of the Lakota Indians was a difficult topic to talk about. He didn't want to step on the elder man's toes by saying something foolish.

Cody was indeed interested in getting to know how the members of the tribe lived nowadays, and how much of their rich culture the younger generations were learning. "Takoda, I hope I'm not out of line. Before this, I haven't heard a Native American talk so openly about his tribe and the difficulties they face."

The man looked him straight in the eyes and answered without hesitation. "When you work for a man like Gary Bradshaw, you don't have to pretend to be someone else. You can speak about all the things that bother you. You can openly say things that you would rather keep to yourself in a different place. Your friend Gary has treated me well from the start, and he has always shown a lot of respect for our culture. I do believe that one can only expect understanding when the person you are talking to knows how you feel inside."

Takoda remained silent for a moment as he carried a cleaned saddle back to the shelf. He turned around, rested his callused hands on his slim hips, and studied Cody's face. "I admit it's always been difficult to talk with white people, especially about the things that happened to my ancestors. It's hard to accept the wrongdoings against my culture. You wouldn't believe how I was treated in school or as a young man. We are outcasts to many, even today. I always think twice before I share information and stories about the old ones." He chuckled. "To be honest, I wouldn't talk with every red brother I meet either. A few of them are as responsible for the downfall of the Lakota culture as certain white people are. Some of us shamed our own heritage in those days, and some still do it nowadays. The government oppresses us along with racists, but sadly, I have to admit that many Lakota repress each other as well. Each nation has black sheep, right?"

He turned around, grabbed the next saddle, and carried it to the work bench. He dipped his sponge into the bucket of warm water and continued to speak as he worked. "I got the impression that your heart is in the right place, otherwise Gary wouldn't have invited you to move here. That's the reason why I speak so openly with you. Once we were a proud people, but much of our culture and traditions have been lost forever. Sometimes my friends ask me if I wished myself back in the glory days of the brave warriors. I admit that I often do. But on other days, I'm not so sure about it. I don't want to miss the comforts and amenities we enjoy today. Everything I need is here at the ranch. I'm not rich, but other than the old ones, I don't have anything to fear. What I really wish for is the opportunity to meet some of our great leaders and chiefs in person and listen to their wisdom. They were brave and wise men. I'm pretty sure that they would feel ashamed if they saw what became of their people. Their hearts would be saddened to recognize that their crusade for freedom was in vain."

Cody checked a bridle. *It must be terrible to live a life torn between two cultures with a devastating past and a difficult present.* It flashed into his mind that he was in a similar situation. Just like Takoda's people, his nightmares caused him to re-experience the horrors of the past, yet his future was uncertain. Similar to many people living on the reservation, he didn't know how long he would have a paying job. He trusted his friend and employer, Gary Bradshaw, but how long could he rely on his body to be strong enough for the challenging ranch work in a state with harsh winters?

Cody's traumatic experiences were nothing compared to those the Lakota had endured through the last two centuries, but still, just like them, he needed to let go of a traumatic past so he could move into a rewarding future. Just like Takoda's tribal members, Cody didn't dare believe in a better tomorrow... not yet.

He glanced at the elder man and spoke no further. With their silence, they had a mutual understanding, and Cody found comfort in the presence of the Lakota elder. *If, against all odds, he can be positive about his life, I might be able to do the same someday soon.*

The older man silently studied Cody across the worktable. Cody felt as if the Lakota was capable of seeing straight into his soul.

"Looks like I'm not the only one who faced a painful past. Maybe you will tell me about it someday when we know each other better."

Cody stared at the older man, confused about how Takoda knew so much about him. Was it so easy to read him, or had Gary told Takoda what happened to him?

The older man resumed rubbing saddle butter into the well-tooled saddle in front of him. "Back to your question about what life is like on the reservation. There are plenty of reasons why I prefer to live in a teepee here on this property. On the rez, we have huge problems with poverty, alcoholism, and violence among our people. The suicide rate among many tribes is tremendously high, but in my opinion, the Lakota and Dakota tribes suffer the most. One of the reasons might be the fact that we once were very proud people. To a certain degree, we still are, and that makes it even more difficult for us to adapt to the modern world. For over one and a half centuries, the government has tried everything to break our will, and sadly, they succeeded. Many men beat their women, either because they're frustrated or drunk, most times both. In the old days, we had a lot of respect for women, as they were the backbone of a strong tribe. To make it worse, a lot of young girls disappear without a trace. Some are found brutally murdered, but the white man's legal system isn't interested in solving those crimes."

Cody watched Takoda skillfully cleaning the saddle. After removing the dirt, he polished it using a rag soaked with saddle butter that smelled of beeswax.

"A lot of our men are involved in deadly accidents. They try to hitchhike when they're drunk and are often run over on the highway. They never come home. Our educational system is lousy, and the young ones don't have much of a chance to get a good-paying job or to go to college unless they're as ambitious as my niece, Winona." Takoda laughed softly, turned to Cody, and smiled. "I nicknamed her *Little Sitting Bull* because she is such a fierce fighter. Winona has achieved a lot in life, but it sure made her tough. Things have never been easy for her, and I'm dang proud of her. She's a true Lakota. The meaning of her name in our language is 'First Daughter.'"

"And your name?" Cody wanted to know.

Takoda smiled. "'Friend to Everyone.'"

Cody laughed out loud. "I sure believe that." He gazed out of the window across the pastures. He was astonished to see the sun sinking behind the hills in the west.

Takoda followed Cody's gaze and nodded. "Time to call it a day. We have done a lot, and I'm sure the boss man will be satisfied." Cody was about to leave the tack room, but Takoda stopped him, his expression serious. "I want to warn you about one man in the crew. His name is Stacey Foster. He brags that his father was a full-blooded Kiowa. He's a good rider but a bad human being. You cannot trust him. He's like a rattlesnake. Stacey thinks he's the boss on this ranch and behaves according to this illusion. Beware of him, he is dangerous. None of us like him. At the moment, he's leading the cattle drive, but when he comes back and sees Gary has hired somebody who might take his place, he'll cause trouble for sure."

"Thank you, Takoda. I appreciate your advice. I just want peace and have no intention of taking anybody's position. It's good to be forewarned. I'll definitely watch out."

The older man slapped Cody on the shoulder, and together they walked over to the main house to wash up and eat their dinner with the other men.

TEN

Time for Confessions

THE REST OF the week went by quickly as Cody settled in at G.B. Ranch. Being able to work again made him feel worthy. He hadn't realized how much he missed the smell of hay and horses around him until he experienced it again at Gary's place.

With the weekend just around the corner, Gary invited Cody to go on a ride with him to the western border of his property. Gary claimed he wanted to check the fences there, but Cody knew better and assumed Gary wanted to talk with him about the events in Cheyenne. He didn't mind. Sooner or later, Gary would know the truth.

Cody checked the cinches of the two geldings he selected for the ride when Gary entered the barn.

He grinned mischievously and pointed to the two well-used saddlebags he carried over each shoulder. "Ruth packed us some tasty provisions. I'm sure we'll be gone most of the day, and it doesn't hurt to carry a delicious lunch parcel along. Nothing better than spending a relaxed day riding and enjoying a decent meal at the campfire, right my friend?"

Cody smiled and tied his canteen to the saddle horn. "Amen to that."

He looked forward to the ride. When he got back home after spending weeks in the hospital, he had difficulty getting back in the saddle at first. His serious accident left him fearful of riding, but time had cured both the psychological and the physical wound. Now he enjoyed riding at a gallop through the fields, forests, and wildflowers. The sense of freedom and harmony with nature on the back of a horse was exhilarating, and he wouldn't want to miss out on it for anything. He felt fulfilled when his heart joined the rhythm of a horse's hooves and the wind smelled of freedom as it tousled his curls.

It was time to head west. They mounted and guided their horses through the gate, Gary leading the way. Both men remained silent for a few minutes, giving in to the wonderful feeling of being in balance with their horses and nature around them. The air was crisp and clear at this early hour. Although it was still late summer, they could feel a trace of fall on the breeze. Wisps of fog caught the sunlight, which turned the mist into a magical golden veil.

The country is so different here compared to Arizona where I grew up, Cody thought. He was glad he had decided on the warm lumberjack shirt and wondered if he might even need the sturdy canvas jacket he had tied to his saddle.

Gary was lucky to call this wonderful piece of land his own. Cody envied him for the green fields and the carpets of blooming wildflowers, which looked like colorful dots added by an artist. But after having known Gary for so many years, Cody was aware of how hard he must have worked for all this. Nevertheless, he couldn't help but wonder where Gary got the seed capital to buy the ranch in the first place. *That's none of my business*, he reflected.

Nevertheless, Cody continued to speculate. He knew Gary grew up in a poor family, but he might have inherited a nice amount of money after he left Cody's father's place in Payson. Somehow, he must have accumulated enough money to buy his ranch.

The two riders reached the western border of the property right around noon. They rode along the barbed-wire fences and checked if the poles were still solid and the wire unbroken. There were quite a few spots where they had to restring the fence using the pliers from Gary's saddlebag and the coiled wire he brought with him. It was tough work to pull the filaments together and splice them. Clearing enough soil to push the loose poles back into the solid ground gave the men more than one bleeding cut on their hands despite their sturdy leather gloves.

Gary stood up and wiped his forehead with his sleeve. "What is it about all the wildlife that they think they have to damage my fences every year? I have been riding and repairing fences my entire life. Last time I found a ten-point stag with his antlers caught in my fence. Sadly, it had died before I got there. Snapped its neck trying to escape."

After maintaining the last section of the fence, they chopped down a sapling to replace a rotten pole. They were finally done and rode toward a stand of aspen to take a well-deserved break. A merry creek gurgled beside some ponderosa pines. The two men dismounted and allowed the horses to graze.

Cody found rocks twice the size of his fist and arranged them in a circle. Gary brought the two saddlebags over, then searched under the trees for firewood. He didn't find more than an armful of branches, but it would be enough for a campfire so they could brew a pot of coffee.

Once the flames crackled, Gary filled the old, dented pot with water from the creek and added a handful of ground coffee beans. While it brewed, the two men sat and sorted through all the goodies Ruth had packed, exclaiming with delight at each discovery.

Cody took a hearty bite of his thick roast beef sandwich. The tangy flavor of mustard and pickles tickled his taste buds. "Mmm. That is exactly what I need now."

"Normally I would have brought a can of beer," Gary mumbled.

Cody remained silent and stared into the flames.

"Hey, there's no reason for a sad face. I actually like this Diet Coke stuff as much as you do, and coffee after lunch will sure taste good. I don't doubt that you got your former alcohol problem under control. I just don't want to make it unnecessarily hard for you."

Cody nodded without a word. He appreciated the thoughtfulness of his friend, but he still felt ashamed about his past as a drunk. "Were you ever scared in life, Gary? I mean so afraid that you had the feeling you couldn't breathe anymore?"

Gary thought about it for a moment. "To be honest, in all the years I worked as a cowboy, I have never been scared. I got bucked off countless times and fell in the dust of the arena or the hard-baked soil of a ranch. I broke so many bones, I quit counting them. I've experienced worries and sorrow, but fear? No, I never felt fear." He stared into the flames, remaining silent for a few heartbeats. His eyebrows came together, and he turned to look at Cody, who was stunned to see tears glistening in

Gary's eyes. "Thinking of it, that isn't entirely true. I was afraid a couple of months ago."

Cody was about to interrupt when Gary silenced him with a wave of his hand.

"I have to correct what I said because there *is* something I'm really scared of. I fear ending up in an old folks' home or in the hospital. Thinking that someday I might have to wear diapers and have a nurse feed me like a helpless child or be dependent on other people for the simplest things is a horrifying thought for me. I don't think I could stand that. I would rather put a gun to my head and pull the trigger than vegetate like that until I take my final breath."

Cody stared at his friend, shocked at his words. He felt the color drain from his face at the thought that Gary would consider suicide—but Cody understood what he meant. Thinking of Gary Bradshaw sitting in a nursing home, staring blankly out the same window with no hope for a better tomorrow, was something Cody couldn't picture either.

Gary's features softened. "You know, I have been watching you all these years, and I know you're an excellent rider. Up to this day I don't understand what happened in Cheyenne. I had the impression that you had that nag well under control. But you seemed confused and unfocused. I remember you looked pale as a ghost, and I wondered if you were sick. What really did happen that day, Cody?"

The younger man pressed his lips into a tight line. Then, he took another bite of his sandwich just for the sake of stalling before he had to answer. Cody collected his thoughts.

Gary didn't push him, but he felt that there was more to the events in Cheyenne than just the accident in the arena. He got up and poured them another cup of coffee, placing a jar of sugar between them. He waited patiently while stirring two spoons of the sweet treat into his steaming coffee.

The horses grazed nearby, snorting from time to time. They warded off the annoying flies with their tails. Gary always loved the *swish, swish* sound it created, and he smiled, obviously content living in the present moment while watching the two beautiful animals.

Cody dumped a spoonful of sugar into his coffee. He was lost in thought and stared into the flames of the campfire. *Well, guess it's about time to lay my cards on the table.* When he started to tell his tale, Cody spoke so softly that Gary had to lean in to make sure he understood what Cody said.

"At the beginning, the rodeo went well for me, at least on Friday. But Saturday everything changed in the blink of an eye, brutally and unexpectedly. Lynn was in a pissed-off mood the entire morning. She was looking for a fight and complained about everything. I couldn't do anything right in her eyes that particular day. Thinking back on it, that argument had started a few days earlier. You know how it is at the rodeo, Gary. One has so much work to do with the animals and the equipment, plus there is the stress of driving from one city to the next one. We were constantly on the road, and I worked my butt off to make it to the finals in Las Vegas. I guess Lynn felt neglected."

Cody shrugged his shoulders in a dismissive gesture. "You know her. Perfect makeup and the newest fashion were always more important to her than participating in the next barrel race. To be honest, I would have appreciated it if she had been a bit more ambitious. We could have used some extra prize money, but instead she preferred to spend my cash rather than earning her own."

Gary poked at the embers of the fire and added a few more branches. The two men watched the flames licking the new wood. "So, the two of you were fighting the day of the accident, were you?"

"I wouldn't call it a fight, but the atmosphere between us wasn't positive. I wanted to make up with her and went over to one of the trader's stalls. I bought a beautiful, handcrafted belt. The buckle was engraved and the belt itself adorned with horsehair stitching. I wanted to make her happy and take things back to the way they were before. I wanted the relationship to be like it was at the beginning when we were head over heels for each other. Hell, I mean, every man wants a relationship to be a blessing and not a lesson, right?"

Gary nodded. He knew the problems that occur in a marriage when the riders entered the rodeo circuit. They trained every spare minute and often neglected their families, spouses, or partners while battling for every point on the way to the finals. And those who loved them felt constant fear because of the financial risk and the danger involved in the sport.

"Didn't she appreciate your gift?" Gary wanted to know.

To his surprise, Cody scowled. "I returned to our trailer, hiding the bag holding the belt behind my back. I wanted to surprise her, but she wasn't there, so I took the gift with me because I wanted to give it to her personally and not leave it on the table."

Cody combed his fingers through his thick curls and seemed to be struggling to keep his emotions under control. "I had to get ready for my next ride, but on the way to the arena, I walked by Tanner's trailer. I wanted to congratulate him for his excellent ride and high score. As you know, he was my best friend, and I never saw him as a competitor. Good grief, I mean, he was like a brother to me."

Gary chuckled. "Oh, yes, you and Tanner were like twins and nearly inseparable." But then he noticed that tears dampened Cody's lashes. He stopped talking, anticipating what came next.

"We never cared about formalities, and I just walked into his trailer because his boots stood in front of the door, so I knew that he was inside. I wanted to tell him that he owed me a beer if I reached a higher score than his. When I saw him, I almost choked on the words. Tanner didn't notice me at first. My wife straddled his lap. She was buck naked, and judging from the way she moaned, he was giving her a lot of joy."

Cody wiped his eyes with the sleeve of his shirt. "I remember stumbling backward through the door and hearing Tanner cussing from inside. I'll never forget that image, Gary. They were screwing each other while I did my job, working hard for a better future less than a hundred yards away from them."

Gary stared into Cody's face and shook his head. "Almighty. I always had the feeling that she wasn't the right one for you. Lynn isn't the kind of woman one should consider getting old with—I realized that pretty quick. Probably a result of my own experiences with women. But the fact that your best friend betrayed your trust like that after all the years you knew each other is something I can hardly believe. I would never have thought Tanner to be such a villain. What in the world got into him? The wife of his best friend. Jesus, that's an absolute taboo, a no go by all means. Why didn't you call the two of them out right there at that very moment?"

"Would it have changed anything, Gary? They betrayed me, and even calling them out wouldn't have undone the betrayal. Even if we had talked about it, my trust doesn't come with a refill. I should have used that belt to whoop her behind. She deserved it. The only thing I remember is that I heard the announcer calling my name and my starting number, so I walked over to the arena. I handed over that dang belt to some volunteer of the organization and climbed onto that backbreaking mare. The only thing I felt was emptiness inside."

"So, you tried to ride that beast literally minutes after catching your wife messing around with Tanner?

"I know I should have canceled the ride because I couldn't concentrate. The first three or four seconds everything seemed fine, but instead of paying attention to the tricks of the horse under me, I couldn't get rid of the picture of my naked wife on top of my best friend."

Neither man spoke but stared into the fire.

Gary shook his head in a helpless gesture. Then, he whispered, "Now I understand a lot better."

Cody shrugged his shoulders. "My left boot got caught in the stirrup. I wasn't even aware of it, and when I realized my mistake, it was too late. That mean beast bucked me off, and I couldn't escape when she reared. I tried to roll to the side, but her left front hoof hit my side with full force. I remember the cracking sound when a bunch of ribs broke, and I couldn't breathe. Then, everything went black around me. That is the last thing I remember of that day in Cheyenne. God, I wished I had never been there."

"As far as I remember one of the broken ribs punctured your lung and it collapsed, so no wonder you couldn't breathe. According to your mother, your injuries were terrible. I spoke to your parents a couple of times while you were in the hospital. If I had known that your wife didn't support you during your rehab, I would have returned to your dad's ranch right away. I was convinced that she was by your side the entire time through surgeries and healing. If only I had known."

Cody scoffed. "She would have been a daisy if she did, but to tell you the truth, the two lovebirds disappeared the following morning right after my accident. I was in the hospital in intensive care. Some of my rodeo friends took care of my two horses and the trailer. Two of them drove everything back to our ranch. A week later, they finally spilled the beans that Tanner's trailer disappeared the morning after I landed in the dirt, and with him my beloved wife." He rubbed his thighs in frustration. "I assume neither one had enough backbone to look me in the eye or to find out if I was going to make it."

"Are you actually telling me that neither Lynn nor Tanner ever visited you in the hospital or during your recovery? You can't be serious." Gary stared into Cody's face, his eyes huge with disbelief.

His younger friend shook his head, and the gesture was answer enough. "After a few weeks, I was released and able to return home. The first thing that awaited me there were countless bills from the hospital and a thick envelope from a Las Vegas lawyer containing the divorce papers. The fine lady traveled to the finals with my best friend instead of with me. I'm pretty sure they must have laughed their heads off over dumb little Cody Ferguson, who would have trusted them both with his life." Cody's voice oozed bitter sarcasm, and his dark eyebrows drew together in an angry frown. His right hand clenched into a fist.

Gary patted the younger guy's shoulder. "Your marriage to that woman never would have been successful. Deep down, you know this is the truth. People say, 'It's better to have a shocking end than a never-ending shock.' I think that Tanner betrayed you worse than this little hussy ever could. Try to leave it behind you and march forward, son. The only thing you need to build a better life is passion, determination, and backbone. Oh, and not to forget, a really good friend you can trust, and you got that in me. I'll always have your back for the rest of my life."

Cody stretched his long legs and brushed the dust off his jeans. "Gary, I wasn't able to pay all those bills because I couldn't work for a long time. When my father passed away from the heart attack, I started to drown my pain and my disappointment in whiskey. I drank more than a sailor in a cheap bordello and made everything worse by doing so. I still feel ashamed about it and blame myself for Father's death because he died shortly after we had that terrible fight. I said some real mean things to him and hate myself for it. He deserved better, and I think I was a lousy son to him."

Gary jumped to his feet so abruptly that Cody jumped in surprise. "Boy, what did I teach you? No whining because it doesn't get you anywhere. Crying about things you can't change will not help you. Once and for all, you got to let go of this whole mess and build up your new life. Be grateful for the things you have. You learned your lesson, and next time you will do better. We have to burn our fingers, or otherwise we wouldn't understand that we are not supposed to touch the hot stove, right?"

Chastised, Cody got up as well and tossed the rest of his cold coffee into the fire, where it evaporated into a cloud of hissing steam. He helped Gary put all their things back into the saddlebags and patted the neck of his horse. He looked at his friend and smiled. "I reckon you're right. I should be grateful that I'm still alive. Thank you for listening. You're a true friend for life. I consider myself blessed to know you." He put his boot in the stirrup and pulled himself into the saddle.

Cody waited until Gary mounted, and they turned the horses to hit the trail back to the ranch. A gorgeous orange and golden sunset rewarded them with its God-created beauty.

Cody felt much better after sharing what happened in Cheyenne. If he had known how much weight would be lifted from his broken heart, he would have done it earlier. To do so, one needed the right listener, and Gary was exactly that. He wasn't a condemning kind of guy. Cody knew his friend was right. He would never be capable of building a better future and a new life if he didn't let go of the past. From the next day onward, that's what he planned to do.

ELEVEN
First Encounter with Lightning

THE FOLLOWING MORNING passed so quickly, Cody could hardly believe it was already time for lunch. He and Takoda finished cleaning up the tack room, and Cody completed his list of items that were worn out. Cody knew a saddle-maker based in Denver who would charge reasonable prices for repairs. He was thrilled his friend would be able to repair much of the minor damage and save Gary good money. Fewer saddles and bridles had to be replaced with new ones, washing away Gary's original worries.

"I'm going to call it a day a bit earlier," the Lakota elder remarked while wiping his hands. "A young girl's puberty ceremony starts today. It's time to welcome her into womanhood. This is a very special moment in the life of a Lakota woman, and we celebrate it with a traditional four-day ceremony. I lead the ritual in my role as the tribe's traditional medicine man. It is very important that our young ones don't forget their roots. I have hope that the more they know about our traditions, the more we can prevent them from choosing the road to Hell. My niece, Winona, will replace me here at the ranch for the next few days. She has worked for Gary before and doesn't shy away from hard work. I am sure you will get along well with *Little Sitting Bull*," Takoda said with a hearty laugh.

Cody nodded. He would love to attend such a ceremony. *I'll have to ask Takoda if it's possible to witness a traditional Lakota gathering someday. Maybe I'll have a chance to learn more about them and their culture.* Cody walked over to Gary's house after waving goodbye to his Native American friend.

Once he finished lunch, Cody walked over to the pasture, where the aggressive and unsocialized stallion named Lightning grazed in the warm afternoon sun. The magnificent animal threw his ears back and stepped away from the fence, putting more distance between him and the intruder walking toward the gate.

The horse's body language made it clear he wasn't thrilled about the former saddle-bronc rider's visit. Lightning snorted and scraped through the dirt with his right front hoof, but Cody didn't respond to his behavior. Instead, he placed an old wooden box in the corral, sat on top of it, and placed old leather chaps in his lap. He opened the tin of saddle butter and enjoyed the smell of beeswax. Then, he scooped out saddle butter with an old cotton rag and casually polished the leather of his old worn chaps. He kept his movements restrained, and he completely ignored the stallion on the other end of the pasture.

Although he turned his back toward the skittish animal, after several minutes he could hear Lightning's hesitant steps toward him. The horse took uneven steps across the field, stopping often, and came no closer than a few yards, judging by the sounds behind him. Cody didn't turn and kept working on his chaps. He would let the horse choose his own pace to come closer to the man.

It took over an hour for Lightning to sidle up far enough and stand right behind Cody, sniffing his hair. He remained seated on the wooden box, still avoiding quick movements. He didn't want to startle the magnificent stallion. He inched his hand toward the pocket of his denim jacket and pulled out a red apple, holding it where the horse could see it. Just as slowly, he pulled a knife from his jeans.

Cody examined the beautiful ornamentation and his initials engraved on the pocket knife. It had been a gift from his late father. *I really miss him*, Cody thought, and sadness settled in his chest. A snort behind him reminded him of his mission, and he cut the fruit in half.

The apple was so ripe the juice ran over Cody's hand. He took a bite, and the sound of chewing with the smell of the apple awakened Lightning's curiosity even more, and he stepped beside the box where Cody could see him. His ears pointed forward in a friendlier manner than Cody had seen before, and the dark eyes framed with long lashes watched the man in front of him attentively. The stallion snorted again, but Cody still didn't acknowledge his presence. He had to be patient and leave it up to Lightning to approach him first.

Very slowly, inch by inch, the restless animal lowered his head and sniffed Cody's sleeve. The cowboy stretched out his hand, offering the other half of the apple. Lightning shook his head nervously and snorted. Surely he could smell the aroma of the apple. After much hesitation, he swiftly snatched the apple between his teeth and trotted triumphantly toward the other side of his pasture.

Cody couldn't help but chuckle. "Good boy. This is a start, I'd say. I'll bring you another apple tomorrow if you like them so much."

The horse listened with his ears moving back and forth. He didn't retreat all the way to the opposite fence but remained in the middle of the field. Lightning swallowed the apple, and when Cody rose and carried the wooden box and his chaps out of the pasture, the stallion didn't run away from him. He stood a few feet away, and for the first time, his posture and body language told Cody he felt more relaxed.

THE FOLLOWING MORNING, Cody helped Gary change the oil in both his pickup trucks. The two men functioned as a well-coordinated team. They bent over the sink with their sleeves rolled up, cleaning their oil-smeared arms with old rags.

"Have you made friends with the stallion yet?" Gary asked.

"I would say... a tiny bit. He's extremely standoffish, but who can blame him after what he's been through? He has a sweet tooth for apples. As we know from the Bible story, a juicy apple is the best way to get the most stubborn male on your side."

Gary laughed heartily. "Speaking of how to seduce a man, Ruth baked a delicious apple cake, and I'm really looking forward to dessert this evening. The entire house smells like a bakery."

Cody grinned, and for the first time in many months he felt content and happy. The heavy burden he'd carried for so long seemed to have lifted from his shoulders. He had no doubt it had been the right decision to accept Gary's job offer and move to his ranch in Montana.

Cody soaped his arms and rinsed them. "When do you expect your men to return from the cattle drive?"

Gary searched for a clean towel. "Knowing the boys, it'll probably be another three or four days. Stacey tends to take advantage of every opportunity away from the ranch to indulge in some private amusement."

"You're talking about Stacey Foster, right?"

Surprised, Gary turned to his friend. "Do you know him?"

"No, but Takoda warned me about him. He described him as, well, let's say not very diplomatic or a team player."

Gary scratched his head and nodded thoughtfully. "Takoda told you the truth. To be honest, I thought about firing him a couple of times, but I need him as head wrangler. Stacey has the boys under control, but he is a quarrelsome jerk. I think Takoda is right when he says that Foster will damage the team in the long run. Don't get me wrong, he does his job well, but I don't trust him as much as I used to in the beginning. The day I hired him, I definitely had a better impression of him."

Cody studied his friend's face. It looked like this Stacey was indeed a problem. He decided to be cautious and avoid the man whenever possible. He didn't need any further complications in his life.

TWELVE
Winona Standstrong

A FTER A TASTY lunch and a generous piece of Ruth's apple cake, Cody walked back to the pasture, where he hoped to further connect with the shy stallion. He was surprised to see a woman leaning against the fence, watching Lightning. Cody only saw her from the rear, but that view was quite impressive. Long, straight hair covered her back all the way to her slim waist. The way her hair reflected the afternoon sunlight reminded him of the glossy wing of a raven. She wore faded jeans and a red and blue plaid blouse on her slim figure.

She barely reached his shoulders, but despite her petite stature, she carried herself with an aura of self-confidence. Her arms rested on the fence post, and she perched one foot on a rock nearby. Although she wore sturdy trekking shoes, her feet seemed quite small.

Cody heard her talking to the stallion in her soft, warm voice. She spoke a language he had never heard before. He noticed the stallion listened closely to her voice, and he didn't seem as nervous as usual. The animal reacted to Cody's presence by snorting and shaking his head as if he didn't welcome Cody's visit.

The woman turned and looked him up and down from head to toe.

Cody tipped his hat and greeted her with a respectful, "Ma'am."

She greeted him with a nod but uttered not a single word and turned her attention back to the stallion.

Cody swallowed hard. He wasn't expecting to see such a beautiful face—almond shaped eyes and full lips. Her skin matched the color of polished copper, and she looked like a fashion model.

He cleared his throat before speaking. "Please beware, this stallion is mighty dangerous." He knew he sounded schoolmasterly, but it was a fact that one should not underestimate the size and power of this animal.

She scoffed and answered without even looking at him. The warm, melodious sound of her voice didn't weaken the sarcasm of her words. "Unlike most white men, you can be assured that we Lakota have known how to handle horses for centuries. You might not believe it, but Lightning and I have known each other for quite a while." Putting her hands on her hips, she looked very much like the clichéd pugnacious Prairie Indian seen in countless Hollywood movies.

"Forgive me, ma'am, but I never questioned your know-how when it comes to handling horses. I simply warned you that this particular animal is not a pony from the petting zoo or one of those trail horses that wait for paying tourists behind the fences of some dude ranch."

Without intending it, Cody's tone had changed from cordial to unfriendly, but he couldn't help it. He was not in the mood to allow any woman to make him look like a dummy. He'd had enough of that for one lifetime.

They stared at each other. She squinted her eyes, while Cody pushed his chin forward in a proud and provocative way. From the corner of his eye, he saw that the stallion pawed impatiently with his hoof, throwing up grass and dirt. He must have felt the tension between the two humans on the other side of the fence and didn't like it.

The dark-haired beauty shrugged her shoulders as if she didn't care and turned toward Lightning. She pulled a carrot from the pocket of her jeans.

Cody had been too distracted by her shapely derrière to notice anything in her pockets.

His jaw dropped as he watched Lightning walk toward the woman standing outside the fence. He bent his head toward her hand and carefully nibbled at the carrot.

Cody muttered to himself, "Now butter my butt and call me a biscuit. Typical male." He couldn't help himself and started to chuckle.

To his surprise, the corners of the lady's mouth twitched as she suppressed her laughter. She caressed the nose of the magnificent stallion and turned toward Cody, who stared at the ground ashamed of his previous rude tone.

He stretched out his hand and introduced himself formally. "Cody Ferguson. I apologize for what I said a minute ago. I didn't mean to be rude, but I just wanted to warn you. It looks like you know Lightning much better than I do."

"Winona Standstrong."

"I admit, you do your name justice." As soon as the words slipped from his mouth, he bit his tongue and blushed, deeply embarrassed about having put his foot in it again. *What in the world is wrong with me? When did I turn into a complete oaf ?* he wondered. *So, this is Little Sitting Bull, as Takoda named her.*

Her rich laughter utterly surprised him. It echoed across the pasture as clear as a bell on Sunday morning. Cody smiled at her. There was a mischievous sparkle in her eyes, and he liked it right away.

"You cannot imagine how often I have heard that, but don't worry. I'll take it as a compliment."

Now it was Cody's turn to laugh out loud.

"My uncle Takoda sent me to replace him for the next two or three days." Without warning, she took Cody's hand and shook it with surprising strength. He looked at her slim, tanned hands. Her nails were trimmed short, and veins stood out on the backs of her hands. Apparently, Winona Standstrong was a woman who knew what hard work was, but her appearance was feminine, nevertheless.

"I planned to give the barn a new coat of paint during the next few days. I'm afraid that the coming winter with its severe weather might further damage the wood. If you feel like it, you can help me paint the building. Sure wouldn't hurt to have some help."

"Excellent. Let's get our stuff for the paint job together today so we can start early tomorrow right after breakfast. Ruth invited me to eat here at the ranch with you all, and honestly, who could ever resist her cooking?"

Cody chuckled. It seemed that Gary wasn't the only one who Ruth easily wrapped around her little finger. "Fine with me. Let's meet tomorrow at the barn at eight a.m. I'll get all the brushes, buckets, and paint together so we can get started right after breakfast."

She saluted him playfully, turned, and walked toward her car. She drove a beat-up, dark blue pickup truck that had seen better days.

Shaking his head, Cody walked back to the main building. "Salutes me as if I was General Custer. I'm afraid she's going to make fun of me plenty during the next few days," he growled, but to his surprise, he looked forward to seeing her the next day.

That evening, he excused himself right after dinner and walked to his cabin. He sat in his favorite rocking chair on the porch and read a book he borrowed from Gary's library in the dining room. He tried to concentrate on the first chapter, but the good-looking Lakota woman sneaked into his thoughts repeatedly. A man could get a clear picture of the once so proud heritage of her ancestors while studying her face. There was no question that Winona Standstrong was a gorgeous woman who possessed an exotic beauty. She seemed to be so different from his ex-wife. Unlike Lynn, her beauty seemed to come from deep within and wasn't shallow or painted over by too much makeup.

Winona didn't look like a woman who liked to show off her figure either. She hadn't worn a trace of makeup as far as he could tell. Her beauty was natural. He liked her melodic voice. Some girls at the rodeo had a rather piercing speech, especially when they sought the attention of one of the cowboys. Lynn was the best example for that. He could still recall the high-pitched voice of his ex.

Cody didn't like that Winona occupied his thoughts so much. He had to be cautious not to develop any kind of interest in her. She was fascinating all right, but he didn't want to repeat the mistake of ever trusting a woman again. That relationship had taught him a bitter lesson, and he didn't want to be hurt again. He was much more cautious now. "Once burned, twice shy," he whispered and stepped back into the cabin, where he put the book aside on the nightstand.

❖

THE FOLLOWING DAY, Cody was supposed to meet Winona by the barn. He ate his breakfast earlier than usual, and by the time Winona arrived, he had already placed everything they needed for the day's job in front of the building. When she walked around the corner, he was surprised to see she wore old, faded jeans torn above the knee. With every step she took, copper-colored skin peeked through the hole. A dark blue flannel shirt and a white T-shirt underneath completed her work outfit. Her long hair was tamed into a braid, and she had prepared for a full day of hard physical work. She walked toward him and appeared as fresh as the sunny morning.

"If only my ex-wife would have been such a reliable person," he mumbled, then he managed a smile, and they set to the task of painting the barn.

The morning passed quickly, and Winona concentrated on her work in silence. She painted like a professional, so they were about to finish the entire north side of the barn shortly before lunch.

Around 4:30 in the afternoon, they put their paintbrushes into a bucket full of water to keep them soft and called it a day. Winona told Cody she wanted to go down to the river to collect a bucket of clay before she went home.

"Now what in the world would you need clay for?" he wanted to know.

"I'm an artist, and I create bronze sculptures, mainly of horses. The clay down at the riverbank is perfect for making the molds I need to model before I can pour the melted metal into those forms."

"I'm sure you could buy some similar material at the local Home Depot without having to crawl through the dirt down by the riverside."

She stared at him silently for a moment. Then, she raised an eyebrow and pointed a finger at him like a harsh high school principal. "You know,

Mister Ferguson, sometimes you have to crawl through the dirt to find something precious to use to create beauty. I believe that is not only the case for a sculptor but applies to everyday life as well. You have to earn beautiful moments. They don't just fall into your lap easily. Sometimes you have to start from the lowest level to achieve better things in life."

He didn't know what to say and shrugged his shoulders. Then, he turned and walked toward the main house. "Just watch out that you don't fall into the water. Nobody will hear you down there if you do. I'll see you tomorrow," he called after her.

He heard her mumbling something behind his back, but fortunately he didn't understand it. "What a stubborn woman," he said and was actually relieved to be alone for the rest of the day. He was just not used to female company anymore.

"Horse sculptures, bah. That's all I need. A wannabe artist who thinks a dangerous rodeo stallion is a pet." *Sometimes I wonder if God was sober when he created women.* He shook his head and entered the ranch house.

That evening, Cody visited Lightning and tried to tempt him with a carrot he pulled out of the pocket of his jeans. He was pretty sure it was because of the particular treat that the horse had been so trusting when Winona fed him.

No matter how he tried to lure the stallion closer, the animal stubbornly remained on the other side of the pasture, keeping as much distance from Cody as possible. *How in the world did that woman get him to eat from her hand like a puppy?*

"You're a traitor. That is what you are," Cody growled, frowning.

He threw the carrot as close as possible to the magnificent animal and watched him trot toward it without hesitation. Shaking his head angrily, Cody walked to his cabin. He pulled up the collar of his denim jacket against the chill. He was annoyed that he hadn't gotten any closer to the stubborn beast. The former rodeo champion wasn't used to any animal rejecting him, especially not a horse. *What if Lightning feels that I am insecure about being a decent rancher?* he mused. Some people believed animals sense the fear of the humans who care for them.

THIRTEEN
In Pain

THE PINE TREES swayed back and forth in the gusting wind that blew the puffy clouds across the early evening sky. He didn't need a forecast to tell him the weather would change within a few hours. His joints ached, his scars contracted, and the hardware holding his shattered bones together felt cold and painful—signs a storm approached. The hard work he'd done in the past few days added to his pain, and Cody knew that a rough night lay ahead of him. He entered his home, started the coffee maker, and hurried to his bathroom, where he kept his over-the-counter painkillers.

For the first time since moving into the cabin, Cody felt cold and decided to start a fire. He arranged kindling on the grate and piled logs over the bark and twigs in a teepee shape. Striking a long match on the rock hearth, he held the flame to the kindling until it burned merrily.

There, that was better. Cody had always loved the crackling sound of the flames. It didn't take long before a cozy warmth filled the cabin. The smell of wood smoke, rather than bothering him, added to the homey atmosphere of his place. He climbed the steep stairs to his sleeping loft.

It was past midnight when Cody opened his eyes. Every time he took a breath, pain stabbed his chest like an iron vice gripping his rib cage, making it hard for him to breathe. He pushed away from the bed, but it was difficult even to raise his torso. He rolled to the edge of the bed, felt for the floor with his feet, and pushed himself upright. The descent to the first floor was torture. He gripped the edge of the bathroom sink while filling a glass with water.

Catching a glimpse of his face in the mirror, a mask of suffering stared back at him. He tossed two more painkillers into the palm of his hand and moaned as he swallowed them. The pain of movement stalled him briefly at the sink. When he could walk again, he poked the embers in the fireplace, then added two logs to get the fire going again. The howling wind whipped around the corners of his cabin and made the flame dance.

No wonder I'm in so much pain. Must be the first fall storm brewing. He sank into the armchair in front of the fireplace and waited for the pills to do their job. Every single plate and screw in his body screamed, and his scars pulled and ached. This was one of the miserable nights he knew well but couldn't get used to.

Cody faced such intense pain every time a storm front came through. Snow or turbulent thunderstorms made the torture hard to tolerate and reminded him with cruel clarity how severe his injuries had been. The accident shattered his sternum, punctured his lung, fractured four ribs, and compressed his upper spine to the point of rupturing three intervertebral discs. No wonder he felt a grid of agony whenever he overdid activities or the weather turned to rain or snow.

He watched the flames consume the fresh wood and listened to the howling melody of the storm. After half an hour, he limped upstairs again, one step at a time. He eased into bed, covering himself with the quilt.

As a teenager, he loved the sound of the wind, especially while enveloped in a warm, soft bed under one of his mom's hand-sewn quilts. These days, he knew that wind meant nothing but torture, and those painful days and nights mercilessly reminded him that only broken shards were left of his once successful life.

Cody knew he would never again be able to enter rodeo competitions, at least not as a saddle bronc rider. The exertions and shocks on a bucking horse were too much for his broken bones to handle. He was no fool and tried to make peace with that.

But he could ride a horse and even gallop along less challenging trails. Although riding brought on bouts of pain, he still appreciated that he was able to enjoy Mother Nature from the back of a horse. He had missed that, especially during the weeks in the hospital when he hadn't been sure if he would ever walk again after surgery and rehab.

As he lay in bed awake, Gary's words about giving it another shot at the rodeo crossed his mind. *Crazy son of a gun. How could I even think of it?* He shook his head and touched the scars on his chest. But then he laughed out loud. *Maybe I should try roping. That could be an alternative event to get back to the rodeo circuit.* He smiled in the darkness. *If I don't try, I'll never know.* For the first time in two years, Cody considered rodeo as a career again. He missed it like a long-lost friend. People said being in the rodeo was like an addiction. It never let go of the folks who got into the life.

In the wee hours, he fell into shallow slumber, but the next morning, he felt absolutely whacked. When he stepped out on the porch, it was clear he and Winona wouldn't be able to continue painting the barn today. Rain fell in a steady drizzle, and although the wind didn't blow as powerfully as it had the previous night, it was still fierce enough to blow the rain sideways against the buildings.

When he entered the dining room half an hour later, he was mildly surprised to see Winona eating her breakfast with the other staff members despite the lousy weather. Everybody greeted him warmly, but Winona watched him in silence as he sat in the empty chair next to Gary. *Most likely she is still upset about my stupid remark yesterday.*

She got up and walked into the kitchen but returned a few minutes later with a cup of tea in her slender hands. When she placed it in front of Cody, he wondered what this was all about.

Cody looked up at her where she stood next to him. "Thank you, but I need my coffee in the mornings, or I'm an unbearable grouch. I'm not that much of a tea person, you know."

"It's the same for me, but this tea is special, and you should drink it after breakfast. It's brewed from willow bark. We Lakota use it as a pain reliever. Try it, and you'll see that it really helps."

Cody was astonished that she had noticed his pain within the first few moments after he entered the room. Gary studied his friend's face. Cody knew that he looked crappy and exhausted. There was no way to hide the condition of his body today, and he felt his cheeks flush from embarrassment.

Gary leaned closer. "Cody, considering today's weather, you can't paint that barn, but you would be of amazing help if you would go over the sales books with me. Maybe you can come up with an idea about how we can maximize our profits on breeding those Black Angus cows. By the way, that tea really helps," he added with a wink.

Cody nodded and tried a sip of the hot beverage. It tasted so bitter that he made a face, and everybody at the table laughed. Winona watched him closely, so he picked up the cup again. He didn't want to alienate her and bravely drained the entire cup.

Satisfied, she patted him on the shoulder and declared that she would help Ruth with the laundry.

Cody asked Winona if she found the clay for her sculptures the previous evening.

She smiled. "Yes, I did, and fortunately before the storm hit. I would have looked like a drowned cat if I went down there half an hour later. I avoid going to the river when it rains because the current quickly turns into a dangerous torrent. If you ever feel like it, you should come by my studio, and I'll show you the different steps from a clay mold to a bronze sculpture. It's an interesting process, at least for me as an artist." She added a hearty peal of laughter that he enjoyed hearing.

Her invitation surprised him, but he nodded. "I would love to see some of your work. Thanks once again for the tea. There are days when the pain is worse, especially when the weather goes crazy like last night."

She tilted her head to the side and looked at him with her dark, almond-shaped eyes. "Some wounds take much longer to heal than others," she murmured. Then, she walked back into the kitchen.

He stood alone in the hallway, waiting for Gary. *What did she mean? Does she know more about me than she admits? I wonder what Gary told her.*

Then he shook his head and walked over to Gary's study. It was time to get started with office work.

Gary and Cody worked for hours balancing the accounts and trying to develop strategies to improve income from breeding the bulls on the ranch. After a while, Cody noticed that the willow-bark tea had really helped. His pain was bearable and more like a throbbing pulse in the background. He would have to ask Winona if she could sell him a pouch of the tea fixings and teach him how to prepare it. Cody planned to limit the use of medication.

The next day, as the sky cleared and the sun peeked through the clouds, he had a chance to talk to her about the tea. Cody caught himself looking forward to working with her on painting the building. The unexpected feeling confused him.

"How are you doing today? Did the tea help?"

Cody stretched into an exaggerated pose, hands behind his head and back arched, and smiled at her. "I admit it worked better than my ibuprofen. What in tarnation is in that stuff to make it work even better than my pharmaceutical drugs?"

"The tea is made from the inner bark of the willow tree. We also add dried buds of its new leaves, which we collect in spring. It is an ancient healing remedy, passed down from one generation to the next. Our ancestors knew about it long before a white man set foot on our land. Wisdom about healing plants is one of the rare things that we were able to save for our culture and children. Otherwise, there's not much left of our traditional ways," she added with a sad face.

FOURTEEN
Reservation Reality

W INONA PRESSED HER full lips together, changing the look of her face from pleasant to hard and unforgiving. Cody understood her bitterness. The indigenous people had lost far too much—too many killed, their territory stolen from them, their culture and identity purposefully destroyed.

Cody was the son of a family that had homesteaded five generations ago, and he had always seen history and the past from the point of view of white settlers. But Cody's family ranch land had been taken from people like Takoda and Winona all those years ago, and his point of view was shifting in their favor. He wanted to learn more about their past and their culture.

"Your family members must consider themselves lucky. I am certain that your knowledge about healing plants often saves them a visit to the doctor's office, doesn't it?"

She stared at him with her eyes wide in disbelief.

Cody wracked his brain for his mistake. *Great. I guess I said something wrong again.* This woman constantly gave him the feeling that he overstepped some unknown personal boundary.

Winona didn't answer at first but picked up the paintbrush and opened the bucket holding the barn-red paint. Without a word, she started applying another coat of paint to the weathered wood. He remained silent, and after a few moments, she spoke. "You don't know much about life on the reservation, do you?"

Cody shook his head.

"We don't have a choice of doctors where we live. To see a general practitioner, we have to drive between twenty and fifty miles. Even if we make the trip despite the price of gas, we encounter the next problem. Most of us don't have health insurance, and the doctors will send us away without treating our illness. And good luck if you need a specialist. That would be hopeless.

We acquired every disease you can name from the white men, but we never qualify to receive the needed remedies or therapies. These days, it's not smallpox, dysentery, or cholera that we battle, but cancer, diabetes, and measles. The result remains the same. Since we can't afford proper treatments or surgeries, and we slip through the cracks in the system that would allow us to qualify for affordable health insurance, our people continue to die. Most members of our tribe don't have a paying job, so you can imagine that they can't go to a pharmacy to buy prescription or over-the-counter drugs."

Cody noticed her flushed cheeks through her dark skin. *Healthcare on the reservation is a topic I should avoid in the future,* he mused. "I'm really sorry. I didn't mean to upset you. I take going to the doctor for granted. It's clear to me that I know nothing about your culture. Frankly, I have no clue, Winona."

She sighed and shook her head. "I know that. And I shouldn't have been so rude to you. It's not your fault. It's just that these injustices, especially healthcare inequality, have frustrated me since I was a little girl. I lost my mom because she had no access to proper breast cancer treatment. The white healthcare system could have saved her, and I'm still bitter about it. But I shouldn't lash out at people who aren't responsible for her death." She looked at the ground and bit her lower lip. "I'm sorry, Cody."

Cody thought she looked like a small child who needed comforting. "It's okay. I can understand why that would be a sore spot."

She looked back up at the cowboy. "Hey, you know what? I have an idea. If you really want to learn something about our history and culture, I would love to teach you. I think my uncle would like that, too. He knows a lot about our legends and the old ones. Besides, I think it's about time we behaved less formally toward each other. My name is Winona. That means 'First Daughter' in our language." She stretched out her hand, obviously wanting to start over again.

"Cody." He took her hand. It was a kind of peace offering from her side, and he would be crazy not to accept it. Takoda's nickname for her of "Little Sitting Bull" made sense to him. This woman was indeed a descendant of the once-so-fierce Lakota warriors. She exuded passion about all things that were important to her.

"Oh, and one more thing about me, I don't have a family. Well, not anymore. My parents both passed away, and my younger sister died when she was seventeen. She was killed in a car crash. My uncle Takoda is the only relative I have left."

"Looks like we have something in common. My father died a few months ago, and I don't have any siblings. My mother has dementia, and I can't even recall the last time she recognized me as her son."

Winona cocked her head and studied him for a moment. But she didn't ask him whether he was married or had a girlfriend. He was relieved she didn't bring up the topic. "Gary told me that you were a successful saddle bronc rider. Do you intend to train Lightning if he ever allows you to ride him?"

Cody was surprised by her interest. He wasn't upset that Gary had spilled the beans because it seemed she was the only one who knew, besides Ruth most likely. None of the ranch boys had asked him yet. "To be honest, I would like to give it a try. Gary is convinced that the stallion has an amazing potential for the rodeo. But I still struggle with the injuries from my last ride in Cheyenne, as you keenly observed yesterday. I'm considering joining the roping competition, which is less wearing on the body, and I believe Lightning would be a good partner in the arena. Well, if this crazy son of a gun ever tolerates a saddle again, and if he allows me on his back. At present, he is not very keen about becoming friends with me."

Winona raised her chin. "Most likely he'll not only be a good partner in the arena for you but could become much more."

"What do you mean?"

She shrugged her shoulders and said, "Well, Lightning must come to terms with old injuries just like you. He has to learn to trust people again.

That stallion has gone through so much pain, Cody, and I guess you did, too. It seems to me that you both have a lot in common, and I believe you can help each other. See, in my culture, a horse is much more than just a working animal."

He put his paintbrush aside and narrowed his eyes at her curiously. "More in what way?"

"A horse was the most precious possession a Prairie Indian owned. Without our four-legged partner, we could never have hunted the buffalo so successfully. It wouldn't have been possible to move long distances from one camp to the next, and we couldn't have become such fierce warriors if we hadn't had our horses to carry us in and out of battle safely. The old ones spoke of legends about horses like Lightning." Her dark eyes twinkled. "Maybe I'll tell you one of those stories the next time I come to the ranch. For now, I have to call it a day because I'm expecting a customer at the studio. He is interested in buying one of my sculptures."

"Of course, I understand. Leave the bucket, the paint, and your brushes right there. I'll take care of it."

To his surprise, he regretted that Winona was leaving the ranch early today. Could it be that he enjoyed her company more than he was willing to admit? She could be quite gruff from time to time, but she could be warm and friendly as well.

Cody watched her drive the battered pickup through the gate and smiled when she wound down the dusty side window to wave goodbye to him. He laughed out loud when he saw the big stain of barn paint on her palm.

That evening, Cody selected a nonfiction book about the Lakota Indians from Gary's library and withdrew early to his cozy log cabin.

FIFTEEN
The Legend of the Spirit Horse

CODY HAD SETTLED into the routine at G.B. Ranch. Today was his day off. He hadn't seen Winona for three days. Spontaneously, he decided to pay a visit to the small town of Dillon. After driving the eight miles into town, he parked his pickup in downtown Dillon. He strolled along the streets flanked by historical brick and stone houses and an occasional two-story log cabin. This part of town looked like a perfect western movie set. The historical buildings hosted a colorful mixture of restaurants, shops, and bars, which he, of course, avoided.

He studied the window of an art gallery on the opposite side of the street. Cody's interest in the arts went back to his teenage years, especially when it was traditional western art, such as Russell's paintings or Remington's bronzes. He liked what he saw in the big windows of the place, so he crossed the street, took in the items on display, and stepped through the front door. The chiming of a bell announced his visit.

As soon as he closed the door behind him and got an idea of the gallery's holdings, he was fascinated. Countless photographs and paintings told their own story with their strong and lively colors. He saw portraits of pioneers and Prairie Indians next to beautiful landscapes and paintings of animals, all classically framed with antique-style wood frames. Each piece of art fascinated the viewer with its own unique style.

Cody slowly walked along the walls, studying each magnificent picture. It was like stepping back into pioneer times—he could imagine his own ancestors in the colorful ranch scenes.

An open doorway led into the next room. Beside it, a single black-and-white portrait stood out dramatically among all the varied pieces around him. Weathered driftwood gave the photo of an old native with an unusual appearance a unique frame. A warm scarf covered the man's head, and he wore a black jacket which looked much too big for him. He lay on his back, and his hands were directed toward the camera as if he defended himself against the lens.

Cody tilted his head. *This is a strange photo. That old man looks like one of those mannequins they use for decorating clothing stores that lies awkwardly on its back.*

Something seemed odd about the old man's legs and the position of his arms. The longer Cody stared at the photo, the more wrong it seemed. With a jolt, Cody understood that the photo showed a dead body lying in the midst of a snow-covered field.

Why in the world did they leave him lying in the snow like this? Only then did he notice the tiny sign under the right-hand corner of the portrait.

He read it, whispering the text softly to himself. "Chief Spotted Elk, Wounded Knee, December 29th, 1890."

Cody had read about the massacre at Wounded Knee River, but to see one of the victims so close, face-to-face, turned his stomach. The picture shook him to his core. When he turned toward the opposite wall, more of the black-and-white portraits hung on display, showing dead women holding the tiny bodies of their frozen children and the photo of a mass grave with countless corpses in it.

"Sweet Jesus, this is awful," he whispered. Although the images shocked him, they also enthralled him, and he was unable to turn away.

Cody hadn't noticed the woman behind him until she spoke. Startled, he spun around.

"Hello, Cody. Did you lose yourself in our town?" He was surprised when he recognized Winona. She wore an elegant red knit dress with an Native American star pattern. She had arranged her hair on top of her head in a fashionable style, and the form-fitting dress emphasized her slender figure. She sported a pearl necklace with red and black beads, matching her outfit perfectly.

Speechless, he stared at her, but after a moment, he cleared his throat and pointed back to the front of the gallery. "What are you doing here? Do you work in this gallery?"

"Yes, actually it belongs to my partner and me. We show art of well-known Native American artists, and my studio is behind our showroom. Of course, you can't compare our gallery with the big ones in Denver or Santa Fe, but we are proud of what we have achieved. Have you looked around?"

"Yes, and I very much like what I see. However, I have to admit that this picture series from Wounded Knee shocked me." He pointed at the portrait of the dead old man lying frozen in the snow.

Winona nodded. "Those portraits document one of the darkest days in our history. U.S. cavalry surrounded a camp of the Miniconjou tribe, which is one of the different subgroups of Lakota. The soldiers had been ordered to relocate the natives to a reservation far from their home with the intention of making their land available to more white settlers. They ordered the Miniconjou to give up all their weapons, so they did. Unfortunately, the colonel wasn't satisfied with the number of collected weapons piled up in the middle of the camp. He asked the soldiers to search through the teepees, assuming that my ancestors hid some of their weapons. When the soldiers couldn't find more rifles, that particular colonel forced his men to body search the Miniconjou, which was very humiliating for them."

Cody shook his head, feeling ashamed about the way the white authorities treated those people. "But why in the world did that massacre take place if the Miniconjou didn't have any weapons?"

"One warrior named Black Coyote tried to hide his Winchester under his clothes. He was scared his family would starve to death if he didn't have his rifle to hunt for meat. It was a hard winter, and game was scarce after the white settlers entered the prairie. The white people killed most of our game and buffalo. By that time, the Lakota and other prairie tribes could hardly find anything to hunt and feed our families, and my people suffered from constant hunger."

She turned and studied the portrait of the dead chief. Sadness lay like a heavy veil over her beautiful features. "A soldier saw the rifle and tried to take it away, but Black Coyote wouldn't let go of it, and a shot discharged accidentally. The soldiers started to fire right away. Historians reported the number of victims was somewhere between one hundred fifty and three hundred Miniconjou, depending on which report you read. Many of the victims were women and children. The old man you see in this portrait was their chief, Spotted Elk. He didn't have a weapon, and as you can see from the way he held up his hands, he had clearly surrendered and didn't want to fight. The soldiers shot many victims in the back as they ran away from the massacre. They must have been scared to death."

"Jesus, how can anyone shoot infants?" Cody whispered.

Winona didn't answer his question directly. "When the shooting was over, a blizzard hit the area, and the storm covered the territory with ice and snow for three days. On the fourth day, the soldiers dug a mass grave then threw the frozen bodies into it. Some of the soldiers took those pictures. I can imagine they felt mighty proud about wiping out an entire band of Lakota families. If you ask me, it was the doing of a bunch of cowards. It's easy to win a battle when your enemy has no way to defend themselves. Nowadays people believe that this massacre was the cavalry's revenge for the loss at Little Bighorn a few years before this incident took place. In any case, there was no reason to gun down an entire tribe for one shot of one single rifle, which wasn't even aimed at a soldier."

"Honestly, I don't know what to say. Of course, I heard about the Indian wars and Wounded Knee and the Battle of Little Bighorn, but it's a totally different story when you see cruelty right in front of your eyes. I mean... I'm devastated. Look at Chief Spotted Elk. It looks like he raised his hands to defend himself with his bare hands from the bullets ripping through his body. They had no chance at all! Who in the world would shoot children and unarmed women? I admit, for the first time in my life I feel disgusted and ashamed about my own race." Mortified, Cody rubbed his hands over his face.

Winona watched him in silence. Then, she pointed to the room at the back of the building. "Hey, would you like to see what I created from the clay I collected at the river the other day?"

Perhaps she wanted to overcome the embarrassing silence between them. Nobody could turn back time and undo history, but everybody had a chance to learn from it.

Cody nodded to her invitation, and relief washed over him to escape the disconcerting photo of the frozen dead man in the snow. He didn't have answers to questions about the heartbreaking past. Nor did he know why certain things were done so cruelly by those who forged the history of this nation when it was young.

He followed Winona into her studio. A big workbench at the rear wall dominated the room. Tools for modeling and carving clay hung from a rack above it. Everything seemed in order and well organized. A modern kiln sat in the opposite corner. A couple of finished art pieces and pottery with traditional Native American patterns lined the shelf close to the door. The room smelled of fresh clay, sanded wood, and paint.

"Welcome to my little kingdom," she said with a warm smile and walked over to the workbench, where a machine bristling with polishing tools waited for her to continue whatever he interrupted when he entered the gallery. It looked like she had been polishing a sculpture. Cody noticed the white apron hanging near the machine, which she must have removed before she entered the front room. He smiled as he imagined her wearing it.

He admired the almost-finished bronze sculpture she pointed to. It showed a stallion with his head held high in a proud gesture. The animal seemed to be looking far beyond this room as he held his ears tilted forward in mild curiosity.

Winona carried the sculpture to the middle of the room and set it on the small pedestal. Then, she turned it sideways. At first, Cody thought she'd forgotten to polish some scratches from the rear legs of the bronze figure. But then he understood that those were not scratches. The fine lines resembled scars.

"Good heavens, that's Lightning, isn't it?" he exclaimed in surprise.

Winona nodded, saying, "I named the sculpture *Spirit Horse.*"

"Why Spirit Horse?"

She didn't answer at first but walked to the modern coffee maker hidden behind the door on a counter. She put one of those capsules into the machine, looking back at him, and asked, "Coffee with sugar, right?"

"Yes, ma'am, which would be wonderful. I can never resist a good cup of coffee," he admitted with a smile.

"Looks like we have that in common. I call coffee my life substitute," she answered with throaty laughter and pushed the start button of the coffee machine, which *peeped* its readiness. A steady humming signaled the brew cycle. After pouring, she passed him a steaming mug and a little clay pot filled with sugar cubes. After she brewed hers, they both stirred their beverages in silence.

When Cody took the first sip, he was surprised at the bold flavor of his coffee. He sat down casually on a stool next to the workbench. The muscles of his upper thigh were clearly visible under the fabric of his tight jeans and spoke of sheer masculine strength.

Winona swallowed, embarrassed when she realized she was staring at his long legs. She cleared her throat and said, "You wanted to know why I named the sculpture *Spirit Horse.* Do you know anything about the legends of spirit horses or ghost ponies?" When Cody shook his head, she pulled another stool closer, sat, and continued. "An old legend of the

Choctaw Indians tells a tale about the so-called spirit horse. A lot of different tribes believe in them, and some tribes like the Apache named those horses 'ghost ponies.' Whatever name they used, they all believed in the same legend. The elders used to tell us that it is the task of the ghost pony or spirit horse to bring a warrior to the land of the ancestors when his or her time has come to leave this world. The Choctaw specifically told the story of a young man whose foot was caught in a mountain man's bear trap."

She took another sip of her coffee, pulled the stool a bit closer to Cody, and set her mug on the scratched workbench as he waited patiently for her to continue the story.

He stared at her sensual lips on her pretty face as she took another sip of her beverage. He quickly looked down at the floor when he realized that he found her more and more attractive with each passing day. *Those lips are made for kissing*, he thought and blushed. He quickly stirred his coffee to distract himself, hoping she hadn't noticed his stare.

"This young warrior was hurt fatally because the bear trap tore off his foot. Scared for his life and slowly bleeding to death, he crawled in the direction of his tribe's camp, knowing he probably would never reach the teepee of his family before he died. Out of the blue, a magnificent horse came trotting toward him. It bent down far enough that the young man was able to pull himself onto the back of the horse by holding onto its neck and mane. It was a ghost pony or spirit horse, as the Choctaw say. But not only that, it was actually the last one of its kind."

Fascinated, Cody listened to the story and wondered what became of the young warrior. *Is this really just a legend, or is it a true story?*

"Normally, the spirit horses separate from their rider after delivering them to the land of the ancestors because they knew that countless other warriors would need their help reaching the Place of Happiness after death. During this ride, the spirit horse was capable of feeling the thoughts and emotions of the human on its back for the very first time in its existence. The animal felt that this would be his last ride, just as it was the last one for the young man."

Winona drained the last of her coffee. "The spirit horse brought the warrior to his camp and to his family. Both heard the lamentations of the people gathered around their teepees. But the horse didn't stop. It galloped through the high buffalo grass, which reached to its belly and tickled the young warrior's legs. He felt the wind in his face but no longer felt the pain. The two challenged the wind and raced against it, free and impetuous. After a while, they arrived at the blessed land of the ancestors."

Winona smiled at him. "Many of those who died before the young warrior came running toward them. He jumped off the back of the spirit horse, smiling happily. To his astonishment, he landed on two feet. He could walk and run as he had in his childhood days. Gone was the fatal injury from the bear trap. The spirit horse stayed by his side because it was its last ride into the land of the ancestors as well. They both were granted the privilege of remaining forever in the Place of Happiness, as many of us call it."

Cody remained silent, lost in thought. The story touched his heart.

Winona studied the sculpture in the middle of the room.

He followed her gaze. "You think that Lightning is such a spirit horse, right?"

She nodded. "I do believe that Lightning is waiting for his personal rider—a person whose destiny is to be Lightning's soulmate. I don't believe in coincidences, and I'm certain that you and Lightning were meant to meet at Gary's ranch."

Cody stared at her. *What if she was right? Could it really be?* He got up and walked toward the sculpture to touch it tenderly. Winona's talent was remarkable. She caught every nuance of the muscles and the way the stallion held his head. It was a wonderful piece of art, and he was sure it would bring a great price when sold. He felt a pang of envy for the person who would own this wonderful sculpture, even though they wouldn't know the true story of the horse.

He turned to her. "Thank you for sharing this with me. It's a beautiful legend and has touched me deeply." He looked at the floor and whispered, "I plan to eat something in one of the restaurants close by. Do you keep the gallery open during lunchtime, or do you think you might close it for an hour? It would be wonderful if we could eat something together. I would like to invite you, Winona."

She didn't answer right away, and he feared she would turn him down. But then she said, "There's an excellent steak house next door. I can keep an eye on the gallery and see if somebody wants to look at the art. All we have to do is take a table by the window. It's time to eat something anyway. Give me a second. I need to get my purse."

"Excellent. I'll wait for you at the front door." A few minutes later, they entered the nicely decorated steak house next door. Cody held open the door for her.

THEY DIDN'T PAY attention to the man standing on the opposite side of the street. He watched Cody and Winona, his face annoyed, his eyebrows knit together. He tossed the half-smoked cigarette angrily onto the pavement in front of him and stomped on it with a scuffed boot. His clothes were dirty, and his cowboy boots had seen better days. His shoulder length black hair looked greasy and uncombed. Many sparing him a glance might judge him untrustworthy.

The man spun abruptly and walked into the next bar. "I'm gone for a few days, and immediately a lousy squirt tries to lay his fingers on my doll face's body," he growled, stomping into the sleazy bar and sitting on a bar stool.

SIXTEEN
Conspiracy

T HE BARKEEPER PUT the glass of cheap whiskey in front of his only guest at this early hour and whisked to the other side of the bar. The guy took a sip from the glass, baring his bad teeth when he grinned at the barkeeper provocatively. The man behind the counter pretended not to see.

Stacey Foster was well known as a roughneck always looking for a fight. Nobody in Dillon wanted to cross his path if they could avoid it. Even the owner of this bar didn't dare get too close to him. He had seen his share of fistfights provoked by the good-for-nothing wrangler from Gary Bradshaw's ranch and knew that he wouldn't hesitate to stick a knife in an opponent.

Before long, a second shabby-looking cowboy entered the premises and walked straight over to Stacey. The men bellowed their orders for a glass of draft beer and a second shot of whiskey for Foster. Then, they walked to a table at the far end of the room so no one could overhear their conversation. The barkeep figured they had something important to talk about.

The man sitting opposite Foster threw his sweat-stained hat on the table and emptied half the beer in one swig. Then, he wiped his mouth with the dirty sleeve of his ragged shirt and belched. The bartender noticed with disdain he was like Stacey, of mixed heritage, with stringy black hair and a nasty scar across his right cheek.

"WELL, FOSTER, WHAT is so important that you lured me away from my woman? We were just about to have a little fun together when you called and disturbed us."

"I been running a cattle drive for the boss man these past few days and met this Lakota fellow up there in the mountains. Guess what? He had an interesting story to tell," Foster bragged, without acknowledging his pal's complaint.

"Listen, I haven't come here to have a useless Sunday-after-church talk with you. I want to get back to my little Mexican Margarita and mess around with her, so you better spill the beans about why for God's sake you asked me to meet you here."

"Listen here. That Lakota boy knows the uncle of my Winona, and he told me a wild tale that some tribal members claim that old Takoda knows something about some gold. They say he knows where the notorious Henry Plummer hid his gold in the old days before his gang got arrested and hung from the gallows."

The other lad scoffed. "Yeah, right. Winona. What a joke. She don't want nothing to do with you, and honestly, I think that girl is way above your league anyway, my friend."

Stacey stared into his glass, his face a mask of fury. He thought about that stranger sitting with *his* Winona in the steakhouse across the street. *I'll take care of that jerk later.*

"So, let me get this straight." His companion leaned across the table. "You're saying that the old Indian fox knows where Sheriff Plummer hid all his stolen gold when he was still a decent outlaw and before he pinned that ridiculous tin target on his vest, claiming to be a man of the law and pretending to have a clean reputation?"

"Exactly. I'll grill the old medicine man and see if he really knows anything. As legend goes, so far nobody has found the box with the nuggets and the gold bars that he stole during the train robberies he committed. Fact is that the Plummer Gang robbed numerous gold transports on the Bozeman Trail. Old Plummer had up to a hundred men riding with him, so my guess is that loot should be of decent size. If we find that gold, we will be stinking rich, and then you can mess around with all your *chicas* as much and as often as you want. Hell, you could even buy an entire Mexican village, and neither of us would ever have to work another day in our entire life. I am done with that job as a cowpuncher anyway. I'm sick and tired of sniffing cattle manure for some boss man who gets richer with each passing month, while I have to sleep in a bunkhouse full of snoring wannabe cowboys."

His companion drained his mug. "Interesting tale, but what I don't understand is why in the world you would need me?"

"My guess is that Takoda might have told Winona about the treasure, and if he didn't, I'm pretty sure that he would be happy to tell me once he finds out that his beautiful niece is our unwilling guest. Since I work at old Bradshaw's ranch, I can't just go ahead and kidnap her from there, can I? They would suspect me right away. I need your help for that task, and also to keep an eye on her while I try to find out what old Takoda knows about the Plummer loot."

The man across from Stacey pushed back his greasy hair and scratched the stubble of his beard. He rubbed his index finger across his scar as if it was a long-established habit. A dangerous spark glittered in his dark eyes. "Of course, I'll watch over the little bird. I suggest we keep her in our hunting cabin in the mountains. Nobody at the ranch knows the place, and I'm dang sure it would be safe enough to hide the girl there."

Stacey frowned, watching his friend, shifting uncomfortably in the wooden chair. His words sounded more like the dangerous growl of an animal than the voice of a man. "You better keep your hands off her, Cliff. The girl is mine. If I find out you touched her, I'll kill you." To emphasize his words, he pointed his left index finger at the man while resting his right hand on his pistol.

Cliff sighed. "All right, all right. I get it. You'd begrudge me the shirt on my back. Okay, I'm in. We have a deal. We share fifty-fifty if we find that treasure."

"Agreed." The two men shook hands, then Stacey twisted his head, looking for the barkeeper. "Hey, soda jerk, bring a bottle of whiskey, and you better make it quick!" He turned back to his new business partner. "This one is on me," Stacey declared generously. "I never doubted that you'd pull your weight, Cliff. After all, you're my best buddy."

❖

IT WAS EARLY afternoon when Cody drove back to the ranch. He enjoyed having lunch and spending time with Winona more than he wanted to admit, especially to himself. Their conversation had been pleasant, and the food was delicious. On his way back to his cabin, he thought about the sculpture she created and how talented she was. Winona had a good eye for every detail and understood more about horses than he originally thought. If not, she couldn't have created the sculpture of Lighting in such exquisite detail. Reluctantly, he admitted to himself that he was fascinated by that woman. *Great, that's all I need*, he thought, but he chuckled when he remembered her subtle humor.

After the big lunch, he skipped dinner and enjoyed the rest of his free evening sitting on his porch with a cup of coffee. It had turned chilly with fall just around the corner, so he wore his favorite wool jacket. It was a warm and cozy one and smelled of hay and horses.

The night was cloudy and damp. After only a few hours of sleep, a terrible nightmare woke Cody. Images of frozen, dead Miniconjou lying in the snow disturbed his sleep. He couldn't pinpoint the cause, but he felt anxious even after the nightmare ended. *Maybe that exhibition about the Wounded Knee Massacre and those portraits shocked me more than I thought.*

SEVENTEEN
Unpleasant Coworkers

WHEN CODY ENTERED the dining room the following morning, three men he didn't know sat at the table. The two younger ones introduced themselves as Pete and Andrew McKenzie. The third one stared at Cody, wearing a half scowl and not introducing himself. Cody disliked him from the very first minute, but he had to work with everybody on the team. He reluctantly stretched out his hand toward the stranger and introduced himself as Cody Ferguson.

The man refused to shake Cody's hand and grumbled a barely understandable "Stacey Foster." Then, he shoveled another forkful of scrambled eggs into his mouth and chewed noisily. His table manners accurately matched his shabby looks and impolite behavior.

So, this was Stacey Foster who Takoda had warned him about when he first arrived at Gary's ranch. Was he mistaken, or had the atmosphere become less relaxed today compared to the past two weeks? But Cody didn't want to be unfair and believed in second chances for everyone, so he decided to meet the guy halfway. *Who knows? We might get along better than I expect.*

An hour later, the two men ran into each other again at the corrals near the tack room, and Cody nodded to Stacey in a cordial manner. Foster, however, ignored Cody's friendly greeting and squinted at him, frowning. Then, he turned away from Cody to show he had no interest in any conversation. Without wasting another look in Cody's direction, the unfriendly fellow walked to the tack room. This rude behavior stunned Cody.

"Wow, that seems to be a real *friendly* fellow," Cody mumbled, his voice dripping with sarcasm. He hated jerks like that. Then, he walked to the workshop. It was time to start the daily cores. He decided to be very careful and to avoid Stacey Foster whenever he could. One thing was sure, Takoda hadn't exaggerated his opinion of the man. Foster oozed malice. The man clearly could cause trouble.

Two days later, Winona and her uncle came to the ranch. A broad smile spread across Cody's face when he caught sight of them. Winona seemed more relaxed in the company of the handsome rodeo rider since their meeting at the gallery.

"I just stopped by to say hi and drop off my uncle. I have an important meeting with a client at the gallery. You remember the portrait series about the Wounded Knee Massacre, don't you? Keep your fingers crossed because it looks like we have a well-known German museum in Berlin which is willing to include the portraits in an exhibition. I am so thrilled upon the fact that the history of our tribe will be explained in Europe. It is so important to keep that part of our past alive and show people that we are still around despite all the hardship and persecution we faced."

She stood before him, the charming blush that colored her cheeks showing how excited she was. She wore tight jeans, moccasin boots with fringes, and a beige pullover adorned with Native American patterns. Her glossy black hair was pulled into a tight ponytail held back by a beautifully carved wooden hair clip.

Her makeup, hair, and clothes emphasized her natural beauty without overdoing things. Cody swallowed hard, increasingly aware of how attracted he was to her. He hoped that she didn't realize how much she appealed to him. He would have been embarrassed to the bone, but more than anything, he feared being fooled by a woman again.

"I'll keep my fingers crossed that you are able to connect with that museum. Who knows, they might be interested in displaying your sculptures one day. Your uncle already promised me that he would help me finish painting the barn. You see, you'll be represented in a worthy manner as a barn painter," he added, smiling boyishly.

"Yes, I know. I only hope he knows how to use that paintbrush as well as I do," she joked, and her clear laughter bubbled through the air. He watched her as she walked to her pickup. Her movements were very different from those of his ex-wife Lynn. Winona didn't need to sway her hips in an exaggerated way. Her stride was fast, almost boyish, but one noticed her shapely rear, even though she didn't flaunt it.

Cody was about to head for the barn when he saw Stacey Foster walking toward Winona. He started a discussion with her that, from a distance, appeared disrespectful. The man emphasized his words with exaggerated gestures, and his face looked rather hostile. Unfortunately, Cody couldn't understand a single word because they stood too far away from him. However, he noticed that Winona stepped back, trying to put distance between herself and Foster. Her body language signaled indignation and self-protection. Cody thought it seemed obvious she didn't want to talk with the head wrangler. She folded her arms across her chest as if to defend herself.

When she turned her back on Foster and tried to put her car keys into the lock of the driver's door, he grabbed her arm and forced her to look at him. Cody didn't like what he saw and took a step toward them, intending to interfere. Then, he saw Winona break away from the moron and angrily open the door of her truck. After jumping into the seat, she pulled the door closed in such a forceful manner that she almost slammed Foster's hand in it. He jumped back, cursing and making fists behind her pickup as it pulled away while his face resembled a demon from Hell.

Now Cody understood Takoda's warning. This guy has a severe anger problem, and Cody instantly knew he would have to watch his back whenever work forced him to be around Foster.

EIGHTEEN
Cruelty

EVERY DAY, CODY tried to gain Lightning's trust a bit more. The stallion gradually allowed Cody to come closer. After another three days of working with him, Cody was able to touch the reluctant animal and scratch him behind his ears. Although he was an experienced horseman, he allowed the magnificent horse to take his own time.

One morning, as Cody repaired the gate to the stallion's stable box, Lightning moved closer and rubbed his head on Cody's flannel shirt. He'd broken the ice—finally. It was a moment that filled Cody with joy and hope.

During dinner, Cody told Gary about the success he had with Lightning. Gary pounded Cody's shoulder approvingly when Foster walked in and rudely interrupted their conversation.

"If you ask me, the dang crowbait's only value is to get shot and pulled out somewhere for the predators. They are the only ones who would have a use for the old hack. Lightning is a waste of time and a mean, unpredictable beast. The best thing you can do with that stallion is to shoot him dead."

Gary regarded his ranch hand coolly. "It would be better if you left it up to me to judge which one of my horses I should consider valuable and which one should be driven to the slaughterhouse. This horse was a rodeo champion, and with Cody's help, I'm one hundred percent sure he will be capable of it again. If he can't be trained for the rodeo, then he's a promising stallion for breeding. So, I suggest you use that mouth of yours for the purpose of eating your breakfast instead of spitting stupid remarks into the room. I didn't ask for your opinion when it comes to that horse, so you better keep your saloon-drenched wisdom to yourself."

Foster's face transformed into an expression of fury, his eyebrows meeting in the middle and his eyes narrowing to slits, staring at his boss. The corners of his mouth turned down, and his lips pressed together tightly, as if he held back a torrent of words. He crossed his arms over his chest and made fists with his hands.

Cody was sure the fellow hated to be corrected in front of others and likely never considered that he might be wrong in his opinion or behavior. It seemed that Foster was too full of himself to accept criticism. The head wrangler rose and slammed his dirty plate so hard onto the sideboard that it was a wonder it didn't break. Then, he strode out of the dining room without another word.

Gary shook his head, but the man's behavior concerned Cody. It seemed as if Foster often looked for a reason to argue or fight. His lack of respect for his employer worried Cody. That wasn't good at all because it suggested Foster had no principles or restraint.

The following day, the ranch hands got all the horses ready for the blacksmith to re-shoe them. While leading three mares into the corral next to the tack room, Cody noticed Foster walking near the pasture where Lightning grazed. Upon seeing Foster, the stallion pulled back his ears and rolled his eyes nervously. He trotted away toward the fence, looking more skittish than Cody had seen him in days.

To his dismay, Foster picked up a rock the size of a man's fist and threw it full force against Lightning's flank. The beautiful animal reared and whinnied loudly, clearly in pain. The whites of Lightning's eyes were visible, and Cody could see the spot where the stone hit starting to swell.

"I'll teach you manners, you lousy beast." Foster shook his fist. Cody could tell the stallion feared Foster from the way he backed up until he was nearly against the rear fence rail. Foster stomped toward the gate leading to Lightning's pasture. His body language appeared threatening, and the man's hands were squeezed into fists. He frowned, his lips pressed together in a thin line.

Cody had seen his share of men who mistreated their animals, and he understood from Lightning's reaction that this wasn't the first painful encounter between the stallion and Foster. He was really coming to hate the man because, in Cody's book, it was absolutely forbidden to mistreat some of the most beautiful creatures God ever gifted to human beings.

"Foster! The men are looking for you. The blacksmith has arrived," Cody yelled toward the pasture.

Foster whirled and stared at the intruder. "Who do you think you are to disturb me during my work?" he yelled back at Cody.

But the former rodeo champ remained cool, standing like a rock, crossing his arms over his chest. Cody was not impressed at all by Foster's short fuse. "That didn't look like working to me. As a matter of fact, only Gary Bradshaw and I are training this horse. I suggest you get going and tend to your own chores. You have no business whatsoever with this stallion, Foster."

The quarrelsome ranch hand stared at Gary's new assistant, whose body language oozed self-confidence. Cody stood there, chin pointed forward, feet planted, eyes wide open, seeming as tightly wound as a cougar ready to spring on its prey.

Cody watched as Foster struggled to control his fury. He didn't want to fight this upstart, but he would if he had to. If the so-and-so started a fight with Cody, Gary would fire him for sure.

But Foster's body language relaxed, and he took a breath. He pulled his cowboy hat off his greasy hair and struck it against the dusty leg of his jeans. "We are not done with each other, Ferguson. I warn you. Don't you dare to get in my way, nowhere, with nothing and with nobody. This ranch is my territory. Understand?"

Cody scoffed. "I think it's my business where I put in my two cents and in which matters I interfere. You don't own this place, and you sure don't have any say in my life. Understand?"

"We shall see, Ferguson." Foster stomped away.

Cody shook his head. Unfortunately, the fight he wanted to prevent from happening had been unavoidable right from the start. The two men had more or less declared open war against each other.

Cody turned and walked toward the gate, thinking about what had just happened. He entered the stallion's pasture cautiously, taking it slow. Lightning stood in the far corner with his flank to the fence, head down, watching him closely. It hurt Cody to see that the beautiful animal trembled with fear. He talked to Lightning softly, trying to calm him.

"It's all right, boy. The villain is gone. I'll make sure that he can't get close to you again. I don't want him to hurt you, but you have to trust me, so I can have a look at the wound. Looks like you're developing a nasty bump where the rock hit you. I have some cream that will help you heal faster. What do you say, can I have a look at it? I promise I won't hurt you."

While he spoke with Lightning, he walked around the horse toward the flank where the rock had hit the stallion. Cody understood an injured animal was as dangerous as an aggressive one. Lightning's behavior showed he knew that Cody protected him and intended to help him. To Cody's relief, the horse hesitantly stepped closer to him, licking his lower lip nervously. Was he debating with himself about whether to trust the new man on the ranch?

Cody felt that this could be the turning point in their relationship, and he remained motionless, allowing the stallion to come closer at his own pace. After several minutes, he stood in front of Cody, lowering his head. The rodeo champ gently caressed the soft nose. Then, he stroked the neck and back all the way to the injured flank, where he examined the bump the rock had caused.

Cody's jaw tensed with anger at what he saw. He wished he could hit that fool Foster in the head with the very same rock. What a bastard! For the time being, Cody had to ensure that the already-confused animal didn't sense anger boiling in him. Whether he liked it or not, he would have to talk to Gary about the incident because the boss man would have to make certain his ranch hand didn't get another chance to threaten or hurt Lightning in any way.

God only knows how he treats the other animals when Gary isn't around or when Foster is on a cattle drive, Cody thought. He could imagine the cruelty men such as Stacey Foster were capable of. He pushed his hand into the pocket of his denim jacket and pulled out a juicy apple. This time, Lightning nibbled at the apple from Cody's hand without hesitation and even allowed him to caress his ear while chewing noisily.

Maybe Winona was right. He and Lightning were injured souls with similar scars, and it was possible that they needed each other to heal. *This stallion might indeed be my personal spirit horse,* he mused.

That evening, Cody waited to eat dinner after the other staff members left the main lodge. Just as he hoped, when he walked into the room, Gary and Ruth sat alone at the dining table. From the number of dirty dishes sitting on the kitchen counters, Cody guessed everyone else had already finished their food. After eating, Cody thanked Ruth for the wonderful meal. Gary hadn't exaggerated on his first day at the ranch. Ruth was indeed a fantastic cook, and Cody had to admit that she even beat his mom on the beef stew she'd served him half an hour ago.

"Gary, I have to talk to you about your head wrangler." Cody stirred sugar into his coffee.

He wasn't the kind of guy who beat around the bush. Gary said he liked that quality in him, and Cody had his full attention right away. They both grabbed their coffee mugs and walked to the fireplace. Gary motioned to the two armchairs. Ruth sensed that Cody had to talk about something serious, and she withdrew into the kitchen, granting the two men some privacy. Cody was thankful for it because he was hoping for a face-to-face conversation with Gary alone.

"Spill the beans, son. What's bothering you?"

"This Foster chap, I think he abuses the horses."

Surprise showed on Gary's features, and he bent forward with his elbows on his upper thighs. "What makes you think he does? That is quite a strong accusation, you know."

Cody took a sip of his coffee and described how he caught Foster ill-treating Lightning this morning.

Gary remained calm, but the pulsing vein at his temple assured Cody that Gary was as furious about the incident as he was. "Did he hurt the stallion?" he asked.

"He has a nasty bump on his flank. The bruise is about the size of my fist, and he will be sore for a few days. Walks with a slight limp, which isn't surprising, but I guess he will be okay by the end of this week. It was a big stone, and that jerk threw it with all his strength. I'm not worried about the injury, but what bothers me is Foster had no reason to throw that rock. He wanted to hurt Lightning on purpose, you know, Gary? This man has a major anger problem. He is brutal and unpredictable. I don't even want to think about the chance that Lightning will never learn to trust a man again if he encounters nasty treatment like he did today."

Gary scratched his chin thoughtfully. Then, he set his cup on the table next to his chair. "To be honest, I've had the same suspicion for the last couple of weeks. We've faced problems with horses who never gave us trouble before. As soon as he gets close to them, they start to buck and act strangely. I didn't want to see the truth, but I'm afraid that he's been beating my horses regularly."

Cody shook his head in dismay. "He threatened me, too, Gary. I don't fear him, but I'm certain that he can cause serious trouble. He is aggressive, and his quarrelsome nature could easily get out of control. Takoda was absolutely right about him. I'm not willing to tolerate any threats from him."

Cody didn't mention the scene he witnessed between Winona and Foster to Gary. He didn't want to be a tattletale. Whatever personal issues occurred between Winona and Foster was their business alone. He had no right to question it, although he disliked it.

"I'll talk to him tomorrow morning. I think it's best for all of us if he picks up his final check and hits the road. I don't believe that he'll change for the better if I tried talking some sense into him. Lowlifes like him never change. I heard rumors that he caused trouble in town as well. He always gets into fights after drinking himself senseless. So far, he hasn't started any commotion on the ranch, but I know it's just a matter of time. The only good thing about that ugly incident is that Lightning understands now that he can trust you."

Cody nodded. Then, he stood up and carried the cup over to the sideboard. "It's been a long day. Time to hit the sack. See you in the morning, Gary."

"See you, Cody. Thanks for your openness and stepping up for Lightning. I know you would have preferred to stay out of it."

With a nod, Cody turned and waved into the kitchen to wish Ruth a good night. Then, he left the main building and walked to his cabin.

That night Cody, didn't sleep well. Pictures of a bleeding and whinnying Lightning hounded his sleep.

NINETEEN
Family Barbecue

EXHAUSTION TROUBLED CODY the next morning, and he sat on the porch with his shirt unbuttoned and his hair still wet from the shower. A loud argument erupted from the ranch's main building, Gary's home. Startled, Cody looked over and saw Gary standing on his porch yelling at Foster, who stood at the foot of the stairs. The two men continued arguing for a few minutes until a furious Foster stomped toward the crew bunkhouse and slammed the door. Gary remained on the porch, his hands on his hips, angrily shaking his head. He looked pale.

Cody buttoned his shirt, tucked it into his jeans, and walked to Gary's house.

Foster strode past him, carrying a shabby travel bag. He threw it onto the passenger seat of his old beaten-up Ford, then whirled around and stared at Cody. He was pale and trembling with anger. He shook his fist threateningly in front of Cody's face.

The pure hate in his eyes surprised Cody.

Foster's voice escaped his throat in a deep growl. "I'm not done with you, Ferguson." His voice grew louder. "You and this old fool who thinks he's still one of the biggest cowboys on this planet—you'll both pay for treating me like scum. I swear to God, I'm going to make you regret this day." He jumped into his truck, started the engine, and jammed the accelerator all the way to the floor.

The old pickup leaped forward, and the tires spewed gravel across the driveway. Stacey Foster disappeared in a cloud of dust and screeched curses.

Cody wasn't the kind of man who wished bad luck on other people, and losing a job was tragic, but it was high time that Stacey Foster was gone from G.B. Ranch.

He sincerely hoped he would never have to meet that unpleasant scoundrel again. Little did he know that their paths would cross again soon and under dramatic circumstances.

LIGHTNING ACCEPTED CODY more than anybody expected after Foster had injured the horse with a rock. A few days later, after the bruise healed, Cody was able to saddle the stallion. Once Lightning was accustomed once again to the feel of a saddle on his back, Cody placed his foot into a stirrup without getting into the saddle. He wanted to give the horse the opportunity to get used to his weight in the stirrup and his closeness without pushing it too far. Again and again, he put his boot into the stirrup, hoisted himself up, and stepped back onto the ground of the pen again.

By now, Lightning knew that Cody wouldn't harm him. One morning, Cody took the chance of laying across the saddle, putting his entire weight onto the stallion's back. He expected him to buck, but to the rodeo rider's astonishment, he remained calm and stood patiently, waiting for Cody's next move.

Three days later, the magnificent stallion was good for another surprise, as he finally allowed Cody to sit upright in the saddle without rearing or trying to buck him off. Cody moved Lightning through the pasture on a walk, and then on a slow trot. The horse's movements were powerful yet well controlled, and the horse obeyed each command Cody gave him through his thighs or the reins. Cody didn't wear his spurs as he didn't want to alarm him. They weren't necessary since the animal reacted perfectly to every little touch of the heels from Cody's cowboy boots. The excellent responsiveness of the stallion baffled Cody.

"What do you think, my friend? Should we try to go a little faster?" Cody's heels pressed against his flanks, and the animal responded immediately, accelerating to a fast trot.

Gary called from the gate, "Look at you two. How wonderful." His boot rested on the lower crossbeam, and his leathery hands grasped the top of the gate. He pushed his old, battered cowboy hat back, and a broad smile lit his face. Cody's boss looked like a delighted child. "Looks like you got the ball rolling," he said cheerfully.

Cody turned his head to look at Gary as Lightning trotted around the paddock. "Yes, I think so, too. I'm quite certain that I can train Lightning to become a great roping horse. Who the hell knows, we might enter the rodeo arena together someday."

Gary punched the air with his fist. "Wouldn't that be wonderful? Honestly, I'm still convinced that's exactly where you two belong. I believed in you from the very first moment, just like I trusted this magnificent boy to be a champion one day. Well, I better let you continue your work. I just wanted to let you know that you have to be ready for dinner on time today because Ruth is preparing one of her award-winning barbecues. We both concluded that it's high time for a great evening with a campfire, country music, and barbecue. I'm sure she is performing magic in her kitchen right now. Her marinated steaks are to die for, and wait until you taste our homemade barbecue sauce."

"Oh, barbecue! If that isn't a reason for mouthwatering happiness. Thank you for the invitation. Of course, I'll come over a few minutes early. I don't want to annoy Ruth and bring one of those threatening Texas tornados on me. Great way to celebrate our small success with our temperamental friend here," he said while patting Lightning's neck tenderly.

Gary winked and turned around. But then he looked over his shoulder and said, "By the way, Winona and Takoda are going to join us for dinner." With a soft chuckle, he left his friend behind in the pasture and walked over to the house, whistling a Marty Robbins tune.

Cody watched his friend. *Now why in the heck would he grin and chuckle like that?* he wondered. For a moment, he listened to the wind whispering in the pine trees swaying back and forth in the soft afternoon breeze. Cody smelled the aromatic pine resin, and for the first time in many months, he felt like he had a home.

Winona was coming to dinner. Without being able to control it, Cody was very much looking forward to seeing her again. Against his better judgment, he was fascinated by her, and he liked her uncle Takoda. The conversations he'd had with both of them were refreshing and uplifting. Also, he wanted to get to know more about their fascinating heritage.

Here I go again after swearing to myself never to let a woman close to my heart again, he mused. *Good grief, I feel like a teenager before prom night because Winona is coming for a barbecue.*

He was sure numerous men had similar problems and were unable to resist Winona's charms. Her beauty had many aspects, and she seemed too good to be true.

That evening, Cody dressed differently. He selected a newer pair of jeans and a starched white shirt. He added to his sporty outfit a blue plaid Pendleton jacket and a finely tooled leather belt with an engraved silver rodeo buckle featuring a bucking bronco. The final touch went on his feet—a new pair of light-brown, ankle-high ropers.

Gary and the ranch hands built a bonfire in the driveway in front of the house. Not a huge one, but it was big enough for the group to sit around as each sipped their favorite beverage before dinner. Everyone, that is, except Ruth, who remained in the kitchen, cooking up a storm.

When they arrived, Winona and Takoda were both dressed in jeans and buckskin shirts. Winona wrapped a shawl with traditional patterns around her slender shoulders. A silver bracelet reflected the flames of the bonfire.

Once the fire in the grill was ready, Ruth delivered a platter of raw meat and chicken and a container of barbecue sauce to Gary, barbecue master extraordinaire. The meat sizzled and sparked as it hit the rack.

The evening was pleasant, and after dinner, everybody complained about eating way too much. It was impossible to resist Ruth's award-winning barbeque, which Gary grilled to perfection. One of the ranch boys filled their beer glasses with cool beer from an aluminum keg. There was a lot of laughter and conversation. Later, Andrew McKenzie picked up his old guitar and played "My Pony, My Rifle and Me," and everybody sang along. One tune after another followed, and the evening passed too quickly for Cody's taste. He couldn't recall the last time he felt so happy.

Around midnight, Winona decided to drive home. He walked her to her pickup.

Cody didn't want her to leave. "This was a beautiful evening, wasn't it?"

"Yes, I enjoyed it very much. Gary and Ruth sure know how to throw a cowboy party. God, I ate so much food, I'll probably roll into my bed," she added, laughing.

"Thanks for coming and sharing your stories with us. You know, I really enjoy your company," Cody said, looking at his boots, thankful for the darkness, which hid his blushing face, making him look like a teenager.

This lady sure confused him. He wasn't at all prepared when she impulsively hugged him and wished him goodnight. For an instant, he felt the warmth of her body on his chest, sending waves of excitement pulsing through him. He caught a whiff of her perfume and the fragrance of her long hair.

Winona climbed behind the wheel and lowered the driver's window. She smiled at him, started the engine, and drove a few yards before stopping the pickup again. "You know, you look mighty dapper tonight, cowboy," she called through the open window.

He smiled back at her. "Well, thank you, ma'am. As a matter of fact, you're never hard to look at yourself."

She laughed out loud and drove off. He watched the vehicle disappear through the ranch gate into the darkness of a moonless night.

The next few days passed without incident. Cody stayed busy, and Gary handed over more responsibility to him. After proving himself as a reliable and hardworking staff member, Cody earned his position as Gary's assistant in the ranch management hierarchy. The ranch hands respected Cody and had no problem when Gary announced his promotion as the new head wrangler. Since Gary fired Foster, the working atmosphere seemed more relaxed among the employees. The only person remaining skeptical was Takoda, who doubted that Foster would accept being embarrassed without causing further trouble.

"That Foster fellow ain't a good loser, my friend. I wouldn't be surprised if we hear from him again, and not in a pleasant way."

Cody looked at Takoda. "You might be right about that, but let's hope for the best. I wouldn't mind if I never see his face again in my entire life."

"He's definitely not the kind of guy who will give up his territory without battling for it. Just saying." The old Lakota Indian clicked his tongue.

TWENTY
The Fire

TWO WEEKS AFTER Foster was dismissed, Gary gave Cody the order to drive to Denver to purchase new ranch equipment and look for potential buyers for three of his most promising breeding mares.

On his way to Denver, Cody thought about his friend's words. He didn't think he'd ever meet Foster again, but one didn't know what was going on in another person's mind. One thing was sure, the rogue was a quarrelsome character, and that was unlikely to change. Cody was certain the fool had already started trouble at his next workplace. Takoda was right about one thing—people like Stacey Foster didn't see any reason to alter their ways. They were rotten for decades and remained a disruption in society.

Cody concentrated on the heavy traffic that packed the highway. After the weeks at the ranch and the remote rural life, he felt uncomfortable weaving among the countless cars and the busy traffic of the big city. The rows of condominiums and enterprise zones seemed intent upon squashing the pedestrians walking between them.

He wanted to carry out his boss man's orders as quickly as possible and return to his tranquil new home as soon as he could. He searched for a budget motel because his appointment with two possible buyers was for the next morning. Gary knew them from past deals, and they had already announced that they were interested in buying some of his mares.

After dinner in a fast-food restaurant, which tortured his taste buds compared to Ruth's delicious cooking, Cody returned to the motel to rest. As soon as he entered his room, he noticed the disgusting smell of French fries and the oil from the deep fryers they used in fast food chains. He wrinkled his nose, undressed, and left his clothes in the tiny bathroom. After taking a shower, he closed the door to the bathroom so the fast-food smell permeating his clothes wouldn't tickle his nose the entire night. *I am a country egg and always will be. I don't like the city. I don't like the crowded streets and can't even stand the smell of the city food. I'm a country boy just like Mama always said*, he thought, smiling at the memory of her words.

Cody got up at first daylight, showered, and dressed in a fresh shirt. He threw his stuff into his overnight bag, jumped into his pickup, and drove to the suburban area where he was supposed to meet the first rancher. Cody was sure he would convince the man to drive to Gary's ranch to buy a horse, or even two. Being the modern rancher he was, Gary provided Cody with a laptop so he could show videos of all the animals for sale. The area where the first client lived looked prosperous, and the neighborhood appeared wealthy.

Cody was about to turn into the customer's driveway when his phone buzzed in his pocket. He fished for it while setting the signal to turn, then checked the number of the incoming call and recognized Gary's mobile phone number.

I'm sure he wants to give me last minute advice, he assumed with a chuckle. Once parked in the driveway, he answered the call. "Good morning, boss. Have you decided to keep those beautiful girls for yourself and not sell them?"

"Cody, forget about the sale. Come back to the ranch right away and hurry up!" The sound of Gary's voice made him uncomfortable. His friend seemed upset and confused.

"Why? What's the matter?"

"A disaster happened at the ranch. Part of the stable and the tack room caught fire. We have an injured person, and we lost some of the saddles and other riding gear."

"But how in the world did that happen?" Cody shook his head, shocked at the unexpected news. The engine of his pickup was still running.

"That's not all. I urgently need your help. Lightning disappeared. My guess is that he panicked when the fire started. Looks like he broke through the gate, and now he's gone. I only hope he isn't hurt."

"Who was injured?" Cody was concerned about the stallion and the entire crew. He considered them all friends.

"Takoda has a few burn injuries. Nothing serious, but I'm sure he's in pain. But besides that, he's insane with worry because we tried to reach Winona, but she doesn't answer her phone. We called the gallery and her mobile phone. She

doesn't pick up, and her friends haven't seen her. She's nowhere to be found. Something is odd that I can't pinpoint, and I sure don't like it."

"Me neither. Something seems fishy. My bet is that someone set the fire on purpose. I'll inform the two clients that we have to reschedule and hit the road again. If I skip breaks and just stop for gas, I can make it in less than twelve hours. Keep trying to reach Winona and leave the pasture gate open. Lightning might return as soon as he calms down. The ranch is the only welcoming home he knows and where he feels safe."

"Take a break if you get too tired while driving. We don't need any more accidents. You go ahead and inform our business partner since you're already standing in his driveway, and I'll call the other guy." Gary sounded utterly concerned, and Cody decided to hit the road as quickly as possible.

"You're talking about accidents, my friend, but I doubt that this was one. And where the heck is Winona?" Cody mumbled to himself, frowning. He quickly explained the situation to the potential buyer, barely catching his breath while talking. Fortunately, the man was very understanding and agreed that Cody should return to Montana as quickly as possible. Gary could send information and videos on the mares later that week.

"Don't worry, son, I've bought from Mister Bradshaw before, and I know I've never gone wrong when buying his mares. We'll just postpone the deal. Let me know when you're ready to sell them, and I'll come to the ranch with my horse trailer."

"Thank you so much, sir, for understanding. I really appreciate it," Cody said and wished the man goodbye. Then, he hurried to his truck.

The day had started well, but now Cody's gut feeling told him that something was seriously wrong. He remembered Stacey Foster's hateful face when he threatened Cody and Gary. Was it possible he had something to do with the fire and Winona's disappearance? He prayed everything was okay with her.

TWENTY-ONE
The Search

IT WAS SHORTLY before midnight when Cody finally parked his pickup in front of the main building of the ranch. He was dead tired and leaned his head against the headrest for a moment. Although it was late, it took only a few seconds for Gary to step onto the porch. Even in the semi-darkness of the porch light, Cody immediately recognized the concern written all over Gary's face.

"Anything new?" Cody immediately wanted to know as he got out of the car.

Gary shrugged his shoulders. "Takoda will stay in the hospital tonight. They want to make sure that his lungs are okay after inhaling so much smoke. When I saw him, he was coughing an awful lot. So far, I haven't been able to talk to him. The good news is that Lightning returned after a few hours, just like you predicted. He seems fearful and nervous. I moved him to a different pasture on the other side of the property to make sure that he isn't smelling the smoke all the time. From what I could see, he isn't injured."

"What about Winona?" Cody asked, feeling a flicker of hope. But when he saw the expression on his friend's face, he already knew the answer.

"That's the bad news. Nobody has seen her. Her truck is parked at the gallery, and she still hasn't answered her phone. Hasn't responded to any of our messages either. That is totally weird and so unlike her. I'm afraid something happened to her, and I have a hunch."

"Foster!" Cody spit out the name.

Gary nodded. "I'm afraid I underestimated the fellow. I'll never forgive myself if something happens to that girl. We all love her dearly."

"We won't be able to find any tracks in the darkness, but we should start looking for a trail at first daylight. Have you informed the police yet?"

"Yes, of course, but they won't do anything about it until she's been missing for at least forty-eight hours. It's so frustrating. I feel helpless. If Foster is really responsible for this, then it's my fault."

"Don't blame yourself. It was the right thing to fire that jerk, and if he's the one who set the fire, it proves what kind of villain he is. If I can lay hands on him, he'll be sorry that he ever crossed my path. I'll make sure of that. We won't stop searching for Winona until we find her, that's for sure."

"Yes, we won't stop. If only I knew where to start with the search." Gary threw his hands into the air in a helpless gesture. Even Cody had no answer to that.

Gary's ranch hand Andrew Mc Kenzie walked toward the two men. He stopped at the porch with his cowboy hat in his hands, seeming insecure.

"Forgive me for interrupting your conversation, boss. I didn't mean to eavesdrop, but I couldn't help but overhear what you said about Foster. Do you really think he's responsible for the disappearance of Winona and for setting the fire?"

Cody shrugged his shoulders, but Gary nodded slowly. "It's very likely, Andrew. After all, he's been harassing Winona for months. He wanted her to be his girlfriend. She told me herself. He must have acted quite intrusively lately."

"Well, I can confirm that," Cody said. "I watched a rather nasty scene when he harassed her trying to stop her from getting into her car. It was obvious that she didn't want to talk to him, and he tried to restrain her by grabbing her arm. Should have thrown the guy into the dirt right then," he added, anger in his voice.

Gary looked at Andrew. "I'm afraid that he is responsible for the fire and likely for her disappearance as well. The fire didn't happen accidentally. I had a closer look at our stable and found a gasoline can behind the building. I am sure this was his revenge for being fired, but I had no choice. He mistreated my horses, and that is something I won't tolerate from anybody on my ranch. Besides, he wasn't a team player, was he?"

"No, definitely not. He would get mad at us for the slightest thing. Being on the cattle drive with him was an ordeal. My brother and I had to do all the work, while he drank himself senseless almost every night. I don't even know where he got all the booze. The only reason we didn't say anything to you was because he was head wrangler, and my brother and I doubted that you would believe us." Andrew looked down, and his face appeared pale in the weak porch light.

Gary shook his head. "I'm sorry I didn't give you more reason to trust me, son."

"Sweet Jesus, I never thought he would go that far," Andrew murmured. He stared at the two men, his eyes huge with horror. Then, he frowned and seemed thoughtful. "If he kidnapped Winona, he most likely took her to his hunting cabin. He built it a year ago. It's about a day's ride from here. At least, that was what I would do if I were in his shoes. It's a place hardly anybody knows about, from what he told me."

Gary stared at Andrew in surprise. "What hunting cabin are you talking about?"

"Well, he always bragged about that hut he built in the woods and claimed that he goes hunting in that territory regularly. Stacey wanted to take me along, but I stick to the rules, especially when it comes to hunting. I didn't want to be caught shooting animals illegally, especially if it's not hunting season. He does it all the time, and as far as I know, Stacey doesn't care about a permit either. I didn't want trouble with the ranchers, so I refused to join. I need my job, boss."

Andrew shook his head. "Besides, he hangs around there with his friend Cliff, and I don't want to have anything to do with that rogue. He's a good-for-nothing man, just like Stacey, and I heard that Cliff is dealing drugs. That is not my kind of scene, so I tried my best to stay out of it and avoid them whenever I could."

"Who the hell is Cliff?" Cody demanded to know.

"Cliff Morales, another boozy roughneck. Part Mexican, part Kiowa, like Foster," Gary explained. Cody saw the flicker of panic in Gary's eyes, and it left him deeply concerned for Winona's safety. Remembering the unpleasant scene he'd witnessed between Stacey and Winona, he was certain she was in the hands of that villain. He seemed quite possessive of her.

"Do you have an idea where that hunting cabin is located?" Gary asked his employee.

Andrew nodded. "More or less. As I said, I've never been there, but he described the route in detail because he expected me to join him one weekend a few months ago. I changed my mind on a gut feeling, and I'm glad that I didn't go, knowing now what I didn't know then."

Cody and Gary looked at each other.

"We ride at dawn," Gary declared, and Cody nodded with a grim face. "Andrew, you will join us. Tell the others to remain at the ranch and to stand guard, changing shifts every four hours, day and night. I want to make sure that Ruth and all our employees are safe. We cannot risk another fire or a similar incident happening. Cody, do you think you can ride Lightning in open terrain yet? It's possible that he can sense Winona and even Stacey much faster than we would find them, so he would be of help."

"I don't think that it would be a problem. The stallion trusts me now, and I'm sure he'll allow me to ride him again. I agree with you, Lightning might sniff out that lowlife. His body language will tell us when he's close. I know that Lightning reacts positively to Winona's scent, so let's give it a try. I hope we find her before something bad happens to her."

Gary nodded. Before they separated for a short night's rest, Gary looked at the two men. "Cody, Andrew, we'll go heeled, so pack your guns and ammunition. We won't take any chances, and we'll do whatever is necessary to save Winona."

The two men looked at their boss and nodded. No more words were necessary. They prepared for a fight without knowing the outcome. The three men went back to their rooms, planning to catch a few hours of sleep before the hunt started in the morning.

Cody collected all his things for the next day's ride before trying to sleep. *God, don't let anything happen to her,* he prayed. He grabbed his six-shooter and loaded it. He added more bullets to his gun belt and placed both next to his water flask.

"I swear to God, if you harm her, I'll kill you where you stand, Foster," he whispered into the darkness of his cabin. Then, he prepared to get four hours of sleep after the long ride. The worry for Winona followed him into his dreams.

TWENTY-TWO
Persecution

WHEN THE FIRST pale daylight crawled over the eastern hills behind the ranch, the three men saddled their horses. Ruth approached them, lunch parcels under her arm. She seemed unusually pale and quiet this morning. Cody murmured his thanks to her and divided the provisions among the three of them. Their canteens, filled with fresh water, dangled from the saddle horns. The men silently checked their firearms one last time. Cody and Gary each sheathed an additional Winchester rifle into the saddle scabbards and folded back the stirrups on top of them.

Gary could see Ruth didn't like their intentions, but when she studied the men's determined faces, she remained silent, not trying to change their minds. She was worried for Winona and for the safety of the three cowboys.

She hugged Gary for a long while and whispered, "Return to me safely, Cowboy."

Tears welled up in her eyes as Gary planted a soft kiss on her cheek. "I promise, Ruth. Try to calm Takoda when he calls. He must be out of his mind with fear for the girl. I promised him I would bring his niece back safely, and I intend to keep my word. Tell him to rest and tend to his wounds first."

Ruth nodded. "I'll make sure he doesn't do something stupid like trying to follow you all."

Gary patted her on the shoulder. "I thank the good Lord for you in my life, Ruth," he said in a hushed tone, then he mounted his horse.

Cody and Andrew did likewise. Lightning's step was powerful—it seemed as if he sensed the importance of this mission. He behaved well and didn't buck or play other tricks on Cody. Even after they left his familiar terrain on the ranch, Lightning obeyed Cody's commands. If the task hadn't been such a serious one, Cody would have enjoyed riding Lightning. He was proud of the stallion. They'd come a long way.

After several hours in the saddle with no break, Gary signaled his ranch hand, Andrew, to come to his side. The young cowboy caught up with his boss.

"I'm sure we're getting closer to the woods where you said Foster built that cabin. I think it's better if you take the lead from here. It's very likely that you'll find the way faster than the rest of us since you have an idea of the approximate location. When we get closer, we have to approach slowly and be extremely cautious because I'm sure he has a gun. We don't want to risk getting shot out of our saddles or Winona getting hurt. We have to surprise him if we can. If something bad happens to any of us, I'll strangle that bastard with my own hands."

Andrew swallowed hard and nodded. "Judging from the distance we rode and from what he told me, I guess we should arrive there in about an hour from now. According to Foster, the place is hidden behind some huge boulders, which gives him perfect cover, so you're right, we have to be very careful. We'll likely make great targets if we don't watch out."

Gary nodded and reined in his horse, so Andrew was able to pass him on his sorrel gelding.

Cody had been quiet since the three left the ranch. He feared for Winona's safety and prayed that nothing bad had happened to her. His ashen face framed half-closed eyes. Lightning snorted from time to time. The horse seemed to sense how nervous Cody was, but he obeyed every move of his rider's thighs and heels.

Lightning responded so well that Cody had the feeling they'd be horse and rider for an eternity. Suddenly and against Cody's wishes, Lightning stopped and pulled his ears back. The unexpected movement startled Cody, but he noticed the faint smell of smoke in the air. He pressed his heels against the flanks of his stallion and caught up with Gary and Andrew. He pointed to the nervously prancing stallion. "He's sensing something, and I smell smoke. It's very faint, but there is definitely a fire somewhere close by."

Gary and Andrew stopped their horses and dismounted. Andrew pointed ahead to a meadow surrounded by large boulders. Since they didn't want to warn Foster, they left the horses outside the meadow with their reins wrapped around the low branches of a sturdy oak. After a few steps, they caught a glimpse of Foster's beat-up truck hidden in some trees.

"I'll be darned. That scoundrel really is in that hunting cabin just as you surmised, Andrew. If not for you, we would have never found him.

Unfortunately, we don't know if Winona is with him, but my gut feeling tells me she is," Gary whispered.

"Shouldn't take long to find out," Cody hissed angrily.

At that moment, they heard Foster's voice arguing with someone else. "You think that wannabe cowboy is better for you, don't you? You wait and see how I teach you manners. You're nothing but a cheap Lakota trollop, and I'll make sure you regret rejecting me. You'll learn to obey my orders and earn money for me, woman. Don't you even think you could continue playing the fake artist in that stupid gallery once you're my wife. You're mine, understand?"

Gary looked over at Cody, who nodded slowly and whispered, "It's Winona."

Gary, Cody, and Andrew conferred on a plan to free Winona without putting her in more danger than she already was. The three men surveyed the lay of the land around the cabin and the doors and windows. They knew Foster was unpredictable in his rage.

Cody and Gary silently sneaked behind the cabin. In the woods, Lightning snorted and stomped the ground nervously. He sensed his old enemy close by.

Andrew walked toward the door of the hunting cabin and knocked, pretending to pay his old ranch mate a visit. "Hey, Stacey, are you there? It's me, Andrew."

Silence lay like a heavy blanket on the meadow, and nobody answered from the other side of the door. However, Andrew heard the soft whimper of a woman. Cody heard it as well, and wanted to storm the cabin, but Gary held him back with a hand on Cody's shoulder. Cody swallowed hard. He knew he had to keep his emotions under control if he didn't want to damage their chances of freeing the Lakota woman.

"Andrew? What in Christ's name are you doing here?" a surprised Foster yelled through the door.

"I quit the ranch. Got into a big fight with old Bradshaw. That jerk claims that I was responsible for a little fire we had yesterday. I have no clue how it started behind the tack room and won't take that nonsense trying to blame it on me. I'm done with that jerk, but I'm without a job now, and I thought I might be able to join you for a while. For Christ's sake, open the freaking door, man. I'm freezing my butt off. This is not exactly a Florida beach out here, dude."

Cody smiled, but his eyes remained cold. Andrew played his role perfectly and sounded very convincing. Gary and Cody pulled their guns from their holsters and pressed their backs against the rear wall of the cabin while they slowly stepped sideways toward the corner. Gary heard Foster pull back the bolt of the door and pointed around the corner.

"Holy crap, is that your way of greeting an old friend? Put that gun down, you fool. I've had enough trouble for one day. Wait a minute, what in the world is Winona doing here, dude?"

Now everything had to happen in the blink of an eye. Cody and Gary stormed around the corner of the shanty toward the startled Foster, who stared at Andrew, disbelief and surprise showing on his face.

"You damn traitor. You brought them here. I swear to God, you will regret betraying me," he yelled and aimed his pistol at young Andrew's chest.

Andrew threw himself on the ground just in time before a slug ripped through the air.

Cody heard the horses whinnying nervously. He saw Foster running toward his pickup as if the devil himself was after him. Before reaching the driver's side, he whirled and shot a couple of rounds without aiming at anything in particular. A shot grazed Gary on his left upper arm, and he and Cody crouched behind the front door of the lodge for cover.

Foster saw his chance and aimed at Andrew, who was still on the ground. The rogue's face was distorted into a mask of hatred and cruelty, his lips curled away from his teeth. His desire for revenge was stronger than his desire to escape from his persecutors. "I'm going to finish you off for betraying me like this," he hissed. He raised the gun and cocked the hammer.

The click of it sounded unnaturally loud across the meadow, and Andrew desperately tried to scramble away from the villain. He saw the intense hate in Foster's eyes and had no doubt that the man would try to kill him right here.

Cody's voice rang as a powerful echo through the meadow. "Foster, you better think twice before you pull that trigger. You will never escape here. You're outnumbered, and if you shoot one of us, I'll make sure that you don't leave this place alive. You would make my day if you gave me a reason to shoot your sorry ass dead. You better give up and do it quick because I ain't bluffing." He checked his pistol.

"I'll take care of you as soon as I've sent this rat straight to hell where he belongs. I owe you a debt anyway, Ferguson." Foster spat out every word. The gun in his hand pointed at Andrew, his index finger toying nervously with the trigger.

Andrew scrambled to rise as he stared at Foster, wide-eyed and pale, knowing he was unlikely to see the next sunrise.

The sound of hooves and a piercing squeal startled Foster, and he whirled to his left. A dark shadow loomed over him. Lightning stood on his rear legs, beating the air with his front hooves.

"How in the world...?" Cody wondered, since he had looped Lightning's reins around a branch. Somehow, the stallion must have freed himself and came to the cabin to battle Foster.

"Wait, you dang bag of bones, I am going to teach you a lesson." That was the last threat the world heard from Stacey Foster. He couldn't utter another word because Lightning's front hooves pummeled his shoulders and head with the horse's half-ton of weight. With a cry of pain, the man dropped his weapon. Again and again, the stallion reared, and his front hooves battered on the man who had mistreated him whenever he had a chance.

Foster's knees collapsed, and he fell to the ground, still using his arms to protect his head from the stallion's onslaught.

Cody watched in horror. It was not the first time he saw a horse getting at a fallen man, but this was not the typical rodeo accident. The stallion seemed to be paying back for all the cruelty experienced by Foster and his former owner.

Blood streamed down Foster's face, and the sickening sound of breaking bone accompanied his shrieking voice. The others stared, not able to understand what was happening. Cody stood frozen in shock, unable to help the man on the ground. Piercing screams filled the air for a few moments longer, but then the screaming stopped. After a few weak sobs, Foster lay unmoving on the ground, not far from the man he intended to shoot only a few minutes ago.

Cody staggered toward Lightning, hoping to calm him with the sound of his voice. "It's okay, boy. Take it easy."

For a brief moment, he was also afraid of the stallion. He grabbed the reins, and the magnificent animal quieted, sweating and trembling. The smell of blood permeated the air. The stallion leaned his head against

Cody's chest as if seeking protection. Repulsed, Cody looked down on the bloody shambles of bone, blood, and brains, which once had been Foster's head. It was a disgusting sight, and Cody tasted bitter bile in his mouth.

He turned slowly and saw Gary leading a pale and shaking Winona out of her temporary prison. Gary supported her. She was bleeding profusely from her nose, and her right eye was swollen shut. The man had beaten her badly, but at least she was alive. When she spotted the body on the ground, Gary laid his uninjured arm around her shoulders and turned her away from the ugly scene.

He shook his head. "Don't look at it, Winona. Lightning broke his skull. It looks terrible."

Cody studied the trembling woman. *Praise the Lord. I thought I was never going to see her again.* The thought alone seemed unbearable for him.

Andrew tried to pull himself to his feet using a nearby branch. He was pale as a ghost. When he saw Foster's pulped face, his complexion turned green, as if he was about to throw up.

A blood stain spread on Gary's shirt sleeve.

"Can you use your arm, Gary?" Cody asked. He tried to focus his mind, to function rationally.

His boss nodded, his good arm still around the shaking Winona.

Cody pointed to Foster's old pickup. "You better take the vehicle and drive Winona back to the ranch. I'll ride Lightning and take your horse alongside. Andrew and I will inform the police as soon as we have cell reception. I'll tell them where to find the body and what happened."

"That's probably the best way," Gary said and led the woman to the beat-up truck. Reluctantly, she climbed into the passenger seat. Winona hadn't spoken a single word yet, and Cody was concerned. Perhaps she was in shock. When he looked at her bruised face, he wondered what else the rogue had done to her. He feared for the worst and prayed that Foster hadn't raped her.

That idiot got the punishment he deserved, he thought and turned, scowling at the dead man lying on the ground.

Lightning still snorted, shook his head nervously, and pawed the ground with his front hoof. The other two horses seemed restless as well, perhaps because of the scent of blood.

"Everything is all right, my big boy. You did well and protected us all. Andrew owes his life to you."

Hearing Cody's voice and feeling his tender touch finally calmed the stallion enough for them to be able to hit the trail back to the ranch. Cody still couldn't believe the stallion had protected them and likely saved his friend's life.

He took Gary's horse's reins in his left hand, climbed into the saddle, and followed Andrew down the trail, leaving the scene of the tragedy behind.

Gary started the old pickup after the two riders and the horses were out of sight. Foster's vehicle made a racket due to its damaged exhaust, and he didn't want to spook them.

Winona sat beside him, wordless and pale. She gingerly touched her swollen right eye. She looked terrible, but she was alive, and that was the main thing. Gary thanked God they were able to save her. He wouldn't have known how to explain it to Takoda if they had failed.

TWENTY-THREE
Unknown Enemies

THE WATCHER SAW the pickup disappear behind the cluster of pine trees as Gary drove along the dirt road, leaving the hunting cabin behind. The body of Stacey Foster, its skull smashed beyond recognition, lay at the foot of the steps to the cabin. The crash of breaking branches interrupted the eerie silence that followed Gary's departure. No living being appeared for a few minutes. At last, Cliff Morales cautiously stepped through the bushes onto the meadow.

He looked down upon his dead friend and shook his head. "You damn fool. You've always been so hot-tempered and full of yourself that you underestimated the people you messed around with. Well, bad luck for you, Hoss."

He gazed in the direction the pickup had taken a few moments ago. Cliff grinned, thinking the turn of events was nothing but good for him. "Well, I prefer not to share anyway. In case the old Indian knows something about the lost gold, and I find it, I can keep it all for myself, now that this jerk is gone for good. Little squaw, I'm sure we'll see each other soon, and this time, your so-called rodeo hero won't be able to save you. I'm sure the old medicine man will spill the beans when I lay hands on him... or on you." The villain rubbed his stubbly face. "You won't have such an easy game with me as you did with Foster, girlie," he whispered and licked his lips.

With a last look of scorn at the dead body, the man turned and disappeared into the woods. "Now where was it I hid my old Jeep Wrangler?"

IT TOOK A few days for Winona to recover from her injuries. Her uncle had hovered close, and he needed time to recover from the shock of her kidnaping.

Gary's arm healed quickly thanks to Ruth's care. She kept a constant eye on him and pampered him in every way possible. Cody felt a twinge of envy over the way Ruth showed her affection for Gary. He felt lonely when he sat on his porch or in front of the fireplace after a long day's work, missing the companionship of a loving mate.

He thought of Winona almost daily. Strangely, she and Takoda had been more reticent than ever the past few days. Cody wondered if there was another reason for it besides the shock over the tragic events at the hunting cabin. He didn't know what to think of their silence. One evening, he sat before the fireplace, watching the crackling flames and reading a book about the battle at Little Bighorn. The plight of the Native Americans struck him hard between the eyes. From his European perspective, he could hardly imagine what it must have been like to have land, possessions, and family ripped away as if their people were nothing. How could he ever sympathize with her feelings?

The police investigation into the death of Stacey Foster was rather brief. Unlike Foster, Gary Bradshaw had a superb reputation in the county, so no one doubted his story of self-defense. Foster, to the contrary, was a well-known troublemaker and alcoholic. Everybody in the town of Dillon knew Foster constantly looked for opportunities to start an argument or fistfight. Nobody was saddened by his death. No one was surprised he ended up like this, and some folks in town openly announced their relief over the fact that the rogue was gone for good.

Both the law and the townspeople excused Lightning's aggressive behavior as a natural reaction to the mistreatment the stallion had experienced at Foster's hands and by his previous owner. Cody was able to prove that Lightning acted normally around other people on the ranch.

TWENTY-FOUR
Living the Dream

DAYS AFTER THE terrible events at the hunting hut, Gary watched Cody training with Lightning. The stallion trusted the experienced cowboy, and Cody was able to ride him without any difficulties.

Gary called him over and pointed to the stallion. "Do you think you are ready to take this to the next level?"

Cody frowned. "What are you talking about?"

Gary smiled warmly. "Well, how about teaming up with this old bossman of yours. I am not bad as a roper, and I was wondering if we could give it a try together. You would surely make an excellent header, and I would be the heeler. Age is not much of an issue when it comes to team roping. To be honest, I kinda miss the roar of the crowd and the atmosphere, don't you?"

Cody stared at his former mentor in disbelief. "Well, I cannot say that I miss it, at least not the way I used to."

Gary shook his head. "Who are you trying to fool, Hoss? I don't expect you to yearn for the past and the days in Cheyenne. I know you got hurt in every possible way that week at the Frontier Days, but how about rodeo in general? How about the energy, the smell of the horses, the cheering crowd? How about the challenge, the way of the cowboy, Cody? What about the pride and the way we all stand with our hats taken off and hand on our hearts as we sing the anthem."

Tears pooled in Cody's eyes. "Yes, sir, I miss that part of it," he whispered.

Gary nodded. "You know I will always have your back, son. This time, you won't be alone in the arena, but if we go for it, we will have to work hard."

Cody looked over at Lightning, a former rodeo champion. "I reckon that dang horse would know better than me when it comes to roping a steer, wouldn't he?"

Gary laughed. "You betcha. He was one of the best out there. I think he deserves another chance to shine. All you two need is a bit of confidence and some practice. So, what do you say?"

Cody remained silent for a long moment. Then, his boyish grin started to spread across his handsome features. "All right. Let's give it a try. Let's practice, and if we can catch us some steers, we can enter a few of the smaller rodeos. Just for fun, no pressure, right?"

Gary slapped his friend on the shoulder. "That is the whole point. We are supposed to have fun and live our cowboy dream. Let's start tomorrow with throwing a few loops over that dummy in the arena."

The two friends started their roping lessons the following day right after a hearty breakfast. Cody was nervous. He knew Gary Bradshaw was way more experienced than he admitted. He was just not the kind of guy who bragged about his skills.

Unlike me when I was younger, Cody thought, and shame blushed his cheeks. He threw his rope a couple of times.

Gary watched him and nodded. "You definitely know the basics. Now, unlike on the ranch, when you have to rope yourself a horse you should keep the loop a bit smaller. If your loop is too big, that little bugger might wiggle out of it before you can pull him along. Plus, it would be a lot of rope to pull back, and don't you pull too early either."

Cody nodded. He felt like a teenager again when Gary had taken him under his wings the first time. Nevertheless, he started to relax.

"Another thing you have to pay attention to is not to pull back too harshly with your arm going way to the left. You hold the reins of your horse in that same hand. You know what it would do if you pulled hard with your arm stretched way to the side?"

Cody nodded. "I would jerk my horse's head around as well."

Gary smiled. "Exactly. And we don't want to do that because you need to keep Lightning in line with the steer."

Having grown up on his father's ranch, it didn't take long, and Cody was ready to give it the first try.

"It's time to have some fun, son."

Cody nodded, and they both walked over to their saddled horses.

"Now when you rope, it is a lot about balance. In the chute, you sit in the center of the saddle, but once you give them the sign to open the gate, you lean forward and put additional weight on the stirrups. It signals Lightning to speed up. Give him some extra rein. He knows what to do. Remember to stay in line behind the steer but a bit to his left. Make sure you give him slight direction toward your team partner, and don't chase the steer to the left away from the heeler."

They opened the gate, and the black steer started to run. Cody chased him, swung the loop in his right hand a couple of times, and threw. The rope landed over the steers horns, and Cody pulled.

"Well done. Now pull him slightly to the left for me." Gary threw his rope and caught the steer by his right rear hoof. "Yeah, baby, we caught us a steer," he shouted and laughed like a happy child.

Cody grinned back at him. He felt like in the good old days and patted Lightnings neck. "No wonder they call you a rodeo champ, boy." The horse knew indeed what he had to do, just as Gary predicted.

The two men practiced almost daily for the next three weeks. Finally, they decided to give it a try at the rodeo in Billings. Gary and Cody drove there with Gary's new horse trailer. They loaded Lightning and Gary's favorite bay gelding, Sergeant Pepper, in the wee hours.

Ruth handed them a basket full of sandwiches and a cooler with beverages. She hugged both men. "Have fun, and don't you guys dare to come back with broken bones," she said like a scolding mother.

"Yes, ma'am," Cody answered and walked away to give his boss and Ruth some privacy to bid farewell.

The drive took around four hours, and they talked about their days at the rodeo and how they both started being cowboys. Gary avoided talk about Cody's family, and Cody didn't mention Cheyenne. They were in a cheerful mood and intended to keep it this way. There was a lot of laughter.

"You know, Gary, I haven't felt this good in a long time. Thanks for talking me into doing this."

Gary smiled warmly. "You are more than welcome, son."

They arrived around ten in the morning and quickly tended to their horses before getting a bite to eat for lunch. Gary registered them ahead and had paid the entry fee, surprising Cody with his ongoing generosity.

The exciting atmosphere of the arena infected them both as they prepared for their first run as a roping team.

Cody tried hard to ignore the memories and the images which pushed themselves mercilessly into his awareness. Lightning scraped his hooves in the dirt, perhaps sensing that his human partner was nervous.

Gary walked by and slapped Cody on the shoulder. "We can do this, partner. No pressure, no championship points to collect for Sin City. Let's simply rope and have a great time, okay?" Gary knew that Cody and Lightning both had to face their fears if they were to overcome the past. "Listen to me, son. You're not here to prove yourself to anybody else or to erase the past. You're here to have fun. Try to see today's ride as a test run for you and Lightning as a team. We will go out there and get a feel for ourselves and our rodeo roots. The favorites will feel the pressure, but you can simply enjoy the ride and have a good time. Nobody expects you to win. Who knows, one day we might both tell stories to youngsters about how we won a cool looking belt buckle or a saddle."

Cody nodded. "Thanks, Gary. I mean, thank you for everything you have done for me. It feels like you freed me from a deep black hole, and for the first time in many months, I'm looking forward to another tomorrow."

"Cody, my friendship and my respect for you will never depend on a rodeo championship rank. I have always considered you family. You convinced me of your quality a long time ago, and that will never change. We all have our dark moments. Who am I to judge you? I've had my failures in life like anybody else, and so have you. The main thing is to cowboy up and get back on your feet. Keep on trying to do your best."

He looked down and whispered, "Yes, sir. I just don't know how to thank you enough or to express how much it means to me that you gave me another chance. I'll try to prove myself worthy of your trust."

Gary nodded and remained silent. No further words were needed between the two men. If Cody had been Gary Bradshaw's son, he couldn't have loved him more. Cody looked up to the man as if he were his second father. In some ways, Gary was exactly that.

"Let's go and get the horses ready. Time to catch us a steer."

TWENTY-FIVE
Back at the Rodeo

THE FUTURE ROPING competitor bent to check the cinch encircling Lightning's belly. He climbed into the saddle, tipped his hat as a last greeting to Gary on the other side, and waited for the announcer to call his starting number. *Who would have thought that I would ride into another rodeo arena someday?* Cody mused. Then, he removed his hat and said a short prayer like he always had before every ride.

He stroked Lightning's neck tenderly. "What do you think, my boy? Shall we catch us a runaway steer?"

Lightning whinnied softly as if to agree to the suggestion.

Cody chuckled. The nervousness was gone. He felt content and happy now. Knowing that Gary roped on the other side granted him the chance to have fun, but not only that, Gary believed in him, and thanks to his old mentor, he called the G.B. Ranch his home now. Cody looked forward to tonight's barbecue with Gary, Ruth, and all the ranch hands. He considered all of them his new family.

Cody saw how the rodeo hands closed the gate of the chute behind the steer. Gary checked the loop of his rope for a last time and nodded over to Cody.

Finally, it was their turn. The announcer called his and Gary's names. Cody pushed his curly dark hair under his cowboy hat. He positioned Lightning inside the roping box. Rider and stallion waited, concentrating on nothing but the steer pushing his powerful chest against the metal gate of the chute, trying to escape his short-term prison. It was about time they released the feller into the arena.

"Ladies and gentlemen, we have Cody Ferguson heading and Gary Bradshaw from G.B. Ranch in Dillon, Montana, is the heeler. This is their first run as a team in a roping competition, so let's give them a round of applause and keep our fingers crossed for them."

Cody didn't hear the people clapping or the announcer's words. A calm feeling spread through his body. It was almost like in the old days as rodeo champion. He heard his own heartbeat in his ears, and it overwhelmed all the other sounds. An eerie silence surrounded Cody as if a huge air bubble surrounded him and his stallion. The cheering audience, the crackling from the speakers, the stomping, snorting animals—everything else ceased to exist. There was nothing else but him and Lightning, with the skin on his flanks twitching nervously and his strong, tense muscles. Lightning was ready to shoot out of the starting box like an arrow leaving a fully drawn bow.

Cody was ready, and so was Gary. He turned slightly and nodded. With a loud clang of the metal bars, the gate in front of the chocolate-colored calf opened, and the animal ran into the arena as if the devil himself chased him, looking for an escape.

Once the gate opened, Cody leaned forward, urging Lightning to chase after the steer who ran into the center of the arena. Cody swung his rope, circling his wrist. Once… twice… and with the third rotation of his hand, he let the rope fly. The lasso shot forward like a striking rattlesnake and landed neatly around the steer's neck. With only a twitch of the reins and a nudge of his heels, Lightning pulled their captive to the left. Cody saw Gary racing toward them from the corner of his right eye.

In the blink of an eye, Gary's rope shot around the right hind leg of the steer and took a dally stretching the helpless animal for a catch. Both men smiled and shook hands while riding side by side, leaving the arena to the next team. Of course, they were far from the top five roping teams with a penalty for the one leg catch, but it was a start, and the main thing was that they had the fun they intended to have.

At the end of the rodeo, the pair stood at a surprising fourth place, and Gary was more than satisfied. "That's not bad for a start—not bad at all my friend," he said while Cody pampered Lightning with one of the sweet apples he loved so well. Horse and rider had both caught the rodeo fever again, enjoying themselves. Gary laughed heartily when Cody explained that he felt as if he had just come home.

"Since you feel that way, I assume the two of us will continue going to competitions. The summer is still long, and we can select a few of the smaller sanctioned rodeos and try our luck. Who the hell knows, once you win over a thousand dollars, you can get your PRCA card again. Nothing is impossible, my friend," Gary said with enthusiasm written all over his smiling face.

Cody shrugged his shoulders. "I'm not sure, Gary. You know how expensive it is to travel from rodeo to rodeo and pay the starting fees. I'm afraid I can't afford to do that."

"Nonsense. Let that be my problem," Gary declared.

Puzzled, Cody looked at his friend. "Are you saying you want to sponsor my rodeo season?"

"Hell, why not? First of all, I cannot recall having had so much fun in a long time. Secondly, if Lightning continues to develop into such an excellent roping horse, I can earn a lot of money with him as a breeding stallion later on. I see it as an investment in the future of the G.B. Ranch."

Cody frowned and studied Gary's face. Again, he wondered where Gary Bradshaw got the money for such costly investments. Cody knew from a conversation with Ruth that the ranch hadn't been cheap when Gary bought it a few years back. He remembered Gary was a man of modest heritage. Cody recalled how much Gary earned as a head wrangler at his late father's ranch, and he just couldn't imagine how his friend found enough money to start and run a big operation like the Bradshaw ranch.

Somehow, all this doesn't fit together, Cody thought, but he wouldn't pry into his friend's finances. He would never do anything to jeopardize this precious friendship. Gary was his best friend and his employer. He remembered his father saying, "Don't bite the hand that feeds you," and he intended to stick to that advice. Besides, he had to admit that competing in the arena with his friend and mentor by his side felt much better than battling against a bucking bronc with the weight of having to achieve high scores to make it to the finals.

❖

THINGS ON THE rodeo circuit started rolling for Cody and Gary. They joined one team roping competition after another on the weekends, traveling all around Montana, Wyoming, and even Idaho. Cody was grateful to learn from his old mentor, and during those days at the rodeos, he felt as if Gary was the father he'd missed so much. It didn't take long, and Cody won over a thousand dollars and was able to apply for his PRCA card again. It felt odd to hold it in his hands, almost as if somebody turned back time for him. But Cody knew certain mistakes couldn't be undone, and he needed to concentrate on his new life in Montana.

ONE DAY, TAKODA and Winona joined him at one of the events, which thrilled Cody.

At first, he was afraid Winona wouldn't want to have anything to do with him now that he had returned to the rodeo life. Who could blame her after the tragedy with Stacey Foster? Cody still worried that Foster had harmed her more seriously than beating her.

When Winona and her uncle appeared at the entrance area of the arena, he was so happy to see them both. This time he had no difficulty admitting to himself that his joy wasn't just about seeing Takoda, but the tingling feeling in his tummy was over Winona as well. The knowing smile on Gary's face spoke clearly—obviously his joy was over seeing Winona.

TWENTY-SIX
Admitting Old Wounds

THAT VERY WEEKEND, he and Winona sat together at the campfire some distance from the other rodeo participants.

"I still don't understand why Foster kidnapped you," Cody said.

Winona took a sip of her Diet Coke before she answered, "He always bragged that I was his girl."

Cody regarded her inquiringly, and she shook her head.

"No, I never gave him false hope. Rather the opposite was the case because I hated him from the first moment I met him at the ranch. You know, a couple of years ago, I was in a serious relationship with a member of our tribe. According to Lakota law, we were married. Sadly, he was very much like Stacey Foster. After he beat me up countless times, I finally got out of the abusive relationship. Don't think he released me or that I just walked out of the relationship because he would have rather killed me than let me go." She stared into the flames of the nearby bonfire.

"One day, he went on one of his famous 'booze around town' tours. He was out with his pals and just didn't return home. Three days later, the Highway Patrol came to our door and asked me to accompany them to the hospital. They didn't bother to tell me why they needed me there. I assumed that he had gotten himself into trouble again, and I remember wondering why the elevator took me to the basement instead of to one of the upper floors of the hospital."

She stared into the flames while Cody waited patiently for her to continue. It seemed as if she had seen as many dark days as he had, perhaps even more. Her voice was hushed when she continued, and he had to strain to understand her with the others talking in the background.

"He must have been drunk and walked across the highway. A truck ran him over like he was a coyote. I had to identify him. He looked pretty much like Foster did after Lightning attacked him because the vehicle hit him at full speed. As a special treat, I received a four-digit hospital bill. Up to this day, I feel ashamed that I didn't feel the slightest emotion. I felt no sadness and no compassion. All I felt was empty and cold inside. Hell, to a certain degree I was even relieved that it was over at last." She shook her head, clearly troubled by the memories.

Cody touched her forearm tenderly as if to convince her that it was okay for her to feel like that.

"At the beginning, I thought I was a terrible human being for being grateful that he was gone, but too much happened between us. Like every human being, I can't change the way I feel. I guess it's natural that if you bend the branch too much, one day it will snap."

Cody gazed at her attractive features. Then, he poked the embers with a stick and added another log. The flames licked at the new wood, and sparks crackled into the cool night air. After a moment, he cleared his throat. He knew it was his turn to lay his cards on the table. If he wanted to deepen his relationship with Winona, he had to be honest and tell her the truth about his failed marriage and the times when he was a good-for-nothing man.

"I want to share my hard times with you. I had a bad accident at the rodeo in Cheyenne."

Winona nodded. "Gary told me about it. He said you were severely injured."

Cody nodded and collected his thoughts for a moment. Then, he turned around and looked into her face. "I was almost killed. One of my broken ribs punctured my lungs, and I almost didn't make it. But there was another injury which was much worse, and it left a bigger scar than the one the surgeons left who operated on my chest." He took a sip of his Coke as if to win precious time.

"I was married. My wife accompanied me to most of the rodeos just like my best friend Tanner did. We were like brothers from childhood on. Tanner's family owned the ranch next to ours, and we joined the rodeo together when we were barely out of high school."

Winona listened silently, and he was glad she did. Cody didn't know if he would be brave enough to continue if she interrupted him now.

"Our marital relationship wasn't perfect, to express it diplomatically. We argued a lot, and it wasn't easy to satisfy my wife, Lynn. Don't misunderstand me. I don't blame her for feeling neglected because I also made mistakes, and I guess I should have known that she needed more than watching me riding through the arena as if she were a groupie. I had a dream that we would participate in rodeos together because she started as a competitor in barrel racing. I had this perfect picture in my mind about us raising kids, running my parent's ranch, and breeding horses together. I was ready to settle down, and being in love with her probably made me turn a blind eye to her questionable character."

Winona passed him another soda and wrapped a warm shawl around her shoulders. She leaned back and made herself comfortable, signaling him that he had all the time in the world to tell her what happened. He was grateful for it—after Gary, she was the second person he opened up to the most, albeit reluctantly.

"We got into a fight in Cheyenne. Well, not really a fight, but Lynn was just so quarrelsome and bitchy about the entire weekend. I wanted to make up with her. I wanted things between us to be like they were at the start when I fell for her. It didn't feel good to enter the arena with this shadow of grouchiness hanging between the two of us. You know it distracts a rider when he has to enter a dangerous sports competition and his mind isn't free of worries."

Cody swallowed, and Winona suspected that much more happened besides the accident that weekend.

"I searched for Lynn everywhere because I bought a little gift for her. Finally, I found her." Cody scoffed and crumpled the empty can of coke in his fist. "My wife sat naked on the lap of my best friend. The picture of them having sex behind my back is burned into my subconscious forever. You know, up to today, I don't know who I hate more. Her for betraying my love and making a fool of me, or my friend Tanner who I trusted with my own life. That was the last time I was involved with a woman," he added softly, his inner eyebrows raised. Tears formed in his eyes, which he flicked away with his shirt sleeve.

Jesus, get yourself together Cody. Winona probably thinks you're a wimp sitting here crying.

But Winona looked him directly in the eyes. All he saw in her face was concern. "Looks like we both carry the same scars from life on our souls, don't we?" she whispered.

"You know I swore to myself to never again give my heart to another woman because Lynn destroyed my trust and hurt my pride. She made me look like a complete fool and destroyed my friendship with Tanner. When I was in the hospital battling for my life, neither of the two cheaters came to visit me. Matter of fact, they sneaked out of town while I was in intensive care. I have never seen them again. Oh, and just like you, I had an entire letter box full of hospital bills when I returned home. But unlike you, I wasn't able to pay them, and losing my parent's ranch to the bank was the ultimate insult in a completely screwed up year," he added bitterly.

Winona remained silent. Perhaps she was thinking about the right words for what she wanted to say next. She looked thoughtful and scratched her chin. "You know Cody, if your friendship to Tanner had such a strong base like you claim, he would have never done that to you. Even more so, he would have been by your side while you fought to recover from the accident. In my book, he either betrayed you worse than your wife, or he was selfish and immature at that time. Forgive me for saying this so bluntly."

Cody nodded. "There's no reason to apologize. I think you're right. I just didn't want to see the truth for a long time. Today, I know that Tanner isn't any better than Lynn, and they probably fit together much better than they did with me, anyway. He should have thought of the possible consequences first."

"Uncle Takoda always says that each wound deserves the chance to heal and build a scar. The scar is a reminder of a lesson learned, but it is also new skin and shows that you're healed. It doesn't mean that the damage never existed, but it can't control your life any longer. One has to learn to leave the past behind for the sake of experiencing a new tomorrow. Yesterday is something we can't change, and tomorrow is something we don't know yet. We can't foresee what's going to happen next, but we can live in the present today with all our heart. I follow my uncle's advice the best I can. I must admit I'm not always successful doing so, but I give it a try every single day."

"I think your uncle is a wise man. When I left my fear behind and rode with Lightning in the arena, I felt free and happy for the first time in almost three years. It was an unbelievable feeling. Still is."

Winona smiled at him. "I'm happy for you, my friend."

Cody had no clue where he found the courage, but he suddenly bent down and gently kissed her lips. When they parted, they stared at each other. Winona seemed as surprised about his daring act as he was. Embarrassed, he cleared his throat and pulled away from her. *Sweet Mary in heaven, what do you think you're doing?* he scolded himself.

Cody rose abruptly. "I think it's time to hit the sack. I'm sure it'll take a couple of hours to drive back to the ranch," he said, not sounding very convincing.

Winona nodded, rose, and looked shyly into his face. "Good night, Cody. Thanks for the talk." She wrapped the shawl tighter around her shoulders as she stepped away from the warming fire and walked toward the trailer which she shared with her uncle.

"Winona!" She stopped in her tracks and turned. "It was a wonderful evening. I really enjoy your company. Thanks for listening."

She smiled at him in the semidarkness. "I always enjoy talking with you, and I'm looking forward to more campfire conversations." Then, she turned and disappeared between the parked trailers and campers.

THE FOLLOWING WEEKS raced by. Cody and Lightning trained a lot, and the roping team achieved a better rank with each passing rodeo. One afternoon, Gary walked over to the round pen and watched Cody and Lightning for a few minutes. Gary looked thoughtful, his forehead wrinkled in a frown.

Cody tilted his head and rode over to his friend. "Hey, boss, what's the matter? You look mighty serious today."

Gary nodded. "Just received a call from an old friend. John McCraw has a successful horse breeding ranch not too far from Denver. The guy is also quite big in the rodeo circuit."

Cody dismounted and waited patiently as he sensed that something was bothering Gary.

"Well, he called me and asked me for help. His roping partner had a motorcycle accident, and it looks like he won't be able to ride a horse into the arena anytime soon."

"Oh, my, that is bad luck. The season is halfway through."

Gary nodded. "John and Roger are a great roping team. Actually, one of the top twenty at present if you ask me."

Cody whistled through his teeth.

Gary kicked around some dirt with his boot and reminded Cody of a nervous horse scraping through the soil with its front hoof.

"What kind of help does he need from you?" Cody asked.

"John is an excellent heeler, and he watched our performances lately. He does not have a header and was wondering if you want to give it a try and step in for his injured partner," Gary said.

Cody scoffed. "Are you kidding me? A top twenty ranked team roping duo, and I should replace one of them? I ain't good enough for that, Gary."

Gary shook his head. "The hell you are not. If John does not have a partner, he loses the entire season and the hard work put into it. Starting at the rodeos with you would at least give him a fifty-fifty chance, wouldn't it?"

Cody studied his friend's face. "You are serious about this, aren't you?"

Gary shrugged his shoulders. "Apparently he believes in you, and so do I. The point is that you have to learn to believe in yourself. Nobody can force you to participate. All I am asking from you is to think about it. John knows that the season is done for him. He just wants to go to this one last rodeo and give it a try. After it, he will likely concentrate on the next year's season."

Cody exhaled and nodded. "All right, I will think about it. Which rodeo would I have to ride with him?"

Gary hesitated before he answered. He spoke so softly that Cody had to strain to understand him. "That is the thing. He is registered for Cheyenne Frontier Days."

Cody turned pale as a sheet. "You got to be kidding me."

"Think about it, son. That is all I am asking from you. Sooner or later, you will have to face your demons, and so far, you have done a darn good job to face and battle them. I am proud of you, Cody. Whatever you decide to do, it will not change my opinion about you." Gary slapped

Cody on the shoulder, turned around, and left Cody standing at
the fence.

He stared after Gary until Lightning rubbed his head against Cody's
shoulders, pulling him out of his gloomy thoughts.

AFTER THREE SLEEPLESS nights, Cody finally agreed to give it a try
teaming up with John McCraw. Cody watched some videos of him and
his partner, and he was deeply impressed by their skills.

"Dang, I will never be able to replace that header. He is freaking
brilliant. You really have a talent to get yourself into a knee-deep mess,
Ferguson," Cody scolded himself one evening. However, it was too late
to pull back his offer. He was a man of his word.

THE DAY FINALLY came when the two entered the regional competition
in Cheyenne.

Cody hadn't given it any thought until Gary prepared to travel there.
Shortly before they drove to Cheyenne, Cody sat on his front porch
alone and pondered how he felt about returning to that specific rodeo
where he lost everything—his wife, his best friend, and a great deal of his
physical ability. He recalled how devastated he had been, his pride
severely damaged, without a chance for the championship title or hope
for a better tomorrow after he left the hospital in Cheyenne.

TWENTY-SEVEN
Cheyenne Frontier Days

OVER DINNER AT the ranch before the competition, Gary watched his friend closely. He knew the drive to Cheyenne would take at least ten hours. To make things worse, he had only two days additional stay to train a few rounds with John McCraw.

Cody seemed pensive, but he was sure it had nothing to do with the journey itself. Gary and Ruth were both certain going to Cheyenne had triggered bad memories for Cody. After everybody else left the dining room, Gary filled two cups with coffee and motioned Cody to follow him to the armchairs in front of the fireplace. He passed one steaming mug to Cody and studied his friend's face over the rim of his own cup.

"You're scared, aren't you?"

Cody stared at Gary, surprised at his mentor's straightforward question. "Yeah, I think you can call it fear. I am mighty nervous about being at the same spot as two years ago. I'm worried that I might disappoint the few people who believe in me, especially John, who is a true champion unlike me. I don't know what's going to happen in Cheyenne, but I'm worried. What if I can't concentrate like I should? What if I drop the rope? Yes, to be honest, I am chickenshit scared, Gary."

"Cody, do you really think that us folks here at the ranch measure our belief in you based on which position you hold in the roping competition? Don't you know that I always value you as a human being? Takoda thinks highly of you, especially after you saved his niece from any worse harm by that monster Foster. He'll never forget that. And Winona? Well, I truly think you have conquered a space in her heart, my friend."

Surprised, Cody bent forward in his armchair. "What makes you think so? Did she say anything specific about me?"

"Not exactly, but the few people who know her well see that she's seeking out your company as much as you're looking for hers. Don't you tell me that you don't enjoy it when she's around. Ruth mentioned how Winona looks at you lately. As a woman, she knows about these things better than me, anyway."

Cody blushed like a teenager. He wanted to object, but Gary raised his hand in a gesture indicating he should remain silent. "Everything needs time. If it's meant to be that the two of you get together, it will happen. You have to learn to let go of the past. Don't think about your last ride in Cheyenne. This is a different year, and you're participating in a different competition with a new four-legged partner and new friends who have your back twenty-four seven. You cannot change the past,

Cody, but it's in your control to make sure that whatever happened back then doesn't have power over your future life any longer. You must start to create that new future, my friend. If I can believe in your talents and personality, you can, too."

The younger man nodded. Then, he drained the last of his coffee and thanked his friend for the advice. "I'll see you in the morning at the crack of dawn. The drive will take the entire day. I better get some shut eye."

"Sleep well, my friend, and try not to overthink everything. Trust in the good Lord. He takes care of us," Gary said and got up to carry the cups into the kitchen.

The drive to Cheyenne was a tough one, and Gary decided on short notice to join Cody on this trip. He claimed that riding along would give his friend a chance to rest and not to have to drive the entire distance by himself. But it wasn't easy to fool Cody, who knew Gary wanted to provide him with some much-needed support.

When everything was packed in the pickup, Cody loaded Lightning into the horse trailer. He placed a net on hooks holding alfalfa hay in front of the stallion's head for him to munch on during the drive.

Hearing a pickup rumbling toward the ranch house, Cody turned around, curious. He wondered who would pay a visit at first daylight. He couldn't believe his eyes when he recognized Winona's pickup and Takoda sitting next to her, grinning like a schoolboy. Cody felt honored that they wanted to wish him good luck. But then he noticed the camper hitched to the pickup, and he didn't dare to hope they would caravan along with him and Gary to Cheyenne.

Winona jumped out of the vehicle. "Good morning, Cowboy. Are you ready to hit the road with that beautiful stallion of yours?"

He stared at her open-mouthed, feeling like a complete idiot. "What in the world are you guys doing here?"

She laughed, and he heard Takoda chuckle through the open side window. "Well, my uncle and I thought you could use a little support to make sure you're not just messing around in that arena. Besides, I don't trust your cooking, so I decided to come along and help Ruth prepare some decent meals while you try to keep from breaking your bones in that city of Cheyenne."

She smiled at him warmly, and a mischievous sparkle gleamed in her beautiful, almond-shaped eyes. Cody didn't know what to say, but his heart hammered against his rib cage with excitement. He was thrilled to spend almost an entire week with his best friends, and with Winona in particular. He couldn't believe they were joining him on that long, hard drive just to support him. He stared at Gary, who walked over to them.

"Did you know about this?" Cody wanted to know.

Gary shrugged his shoulders. "You know how it is. One never knows what the Lakota are up to," he said with a deep laugh.

"Amen to that," Andrew said, coming around the corner of his bunkhouse with a beat-up travel bag in his left hand. The ranch hand would join them on this trip since he planned to participate as a bull rider, the most dangerous discipline in the entire rodeo circuit.

They were all supporting each other, and for the first time in years, Cody knew he had a real family. Despite being nervous about driving to Cheyenne, he was now looking forward to it because he knew his friends had his back. This time, he wouldn't be abandoned in Cheyenne. He turned around and saw Ruth walking briskly toward them, two baskets with provisions dangling on her arms. "Good morning, everybody. I prepared sandwiches and cookies. I am ready to roll. How about you all?"

Cody stared at her in disbelief, and she chuckled. "Well, did you think we'd leave you alone with the wild Frontier Days?"

Cody shook his head, tears pooling in his eyes.

Ruth put the two baskets into the pickup and patted Cody's arm. "It's all about family, Cody. That's all one needs in life."

"Yes, ma'am," he whispered and got behind the wheel. They were ready to drive to Cheyenne.

It was already dark when they arrived at the arena where the Cheyenne Frontier Days rodeo would be held. It was the biggest event of the year, and it seemed that the city breathed excitement. The entire population of Cheyenne was thrilled about the annual event. This weekend, people would flock into the streets by the thousands to watch the parades. Additional cowboy-oriented competitions apart from the rodeo would take place during the entire week. The City Council planned concerts and beauty contests to select the new Miss Frontier Days.

Once the horse was watered and fed, Cody walked into the arena and looked around. He turned full circle, observing the nineteen thousand seats around him. He recalled the unbelievable noise level created by the audience as if it was yesterday.

Cody closed his eyes for a few moments and recalled Gary's words. He repeated them and whispered, "It's time to think about the future. Let go of the past, let go."

He opened his eyes, turned, and saw a man walking toward him. "Cody Ferguson?"

Cody waited until the stranger came closer. He recognized him from the videos. "Mister McCraw, what an honor to meet you." He stretched out his hand, and John McCraw shook it heartily. "Listen, I am grateful for the chance given, but after watching the recordings of you and your partner this season, I don't think...."

But McCraw shook his head. "I know we literally threw you into ice cold water. What happened to Roger was a truckload of bad luck. I am grateful that you are willing to give it a try. That's all I am asking for. I cannot expect you to perform like Roger. It takes backbone to even consider riding into this arena with me. I have a hell of a respect for you, man."

Cody smiled. He liked John right away. He seemed like a decent man. One to ride the river with.

"A friend of mine has a small ranch with an arena about eight miles down the road. We can use it for training tomorrow and the day after. We will have our first run Thursday. Hey, I know you had a long drive, and my folks are preparing a small barbeque. You are more than welcome to join us for a bite."

Cody smiled warmly. "I am sorry, I think that our ranch cookie has dinner ready already. Maybe tomorrow?"

John McCraw nodded. "See you tomorrow then. Let's start around eight in the morning."

GARY HAD RENTED a premium space near the arena reserved for campers belonging to the rodeo participants. Cody walked toward his friends' trailer, where Winona placed a plate of sandwiches and fresh potato salad in front of him. They all ate in silence and withdrew early, tired from the long drive and anxiously awaiting the following day.

Cody started up, awoken by a terrible nightmare of a bronc dragging him around the arena. He touched his chest in the darkness and drew a deep breath, trembling. *Where am I?* He reached over and searched for the button that lit the lamp beside his bunk bed. He rubbed his eyes and stared at the alarm clock. Four o'clock in the morning.

Slowly, the memory came back. He was in Cheyenne. *Oh, man, I'm at the rodeo. It's Frontier Days Week.*

He still had another hour before he had to get up, so he stayed in bed a bit longer. Closing his eyes, he crossed his arms on the pillow and rested his head on them, trying to chase away the images from the nightmare. He wished the memories of yesteryear would leave him alone once and for all.

Cody was upset that he still had bad dreams about the past. Sighing, he rubbed his forearm across his hairline. Then, the gentle face of Winona entered his mind, and the feeling which her soft lips had triggered on his own lips. It had only been a quick kiss, but it caused real turmoil in his heart. A gentle smile spread across Cody's face. He pulled the covers all the way to his shoulders and snoozed happily for another hour.

Shortly after five, he rose and took care of Lightning. Then, he enjoyed scrambled eggs and bacon, which Winona prepared for all of them. The coffee was strong and hot just like he preferred it. He secretly watched Winona and Ruth working at the primitive camping cooker, and the sight of Winona warmed his heart. Even with her hair pinned up, wearing faded jeans and an old T-shirt, she still looked gorgeous. He couldn't recall having seen any woman as beautiful who had as good a heart as Winona.

A FEW HOURS later, the excitement of the event grabbed Cody. He didn't remember when he'd last felt this good. Training with John McCraw worked better than expected. The man constantly reminded him that he knew Cody was trying his best. He assured Cody that he didn't expect the same performance as his partner Roger would have put into this competition. Cody was aware that he owed the chance to participate once again in Cheyenne simply to the fact that John was already entered in the event and that he, Cody, held some credibility from his former rodeo career and the score and prize money he and Gary had won the past months. Fortunately, he had achieved his PRCA card again.

Once Cody sat in the saddle, he concentrated on roping the steers. He blocked the thoughts about the past, and some of his old ambitions returned. Cody wanted to prove himself worthy for the chance and trust given by John McCraw, plus he wanted to impress the one man who had become a second father to him. The one human being who gifted him a new life, a better life.

During dinner, Cody discussed his competitors and their horses with Gary, Andrew, and Takoda. Gary gave his opinions about who was the fiercest competition.

While he enjoyed the last cup of coffee with a delicious peach cobbler dessert Ruth presented to them as a surprise, Cody listened to Winona's cheerful report about the superb Western art gallery she found in the town's center.

Cody felt content. He had the people he loved around him, supporting his ambition to become a leading roper. Before he went to sleep, he brought an apple to Lightning and scratched his ears. The stallion rubbed his head against Cody's chest. Cody felt the deep trust the horse built up for him. And that trust was mutual. "Yes, you're indeed my spirit horse, my friend," he whispered.

TWENTY-EIGHT
Ghosts from the Past

THAT THURSDAY MORNING, Winona announced that she wanted to watch the rodeo competition, especially Cody's run. Gary arranged for her to have a good seat near the roping chutes where she could see everything up close. Gary had been making it a priority to give Cody as much support as possible, and he knew his friend would be thrilled to have Winona close by where he could see her.

While they searched for their seats, Cody checked the cinch of his saddle for the fourth time. He was nervous, and his stomach felt as if a flutter of butterflies were buzzing around in it. If he and John did well today, they might be able to enter the semifinals Friday or Saturday. Cody barely dared to hope for it, but he sure as hell would love to achieve that, not only for himself, but also for John because Cody knew from firsthand experience how devastating it was to lose the chance to participate in the finals only a few months before that big event in Las Vegas.

Cody and Lightning stood near the gate that led into the arena. The gate they would pass through to face off with the steer and do their best to achieve a top rank position in today's competition. The excitement in the arena was intense and palpable. Cody reminded himself repeatedly to stay calm, but his pulse increased with each passing minute. He swallowed nervously.

A voice behind Cody called out his name. "Good morning, Cody."

Startled, he turned around and was shocked that his ex-wife Lynn was standing right in front of him. He hadn't seen her in two years and hadn't expected to ever see her again, especially not in Cheyenne.

He gaped at her, and the world seemed to shift for a moment as he adjusted to her presence. She was still a looker all right, her wavy hair and large breasts reminding him of the typical blonde cheerleader. But the closer he looked, he noticed her figure had filled out, and her face wore a calculating and hungry expression, which even her fake smile couldn't disguise. The corners of her mouth pointed downward. All in all, she appeared much older than two more years would have added, and the thick makeup that covered her face settled in the fine wrinkles at the corners of her eyes and above her lips.

"Lynn, what do you want?" Cody's voice sounded cold and self-confident, but his heart beat wildly in his chest.

"I read the starting list yesterday, and to my surprise, I saw your name in the group of ropers. I just wanted to drop by and say hello. After all, we haven't seen each other for quite a while."

"Well, you've said hello, so you might as well leave now."

She stared at him indignantly. "Hey, there's no reason to be so unfriendly, Cowboy. I just wanted to be nice."

"You have some nerve, woman. You screw around behind my back with my so-called best friend, then while I was fighting for my life in a hospital, you and that phony jerk disappeared from here and left me behind, not giving a rat's ass about how I was doing or if I was going to make it. I could have died of those injuries, and neither you nor Tanner cared about it. Don't expect any kind of friendliness, or me being pleased about seeing you again. If it was up to me, I could do very well without ever having to see you or that other sorry ass for the rest of my life. Get along with you, hussy! I don't need you to wish me luck."

Cody turned and continued to check his saddle, not paying any more attention to the woman behind him. His fingers trembled with anger. His wildest dreams couldn't have prepared him for this unwanted encounter. Damn, why now? *I am going to mess up this run because of that trollop*, he thought, frustration clouding his handsome face.

"Listen to me, Cody. Tanner seduced me. The entire situation wasn't my fault. Besides, you had nothing but the damn rodeo in your head, and you neglected me every day. My needs and my dreams were of no interest to you."

Cody whirled around and stared at her. He was pale and shook with repressed rage. "You should hear yourself talk. You're the same liar as you were those days. Seduced? What a joke. You were riding his naked lap, and it didn't look or sound as if you weren't having fun doing so. I tried very hard to build up a prosperous future for the two of us. I wanted to develop Father's ranch into a successful cattle operation so we would have a great income and a good life. For Christ's sake, I even wanted to raise children with you."

Lynn's expression changed to a simper. "But we can still have all that. I separated from Tanner. Come on, darling, give me a chance to make up with you." She stepped closer and wrapped her arms around him, resting hands provocatively on his buttocks. She rubbed his derriere seductively, trying to arouse him.

He pulled his head back and stared at her, his nose filled with her cheap perfume. He felt disgusted by her and was close to pushing her to the ground when he heard a well-known, tender voice behind him.

"Cody?" Winona's soft voice rang out of nowhere and seemed to him like a lifeline. Pushing Lynn's hands away, he turned to look at Winona. Her dark eyes searched his and held his gaze. Their warmth felt like a caress to him. Cody didn't know how much of the conversation Winona had overheard, but he was mighty sure that she had figured out who the overbearing blonde beside him was.

He stepped toward the beautiful Lakota woman and lay his arm around her shoulders, holding Lightning's reins with his left hand. He withdrew his attention from Lynn. The face of his ex-wife clouded over into a frown, her eyebrows knit, and the corners of her mouth turned downward. None of the well-studied seductive moves remained.

She jeered at Cody. "A redskin? You got to be kidding me. Don't tell me you picked yourself a hussy from some God-forsaken reservation and prefer her over me?"

Cody whirled around and took two steps toward Lynn. His whole bearing changed as his fists came up and his jaw tensed. He towered over her, his feet planted in a wide stance. He looked dangerous, ready to beat her.

When he spoke, he spit the words in her face. "I would prefer any human being on this entire planet over you. This woman especially. Get out of my sight, you cheap whore. I don't want to have anything to do with you for the rest of my life. I'm done with you. You wish you had as much grace, dignity, and intelligence as she does. You're nothing but a lowlife floozy with a deceitful character, and I pity every man that is unlucky enough to run into you."

Lynn whirled around. Hate distorted her face, her cheeks flaming through the makeup. Her eyes became slits, and her lips pressed together. She stomped away cussing worse than a drunken sailor.

Winona studied Cody's face. "Was that…?" She didn't dare finish the question.

"Yes, but it doesn't matter. God only knows why in the world she came here. I'm happy that you're here with me in Cheyenne, and that's the only thing that counts for me. I'm sure glad you showed up before I did something foolish. I really hate her, you know. I can't believe how rotten she is. Thinking I once was in love with her really makes me wonder if I was out of my mind when I married her."

"Maybe the two of you might have a chance to talk things over and make up. Have a new start—"

"Hush, beautiful!" He placed his index finger on her lips tenderly. "Don't even think like that. I would never be able to forget what she did. My trust doesn't come with a refill. Once it's gone, it's gone for good. And besides, I don't want to give it another try because she was never the right woman for me. I know that now. It's exactly like your uncle said. We can't undo the past, but we can definitely learn from it. To do that, we have to leave the past behind. That's the only way to start a new and better life. Takoda is a very wise man, and I listened to his words and took them seriously."

"Do you think your friend Tanner is here as well?"

Cody shrugged his shoulders. "I hope not. To face both in one day might be a bit too much, even for me. I mean, we don't have to exaggerate the *face-the-past therapy*, right? Besides, he isn't my friend anymore. Now, my talented artist, would you prefer to wait at the roping box until I'm done with my ride, or are you ready to join Gary up there in the premium seats? I think John and I better get ready. I am sure we will have our run within the next fifteen minutes or so, and I better get ready and concentrate, especially after meeting that phony witch."

"I'll join Gary because I'll get so excited that I'll probably need his hand to hold on to until you guys catch that steer."

"All right then, I'll see you later. Wish me luck." He wanted to turn around, but she caught his sleeve and held him back. She took a step closer and stood on her toes to reach up to him. To Cody's surprise, she kissed him on his mouth. Her lips were warm and soft, but he felt their increasing pressure. He reluctantly returned her kiss because he hadn't expected it.

He wrapped his arms around her and felt the body of this wonderful woman press against his torso. It aroused him beyond expectations, and the play of their tongues got more insistent. For a few moments, the rodeo, the audience, and the noise ceased to exist. All he felt was his own heart hammering against his ribcage and the softness of her long hair covering his hands.

When they finally separated, he was breathless, and his voice sounded hoarse. "Wow, how did I deserve that?"

"Well, let's call it a pre-taste of the future and my way to wish you luck when you enter this arena. Now, you better go and get that steer, Cowboy." She patted Lightning gently on his neck, and the stallion rubbed his head on her denim jacket. Then, she waved at John McCraw and gave him the thumbs up sign.

Lynn remained close enough to overhear their conversation, although neither paid attention to her. She watched them with flared nostrils and tensed jaw, her hands clenched into fists.

She muttered under her breath, "I'll make you pay for treating me like this, Cody Ferguson." She stomped to the trailer of the good-for-nothing bull rider with whom she shared her bed at present. Lynn had never been the kind of woman to take no for an answer and was well-known for it among the rodeo circuit. She wouldn't let Cody push her away for a cheap Indian hussy. While walking to the shabby camper, she swore bitter revenge, oblivious of the fact that she deserved exactly that kind of treatment since she was the one who had mistreated Cody in the first place.

Tanner had chased her out of his life barely two months after Cody's accident. The sentimental fool felt guilty about letting his friend down. He complained that she destroyed the friendship between the two men and that it was her fault he lost his best friend. He missed Cody, but she made it clear he found his way between her legs of his own free will. She insisted she hadn't forced him to start an affair with her. Tanner had been more than willing to succumb to her feminine charms.

A few weeks later, Lynn grabbed the next wannabe rodeo hero who would pay her bills and save her from having to go to work. She had never wanted to work for her own money. The people who knew her among the rodeo circuit nicknamed her the "Black Widow." She was like a poisonous insect who created a spider's web to lure men ruled by their desire into her fangs. She would chew men up and spit them out, if they didn't rid themselves of her first.

TWENTY-NINE
Nasty Plans

WHEN WINONA FOUND her seat next to Gary, she told him about the encounter with Cody's ex-wife. He was furious when he heard the story. He was afraid meeting Lynn could distract Cody and put him in danger of another serious accident.

"I wish the devil would take that rotten tramp where she belongs. God only knows what might be going through his mind right now. Why, for Christ's sake, does she have to show up at all? Why, of all places, here in Cheyenne? I wish she'd gone straight to hell." Gary slammed his fist into his open hand. Ruth sat beside him and looked utterly worried.

Winona touched her friend's arm tenderly to calm him down. "You should have seen the way he sent her away. There was nothing but coldness and hate left. I think he is really letting go of the past and is ready for a new life. She doesn't control his feelings any longer."

"From your lips to God's ears, my beautiful friend. I really hope so because he deserves much better than that spoiled brat. I pray he can move forward to a happier future. It's about time he started a new life."

Winona hesitated to tell him the rest, but when she realized how worried he was about Cody's encounter with his former wife, she took the risk. She smiled at him and said, "We kissed each other. I think that's a step into the future, wouldn't you agree?"

Gary stared at her curiously, then a broad smile lit up his face and gave him an almost boyish expression. "Well, butter my butt and call me a biscuit. It's high time that one of you took the first step. I was afraid it would never happen. Now that is indeed good news. There is hope."

Ruth laughed and gave Gary a quick kiss on his cheek. Then, she winked at Winona.

Cody watched the trio and waved at Takoda, who took his seat next to his niece. Cody noticed Gary leaning closer to Ruth. It looked like he was explaining something to her, and she smiled warmly at him. Gary had his arm around her shoulders. Her concern for Gary's safety after the incident at Foster's cabin had further strengthened their relationship.

I wonder how much longer you will successfully battle those wedding plans, my friend, Cody thought, and a boyish grin spread across his face.

John McCraw nodded at him. Both were ready to give their best as they bathed in the roar of the audience around them.

In the first steer-roping round, Cody and John succeeded with a low time. McCraw grinned when they rode out of the arena. They would get a second run the following day. Both men were realistic enough to know their chances to enter the finals on Sunday were less than meager, but they were thrilled, nevertheless. This time, Cody didn't put pressure on himself. He was already satisfied because he and the magnificent stallion got further in this year's rodeos than he dreamed they would. To participate in a rodeo at all and even stand in the arena of Cheyenne was something he would have never thought possible again.

He waved at Gary because he knew he owed his old mentor credit for this new start in his life. He had come a long way in a short amount of time when he least expected it.

A smiling Winona walked toward him with Gary right behind her.

"Well done, son. I am so proud of you," Gary said.

John McCraw nodded. "I'll be darned. We get a second run tomorrow. That is way more than I expected. Just imagine if we could train a few months together."

Cody smiled at Gary and John while he unsaddled the stallion. "I am sure glad I didn't mess up this run." He winked at Winona. Of course, the kiss they shared crossed his mind, and Cody could barely hide how thrilled he was. It was hard for him to put in words how much her company meant to him, but words weren't needed right now.

He had the feeling that something had changed significantly since he saved her from the brutal jerk, Foster. It seemed something very special developed between the two of them. She laid her hands on his shoulders or arms more often, and she didn't seem to avoid touching him any longer like she used to in the beginning. Winona's smile was heartwarming, and her eyes sparkled when she looked at him. *Who knows, maybe life has beautiful dreams for me after all,* he mused while he watched her preparing a light lunch for them. He didn't waste a second thought on the encounter with his ex-wife.

It didn't take Lynn long to find out where Cody's trailer was parked. She stood off to the side between the pickups watching the peaceful scene of them all having lunch together with narrowed eyes. Lynn's face was pale, and her eyebrows knit together in anger and jealousy.

The only people she recognized were Cody and that native woman at first. There was an elder tribal member and two other cowboys, one younger. But then she recognized old Gary Bradshaw. Her face showed dismay.

"I bet all of these people are his friends. Looks like he has more friends nowadays than when we travelled together on the rodeo circuit," she whispered.

Movement behind the pickup to her right caught her eye. At first, she thought one of the rodeo participants was getting ready for a relaxed afternoon or his next ride, but to her astonishment she saw a shabby looking character spying on the same group of people she did. He watched the two Indians in particular, and when he studied the girl carrying plates to the table, the tip of his tongue flicked over his lower lip, as if anticipating a sweet treat. He didn't notice Lynn since she crouched behind a vehicle out of his sight.

Lynn studied the shady character for a few minutes. From the way he looked, she judged him to be a good-for-nothing. "Now, that is interesting. What in the world would he have to do with Cody and his bunch? He doesn't seem to be welcome, or he would have walked over to them," she whispered to herself.

Whatever business that crook had with Cody or any of his friends, Lynn was determined to find out why he followed them. It would be easy for her to catch the man's attention, and if he was up to causing trouble for Cody or that woman, she was more than interested in joining him. It was always good to have an ally. When the man turned and walked away, she followed him. She forgot the other bull rider who was waiting to have a cheap meal with her.

The stranger stopped at one of the food trucks and ordered a pulled pork sandwich and a can of beer. He sat on one of the wooden benches close by, and Lynn walked over to him with two bottles of cold Budweiser.

"Mind if I join you, Cowboy?" she asked, sporting her sweetest smile and pushing her immense breasts closer to his face. At first, the man looked annoyed, his brows furrowed. Then, he looked her over and saw to his surprise that she put another bottle of beer in front of him.

He reached for the beer. "What do you want from me, lady?"

She studied his face and tried not to flinch at the ugly scar on his cheek. "Oh, hell, I'm no lady. Trying to behave ladylike is way too boring, don't you think?" She smiled at him and playfully wrapped a strand of her long blonde hair around her finger, a gesture she had used a thousand times since her teenage years.

He finished his sandwich and pushed the empty plastic plate aside. "What's your name?"

"I'm Lynn, and you?"

"Cliff. So, what is it that I can do for you?"

"Do you happen to know Cody Ferguson? He participates in this rodeo."

Cliff squinted his eyes. "Now why would I know that guy?"

"Maybe because you were watching him a few minutes ago," she answered with a sly expression on her face.

Cliff pulled over the second bottle of beer and took a long swig. "Is that so? Seems you like to spy on folks yourself, is it? Nothing wrong with watching people, I would say." He looked rather annoyed.

"Oh, I was just wondering if you have similar problems with that dude as I have because if that was the case, we could maybe partner up and teach him a lesson or two."

Cliff leaned forward. She had his full attention now. "Partner up, you say? What partnership do you have in mind, missy?" he asked while staring directly at her breasts.

"Well, let's call it a deal with benefits, if you succeed," she said provocatively, opening the first two buttons on her blouse.

"I'm not interested in this Ferguson fellow. I'm after the old Indian because he owes me important information. I might have to get a little rough with him or his niece to get what I want from them. I'm wondering what's your business with them?"

"I have an open bill with Cody Ferguson, and I think it would play into my hands if you took care of his squaw. It looks like we have a common goal."

Cliff studied her face for a moment, and then he grinned, showing his yellow, broken teeth. "I'll be darned, you're jealous of her, aren't you? What happened? Did he tell you to hit the road and replaced you with that Lakota girl?"

Lynn scoffed. "Nobody replaces me, darling, because I offer much more than other women do. But, yes, matter of fact, we had a falling out two years ago, and when I tried to be nice to him, he was mighty rude. I don't like to be treated like that."

"I tell you what, why don't you stick with a real man instead of that rodeo cowboy?"

"And I assume that real man is you, right?" Lynn smiled at him, but the coldness in her eyes remained.

Cliff stared at her and licked his lips. "Why don't you come to my camper with me, and I show you right now what a real man is? I don't need to ride a bull or wild horse to prove my strength and skills. I'd rather play with women than fool around with livestock. More pleasure in it, and I guarantee you that my rides take much longer than the famous eight seconds in that arena over there."

"So, what do you say? Do we have an agreement that you go after the two Indians for the sake of getting even with that conceited bastard?"

"I was planning to do that anyway, and if I gain a little affection from you, why should I disagree? Looks like a win-win situation for both of us."

"So, where did you say your camper is parked?" she whispered seductively.

Cliff grinned and tossed the empty beer bottle into the trash can close by. "I'll show you the way, then I'll show you what I can do," he bragged and walked ahead.

Lynn followed him with a shark's grin. It seemed she would do whatever was necessary to hurt Cody for the dismissive way he had treated her earlier that day, even if she had to share a dirty bunk bed with the scumbag walking ahead of her. She would sink to any depth to reach her goals.

LATER THAT AFTERNOON, Gary and Cody met with some other ranchers to discuss the possibility of selling some cattle to them. Winona and her uncle investigated some of the attractions around Cheyenne.

In the early evening, Cody walked back to his camper and met

Winona, who prepared some steaks on the open fire. The smell of cornbread baking in a Dutch oven filled the air, and his stomach growled loudly. Before long, they all gathered around the campfire, waiting for the delicious meal and some fresh coffee.

Winona looked around, frowning. "Where is my uncle? When we returned from town, he told me he wanted to check out the saddle maker who has a booth on the other side of the arena. Have you seen him, Cody?"

"Unfortunately, no, but I can look for him if you want me to," Cody offered.

Winona shook her head. "No, let's eat first. Steaks and cornbread are almost done. I'm sure he'll be back in no time."

They sat at the picnic table and enjoyed the food together with Gary, Ruth and Andrew. They all chatted about the day's events, and after they finished their steaks, they relished a cup of steaming coffee and peach cobbler freshly made in a skillet over the fire.

THIRTY
Where is Takoda?

"T HAT WAS A wonderful meal, Winona. Thank you so much for preparing it," Cody said.

"Couldn't have done it better," Ruth agreed.

Winona didn't acknowledge Cody's compliment. "I don't understand what is taking Takoda so long. Normally he's always on time for meals. I'm getting worried. Maybe I should have a look around the camp to see if someone is bending his ear for too long."

"I could use an evening stroll after so much food. I'll accompany you, if you don't mind. Sometimes the boys get a little rowdy after drinking too much, you know. I want to make sure that no one harasses you." Cody let her know his motivations.

"That is sweet of you, and yes, I would appreciate it very much if you came along. After all, you know some of these people personally, and I don't. Maybe somebody has seen my uncle."

They walked through the many lines of horse trailers and pickups and spoke to people at the campfires, but Takoda was nowhere to be found. Winona became more and more nervous with each passing minute. Even Cody suspected something wrong.

When they passed a shabby-looking trailer, a guy stepped out and bumped right into Cody. "Sorry, man, doesn't seem to be my day. My chick just ran off with some dirty looking half-breed and an old Indian dude. As if I wasn't good enough for that whore. Miss barrel racer wannabe, huh, what a joke. Didn't mean to bump into you."

Cody wheeled around and grabbed the man by his shoulder. "Are you talking about Lynn?"

"Yes, brother, that's her name. How do you know her?" The man raised his finger in a warning gesture. "I can only warn you, she's a good for nothing floozy."

Cody took his hand off the man's shoulder. "What do you mean, she ran away with a half-breed and an Indian? What did the Indian look like? We're searching for one."

"He was an older dude. Long gray hair, braided. He looked like a decent guy, unlike the other one, who was younger. That feller looked like a mixed race to me. Medium length hair, scruffy and dirty. He probably hadn't shaved or bathed for days. He sure smelled like it, even from a distance. Had a nasty scar across his right cheek. If Lynn got involved with that one, she's going to get what she deserves. The fellow looked like the brutal type, if you ask me. Well, let him take care of her then. She was only good for spending my money anyway."

A note of panic entered Cody's voice. "Did they say where they were going?"

"If I'm not mistaken, they talked about going to Restway Travel Park campground, but I'm not sure about that. I only followed part of their conversation until I realized she was about to dump me for this jerk. I had no reason to hold her back. Excuse me, partner, but I need a shot of whiskey. This has been a crappy day for me." The man turned around and stomped toward his pickup, likely on his way to one of the saloons in town.

Cody furrowed his brow.

Winona was pale and her lips quivered.

"Don't worry, dear. It's probably all right." But Cody didn't even sound convincing to himself. He put an arm around her while he wondered what Lynn was up to. He was sure it was no good.

"Cody, I think I know who that man is who this bull rider described as a 'half-breed.'"

Confused, Cody studied her face. "Why would you know who it is?"

"When Stacey Foster kidnapped me and took me to that mountain hut, he wasn't alone. Foster had a partner in crime who shackled me and drove me to that place in the mountains. He called him Cliff, and they seemed to be friends. The way this man just described that half-breed sounds a lot like Cliff. He had a scar on his right cheek and shoulder length hair. I thought that after Foster's death he went his own way."

"Why in the world would he be interested in Takoda? I thought the kidnapping was to force you to get involved with Foster."

"I think that was only part of the reason. I overheard them talking about wanting to blackmail my uncle into telling them specific knowledge about the history of the territory."

"What in the world are you talking about, Winona? What knowledge?"

"I can't tell you. I had to promise my uncle to never speak about it to anybody. Maybe you should talk to Gary about it."

Cody stared at the beautiful Lakota woman and shook his head. He couldn't believe that people he was fond of were keeping secrets from him again, unwilling to tell him the truth. History seemed to repeat itself.

Then, another thought crossed his mind. What if Lynn had teamed up with that Cliff to hurt him for turning her down? He knew Lynn could be vengeful, and it wouldn't surprise him if she had something nasty in mind. The thought worried him.

"What do we do now, Cody? I'm afraid my uncle is in danger. God, I can't believe that this trouble followed us all the way to Cheyenne."

"I know that Restway Travel Park the guy mentioned. It's very close to here. Let's take my pickup and drive there right now to look for Takoda. I know that Lynn has a shady character. In case she's teamed up with this villain who helped with kidnapping you, there might be something brewing. Come on, let's go."

When they returned to the camp, Gary and Ruth were nowhere to be seen, so Cody wrote him a quick note and left it under his coffee cup on the table. He opened the door of his pickup for Winona, walked around the vehicle, and jumped behind the wheel. It took them less than fifteen minutes to reach the travel park.

It was dark, and the park wasn't well-lit. The rental fees were low, and the park didn't have the best reputation. Thanks to Cheyenne Frontier Days and its cheap RV fees, it was filled with campers of every imaginable model. A few guys sat around the bonfire in the center of the park.

Cody motioned Winona to wait next to his pickup out of the men's view. He strolled over to the fire, wanting to appear casual, and greeted the guys in a friendly manner. One gander at them told him they weren't the best quality of people, so a direct approach was unlikely to be successful. He had to play a trick and pretended to be searching for a little adventure.

"Hey, folks, a sexy, curvy blonde gave me this address and invited me for a threesome adventure along with her girlfriend. Unfortunately, she forgot to mention which camper she and her lover stay in, but maybe you guys can help me with that."

One of the fellows around the fire pointed with his beer bottle to an old, beat-up camper. "If you're talking about a cheerleader type of woman with impressive cleavage, you'll likely find her in that camper over there. But she's with a dude, not a woman. I think she misled you. I'd like to watch the fun, but unfortunately, we're going to one of the topless bars in town. So, you're on your own. By the way, the guy she is staying with didn't look too friendly. I hope he knows about her invitation, or things might not end well for you. Enjoy the ride, cowboy."

The others laughed, and one after the other got up and walked to their cars. In a couple of minutes, the other people left, and that part of the RV park seemed unusually empty.

Cody strode over to Winona. "Looks like most people have gone into town. One of the guys mentioned that a blonde stays with some guy in the camper over there. The way he described her, I'm quite certain it's Lynn. I'll walk over and see if I can find out something. At this point, I don't know if Takoda is there, or if Lynn's new friend is armed. I'd rather have you wait here, which is safer for you, especially since the guy would recognize you immediately."

"This is my uncle who might be in danger. There's no way I'll wait here doing nothing."

Cody sighed. By now he knew Winona well enough to understand that once she decided on something, he didn't have a prayer of changing her mind. *Oh, that stubborn Little Sitting Bull,* he thought. Yet her fierce and strong will was one of the qualities he was falling in love with, so he gave in to the inevitable, nodded, and accepted her decision.

THIRTY-ONE
The Time of the Warriors

T HEY SNEAKED OVER to the camper where they assumed Lynn was. Winona and Cody pressed their backs against the metal wall of the flimsy structure, listening to the voices inside.

"Listen, you old fool, I'm mighty sure you know more about that gang's gold than you let on. Don't think that I can't make you talk. I have my ways of making you. Even if you don't spill the beans, I might lay hands on that pretty little niece of yours. Wouldn't it be a shame if that beautiful face of hers gets cut up with my Bowie knife?"

His ex-wife's shrill laughter made the hair on Cody's neck stand on end. So, he'd been right—she had indeed teamed up with that rogue. *What is this gold they're talking about?* he wondered.

When they heard Takoda's voice, Cody had to hold Winona back.

Takoda spoke loudly to his captor. "You're nothing but a coward. You and that Foster guy who threatened and kidnapped my Winona will both rot in hell. He already got what he deserved, and you're next. And as for you, lady, you're likely the rottenest piece of crap a man could ever run into. I know the story of your marriage with my friend Cody, and the way you treated him. You're a cheap hussy who sells herself to the man who'll pay the highest price. You've never deserved a decent man like Cody, and you lost him forever. He won't even look at you any—"

Lynn's high-pitched objection interrupted Takoda. "Who do you think you are, dang reservation dog? You think you and the girl are something special? Cliff, hit him for talking to me like this."

"Listen to me, woman, nobody, including you, gives me orders. Do you understand?"

If the situation hadn't been so threatening, Cody would have laughed about Lynn standing corrected by a lower-life character than herself. He was a hundred percent sure that she didn't like it at all. He could just imagine her sour-faced expression. *Serves her right*, he thought. One of these days, she will run into the kind of man who'll teach her manners in the most unpleasant way one can imagine. But Cody didn't feel sorry for her. The only emotion he had left for her was revulsion.

Standing outside the trailer, his mind raced as he worked on developing a plan that would lure Cliff out of the camper. As long as he and Lynn were inside the trailer, Takoda was in danger.

Winona pointed to him and motioned over to the door suggesting that she would go in, but he shook his head vehemently. The thought that she would place herself in danger was unbearable to him.

"It's our only chance," she whispered. "That fool likely thinks that I'm looking for my uncle alone. He surely assumes that you're busy with the rodeo and preparing for tomorrow's performance. When he opens the door and steps outside, you might be able to surprise him if you sneak around the corner behind his back."

"You heard him threatening to cut you with a knife," Cody hissed at her.

But she shook her head. "Remember what I told you about my ex-husband? Believe me, I know how to protect myself and how to fight when I have to. We need to get my uncle out of their clutches immediately before that jerk loses his patience and hurts my uncle."

Cody stared at her. He didn't like this at all. He was terribly scared for her safety. But he couldn't think of a better plan, so he nodded and motioned her to go ahead. He knew she was right that they had only this one shot. He wished he had brought his gun and blamed himself for not having done so.

Winona walked closer to the door but instead of knocking, she surprised Cody by shouting, "Uncle Takoda! Uncle Takoda, are you in there?"

The conversation inside the camper was immediately hushed. Since her uncle didn't answer, Winona was sure that Cliff or Lynn threatened him with a gun to make sure he remained silent.

"Uncle, are you in there? Answer me, please."

The door of the camper opened, but only a small crack. "Who is causing that commotion out there? What do you want?"

"I am Winona Standstrong, and I'm looking for my uncle Takoda. Some folks at the rodeo told me that I would find him here. Don't even think of denying it because I heard his voice a few minutes ago. I want to know why you're holding my uncle hostage in that camper of yours."

The door opened, and an extremely self-confident Cliff stepped out of the trailer. "Look who we got here. Now if that isn't the little squaw that got my friend Stacey Foster killed. What a pleasant surprise. We are having a little question-and-answer game going on in here. Maybe you'd like to join us."

Winona shook her head and backed away from the camper's doorway.

Cody remained pressed against the side of the trailer, hidden behind the opened door.

At a safer distance, Winona drew herself up to her full height. "Foster was a criminal, and it wasn't me who got him killed but his own actions. He got exactly what he deserved. You guys kidnapped me, and now you've taken my uncle as prisoner. I don't understand what this is all about, but it's the second time you've threatened me or my family." She raised a finger to scold him. "If you think you'll get away with it, you're deadly mistaken just like that other idiot was. If you harm my uncle in any way, I swear to God I'll get even for it even if I have to chase you across the entire country."

Cliff laughed, but it was a demeaning laughter, and a dangerous spark filled his eyes. "Now listen to you, little girl. You got some backbone and nerve. I grant you that. I like women with spirit," he said, licking his lower lip provocatively with his tobacco-stained tongue. "Nevertheless, it's amusing that a little girl is trying to threaten me. Don't mistake me to be such easy prey as Foster was. Stacey was never the brightest bulb in the chandelier anyway. As far as I can see, you aren't even heeled. Why do you think you're in a position to threaten me?"

"I am a Lakota. I don't need a gun to get even with you. We learned to defend our lives and those of our loved ones with our bare hands if we have to."

"Oh, don't get me wrong. I wouldn't mind feeling your hands all over my body, but we might consider that for a later time. For now, I'm rather busy with your uncle because he's mighty stubborn. You know, good old Stacey told me an interesting tale before you killed him, or let's say before that damn dobbin trampled him to death. He mentioned that your uncle knows the location of the lost Plummer Gang gold, and I intend to find out if that's the truth. It might loosen his tongue if he knows that you're here within my immediate reach."

As Cody followed the conversation, he stood frozen in shock. Was that really possible? He remembered reading in an Old West book about the old legend of Plummer and his gang and their railway robberies. He never considered that the gang might have hidden their loot somewhere in the state of Montana. Cody stared at Winona, who to his surprise didn't look shocked at all. Did she know something about that tale? Cody recalled that she mentioned her kidnapping might not only have been triggered by sexual desire for her.

I'll be darned, she looks as if she knows exactly what that reprobate is talking about, he thought while listening to the conversation from his hiding place. No wonder that jerk followed them all the way to Cheyenne. With Foster gone, he wouldn't even have to share in case he found the lost treasure.

In Cody's opinion, this man was more determined and more controlled than Foster ever was, which meant Cliff was much more dangerous. He'd met a few men like Cliff before. Where Foster was a loose cannon with a bad temper, Cliff was a calculating sociopath who thought ahead. Knowing that, he was even more concerned for Winona's and Takoda's safety. Cody couldn't afford to fail because they would have only one opportunity. Foster had been outnumbered at the cabin in the woods, but this time it was two against two, since Lynn was still in the camper and also an immediate threat to Takoda.

"Why don't you join me and my new friend in my camper. We could have all the fun in the world together. If you're nice to me, I'll make sure that your uncle won't be harmed. All either of you have to do is to tell me where old Plummer hid his treasure box. Since you're already here, there's no way I can let you go back to your friends so you can let them know about me questioning your uncle. He will likely talk now that I have you under my control."

Cliff slowly walked down the two steps to get closer to Winona. Her eyes grew larger when she realized that he was holding a gun in his hand, but she tried to remain calm. "Threatening me with a firearm doesn't sound like an invitation, does it?" she said to warn Cody about the weapon in the villain's hand.

Cody immediately grasped that he had to act quickly. There wouldn't be a second chance. He slammed the camper door as hard as he could into Cliff's shoulder.

The man screamed in pain, taken by surprise, and stumbled forward. Then, he whirled around to see who had attacked him from behind. He pointed his gun at Cody's chest. "You think you're smarter than me, don't you? I'll finish you off right here. Your little ex-wife inside my camper will probably be thankful if I do." His face turned into a cruel snarl, and Cody felt like bashing his fist right into it.

Cliff cocked the hammer of the six-shooter, his index finger dancing nervously around the trigger. He turned his head to call over his shoulder. "Say goodbye to your ex-hubby, Lynn. I'm about to shoot his sorry ass."

Lynn stood in the doorway of the camper, her hair disarrayed and her blouse open. It wasn't hard to guess what she and Cliff had been up to before they set to threatening Winona's uncle. She grinned at Cody, a cigarette dangling from the corner of her mouth. She looked like the cheap whore she was, and Cody's stomach churned to look at her.

"Well, well, Ferguson, that's how fast we meet each other again, hmm? You should have been nicer to me, Cody. What a pity that you won't be able to enjoy neither my company nor that of your little squaw over there any longer. You have always been a loser. Obviously, that hasn't changed."

Cody glared at her, pure hatred radiating from his face like a flame.

Lynn's mouth dropped open, and her cigarette fell to the ground when she saw his look. He was ready to kill her with his bare hands, and she took a step back into the camper. Despite all the meanness she carried in her dark soul, she had never been brave enough to face the consequences of her wrongdoing. Cody's lack of fear confused and frightened her—indeed he looked determined to fight until the bitter end.

She glanced over to the beautiful Lakota woman and saw the same resolute expression. Winona's jaw was set, and her glower shifted back and forth between Lynn and Cliff. She shifted her position closer to the trailer.

Cody saw fear gleaming in Lynn's eyes. His gaze shifted from Lynn back to Cliff, who still aimed his gun at him. He studied his opponent's eyes. Cliff's gaze steadied on Cody's chest, indicating that he was about to pull the trigger. Cody suppressed a laugh at the absurdity that, for a second time, he was in a life-threatening situation here in Cheyenne, but this time it looked like he wouldn't survive.

In place of fear, overwhelming rage bubbled to the surface of his consciousness. Cody was so sick and tired of being the victim of other people's little plots. The hate was about to erupt like a volcano. Even more than his rejection of victimhood, Cody refused to allow his hated ex-wife to win in the end. He glared at the barrel of the loaded gun and hoped that Winona would get away in time.

He closed his eyes for an instant, waiting to hear the shot and feel the pain. He surrendered to his circumstances. The seconds ticked on, but no shot rang out. Instead, Cliff staggered forward with a surprised, stupefied expression, eyes wide, mouth open.

Before Cody could figure out what was wrong with him, his enemy crashed to the ground like a hewn tree. His head landed near Cody's boots, the shaft of a Bowie knife protruding from the middle of his back. The man who'd had the upper hand in this game less than twenty seconds ago struggled to draw each breath. Then, he breathed no more.

"What in the world?" Cody stuttered. Then, he looked over to Winona and saw her standing, one leg forward, hand still stretched before her. Cody understood that the Lakota woman had saved his life and killed the man with an expert throw of a long-bladed knife.

She pointed down to her knee-high moccasin boot and took a deep breath. "As a Lakota, I am used to carrying a weapon on my body when I enter a dangerous environment. I had no choice because he was about to kill you."

"Holy cow, that was mighty impressive. Remind me never to get on your bad side, lady." Movement close to the camper's door caught his eye, and he saw that Lynn was trying to sneak away from them. Cody shot forward and grabbed her arm, yanking her back roughly. "Now, where do you think you're going, you rat?"

She yelled at him to let go of her as she tried to tear herself away from his grip, but he was too strong for her. She stared at him, pretending to blink away fake tears. "Cody, please, I never meant to harm you. I was just so sad that you would send me away the way you did. I still love you. Please give me a chance."

Cody's lips curled in disgust when he heard her phony words. "You dare to talk about love? You're the worst liar I ever encountered in my entire life. You're good for nothing, and I pity every man who has the bad luck of meeting you, even that ruthless criminal lying over there. You're like a curse in every person's life, and you don't deserve any mercy. I'll hand you over to the authorities for kidnapping and probably more."

"You can't be serious about having me arrested. I haven't done anything bad." She continued trying to wriggle out of his grasp. "Your little squaw over there will get arrested for murder, that's for sure. I hope they lock her away for the rest of her lousy life."

"One more word, and I might forget myself," Cody growled, but Lynn laughed in his face.

"You would never harm me. Besides, you don't have the backbone to stand up for your own rights." Her tone of voice softened. "I know you still want me. Let go of me and tend to that old injun inside the camper. He might have a broken nose, but what the heck, he's only an Indian."

The moment Cody saw Winona go inside the camper to check on Takoda, Lynn pulled herself free. But this time, he would not allow her to get away so easily. It took Cody only a few quick steps on his long legs before he caught up with her. He grabbed her shoulder and twirled her around, forcing her to look at him.

She struggled in his grasp, but he held her arm in a steely grip.

"Do you really think I'm just going to stand here and watch you run away after trying to destroy my life a second time? Last time I couldn't stop you and that other coward, but this time, Lynn, you will pay for your sins. You will stay right here with us, and I will call the police. It is time for you take responsibility for your actions."

Lynn tried every trick she knew to tear herself loose. Stomped on his boot with her high heels and tried to bite his arms. She looked frightened, perhaps not so much of Cody but of having to face consequences for her wrongdoings. So far, she had always gotten away without punishment. This time she knew it looked bad for her. She tried to kick him and scratch his face with her artificial fingernails, but Cody was too strong for her.

"If I were you, I would stop fighting me. Don't make me do something I'll regret later because I don't want to sink to your level."

Cody tried to catch his breath. It was the first time he had ever threatened a woman, and he prayed it was the last time. He'd never beat up a woman, but Lynn had provoked him to a dangerous extent. Her words were like painful thorns in his heart. He didn't even pity her because she might end up in prison—to him Lynn wasn't a woman anymore but a merciless enemy with a rotten character.

When he turned, he saw Winona standing in front of the trailer with her arm wrapped around Takoda's waist to steady him. He bled heavily from his broken nose, and one of his eyes was swollen shut.

Cody shook his head. "I'm so sorry that we couldn't be here earlier. When we realized you were missing, you were probably already in deep trouble."

"Don't worry, son. You were here right on time. I have seen worse beatings in my life. The main thing is that we are all safe." He looked over at the dead man lying on the ground and sighed. "Looks like those knife lessons I taught you finally paid off, huh? Well done, First Daughter. You're a true Lakota warrior, and I'm proud of you."

Cody spoke up. "We better call the authorities. This was a clear case of self-defense, and as well as I know that brat over there, she'll likely be a witness to it for the sake of getting a deal with the prosecutor to save her own sorry ass."

Winona walked over to Cody with the rope in her hand. "They tied up my uncle with it, so you might as well use it on her to make sure she doesn't try to run away again."

Cody looked her in the eyes. "Please, don't think badly of me. I am not the kind of man who threatens a woman. My parents taught me better than that. But in her case, I had no choice but to be rough with her. Lynn ran away once, and she would have left me lying in the dirt just like she did two years ago in that arena on the other side of town. It is not my style to mistreat a woman, and I would never do it to you. But this floozy doesn't deserve to be treated with any respect. She's a criminal."

Winona touched his cheek with a warm and tender gesture. Then, she glared coldly at Lynn. "If I had been the one to stop her, I would have done something much worse to her." She chuckled.

Cody smiled back at her, then gazed over at Cliff's body. "I don't doubt that at all, Little Sitting Bull."

Lynn scoffed at their exchange, but her resistance was broken.

"Thanks for helping me save my uncle. We both owe you a lot. You didn't think twice when you saved me from Foster, and you never hesitated to risk your own life now. I'll never forget that, and neither will my uncle."

Cody pointed to the dead body on the ground. "Looks like you saved my life, too, so I guess we're even. I have no doubt that he would have shot me if you hadn't stopped him. You have mad skills, not only as an artist but also as a warrior."

Cody forced Lynn to turn around and tied her hands behind her back. He shook his head because it annoyed him deeply that he ever loved her.

Lynn had overstepped every boundary possible, and she had also become a danger to the woman he was falling in love with, as well as to the old Lakota he called a close friend. Cody would protect the people he called family even if he had to risk his own life.

THIRTY-TWO
Free to Ride the Rodeo

C ODY FISHED IN his pocket for his mobile phone and dialed 911. When the dispatcher answered the call, Cody explained the situation and the location where to find the body. Then, all they could do was to wait for the police to show up.

It didn't take long before two police cars pulled into the RV park. They questioned Cody and Winona, and both declared that the killing of Cliff was a matter of self-defense. Although they shared every detail of the evening's events, the officers remained skeptical. One of the cops walked back to his vehicle and checked their IDs along with that of the victim lying on the ground with Winona's knife still sticking in his back.

Meanwhile, Cody, Winona, and Takoda gave their testimony of the events separately. The bruised face and broken nose of Takoda spoke clearly and supported their story. Since Cliff didn't have any signs of assault on his body or face apart from the blade in his back, and Takoda's wrists still showed the imprints of the rope they used to shackle him with, it was obvious that Takoda hadn't been in a position to attack anyone.

After some time, the other police officer returned to the crime scene and shook his head. He handed them their IDs while the three friends stood close together waiting for what he had to say. "Your records are clean, unlike those of the gentleman over there and that woman." He pointed to Lynn and Cliff's body lying under a tarp.

"The lady's record includes a list of criminal charges as long as her arm. One for insurance fraud, several DUIs, and multiple receiving and concealing charges. Not really what I would call a blonde angel," he added sarcastically.

"I'm not surprised to hear that, and yes, sir, she is as far from being an innocent angel as Cheyenne is from Mars," Cody said.

"As for the victim on the ground, Cliff Morales is wanted for several crimes in Montana and Colorado. Our computers show him as a suspect in multiple rape cases, drug dealing, physical assault, and numerous car thefts in different states. More charges will probably show up if we dig deeper. Apparently, he doesn't have a blank slate when it comes to crime, so your version of self-defense appears believable. However, you'll need to remain in Cheyenne for the next two or three days in case we need to question you further. We also need your written statement after the rodeo."

Cody nodded. "Definitely, sir. I am to participate in the semifinal round tomorrow, and my friends will stay here as well. As soon as the rodeo is over, we'll drop by the station and give you a written statement.

We have nothing to hide and will do whatever is necessary to help you close the case."

The coroner arrived at the scene, and after a quick examination of the body, they loaded Cliff's corpse into the hearse to haul it over to forensics. The cause of death was no mystery, and the coroner didn't expect there to be any delay in releasing the body for a funeral.

One of the police officers removed the rope around Lynn's wrists and handcuffed her instead. She refused to give a witness statement at first, glancing over at Cody hatefully. But when the police officer told her they knew about her criminal charges, she looked fearful, knowing additional charges of kidnapping and attempted murder would weigh heavily on her shoulders when she had to go to court.

She broke down immediately and admitted Cliff's death was the tragic result of self-defense. Cody wasn't surprised at all when she tried to put the main blame on the dead man being transported from the crime scene that very minute. It was hard for him to understand how he had ever been able to love a woman of such dishonorable character.

After writing down their phone numbers and the location of their camper, they said goodbye to the police officers. Then, Cody, Wynona, and Takoda drove back to their RV park, where they ran into Gary, Ruth, and Andrew.

"Where in the world have you guys been? I was getting mighty worried," Gary exclaimed.

Andrew stared at them and gasped when he saw Takoda's broken nose and swollen face in the light of the campfire. "Jesus, Uncle, what happened to you?"

"That is a long story, son. This old warrior is a little tired. Let me tell you the tale tomorrow."

Ruth walked over to Takoda. "Let me get you something for the swelling, Uncle. I have some painkillers with me as well, and you should eat and drink something before you go to bed."

Winona smiled at Ruth gratefully. "Are you sure we don't need to get a doctor to have a look at that nose?" Winona asked, trying her best to tend her injured uncle.

"I'm fine, Winona. Don't worry about me. I've had worse injuries than a broken nose and a black eye. A little dinner and a well-deserved can of cold beer are what I need, then I'll hit the sack. Tomorrow, we must cheer on our cowboy and keep our fingers crossed that he and John get a good time. That is more important," he said, pointing to Cody with a warm smile of paternal affection.

Gary pulled Cody aside, and the young rodeo cowboy told him quickly what happened.

Gary was shocked. "I don't believe it. So, you're saying that this good-for-nothing woman tried to have you killed? Jesus!"

Cody shrugged his shoulders. "That is likely what she was after, or some form of revenge. What I can't understand is why Cliff followed us here, threatening Takoda and Winona. According to Winona, he was a close friend of Stacey Foster and was involved in her kidnapping. You know, they tried to find out certain information about the lost treasure of the Plummer Gang. You don't happen to know anything about that tale, do you?"

Gary's face betrayed no emotion as he looked at the ground, hesitating before answering. For the first time since he had known Gary, Cody wondered if he had a reason to distrust his old mentor.

He looked Cody straight in the eyes and nodded. "I probably know what they were looking for, but I would prefer to tell you all about it once we get back home. Right now, I think you should concentrate on tomorrow's run. I'll not withhold any answers you're seeking, but I want to give them at the right time. Believe me, it's not easy for me to see that my friends almost got killed over an old legend."

Cody wondered what this mystery was all about, but he wasn't in a position to force Gary to talk now. As a matter of fact, his friend was right when he said he had to concentrate on tomorrow's run in the arena. "All right, Gary, let's talk about it when we return to the ranch. I expect you to be honest with me because my friends got into deep trouble twice, and I almost got shot over this, whatever it's all about. I prefer to know what I'm dealing with so I can be prepared if I need to defend myself or my friends. But I agree with you, now it's time for the rodeo, so we'll talk about it later, after Cheyenne."

Gary nodded and patted him on the shoulder. "I took care of Lightning, so you're free to shower and go to bed. I'll see you tomorrow morning. Goodnight, Cody. Thank you for saving Takoda. We all owe you big time."

Cody remained silent. Then, he walked over to Winona, who had just stepped out of their camper. "How is he doing?" He was still worried for his elder friend.

"He'll be okay. He ate a little and drank a cold one and is trying to get some sleep now."

Maybe I should ask her about that gold treasure story that jerk was talking about, he thought, but then he decided against it. There would be a time to talk about it, but not today. This beautiful woman had faced more than enough for one day, and he had no intention of adding to her discomfort.

He sat down at the campfire and opened a can of Diet Coke. Cody took a long swig and stared into the flames. Winona sat down next to him, and Cody put an arm around her shoulders. The softness of her long hair swept over his rough hand, and the warm scent of her skin tickled his nose.

After all the crazy events of this weekend, he finally felt that he was able to close one chapter of his traumatic past. The damage and pain Lynn had caused him didn't control his life any longer. He was able to let it go, and his feelings for his ex-wife simply ceased to exist. Now he saw the truth about her—she was a much worse human being than he ever imagined. Leaving him for his best friend was no longer a tragedy but a blessing. Cody was much better off without a woman like her in his life. But despite the hurt she and Tanner had caused, Cody still missed his childhood friend. He and Tanner had shared many years of an incredible friendship, with all its laughter and tears. It wasn't easy to let go of the many years they'd spent growing up together.

He glanced at Winona's delicate profile and smiled. For the first time in over two years, he had the feeling that a happy future lay ahead of him, and he would do everything possible to create that happy new life for both of them. Yes, Cody was starting to believe in love again.

THIRTY-THREE
A Letter from the Past

THE FOLLOWING DAY, the entire camp seemed to be sizzling with the fever of anticipation. Today's competitions would decide which bull rider, which barrel racer, which saddle bronc rider, or which roper would win the prize money, and who would move closer to the top twelve and a trip to the finals.

Cody was up at the crack of dawn, and so was Andrew. Both men tried not to get too nervous about the rides ahead of them. Cody admired Andrew for his bravery as he tried to succeed as a bull rider. He knew how dangerous that particular rodeo discipline was, and how many young men lost their lives trying to become the one champion who was able to ride well enough to be the top money winner. Although the safety equipment was much better than it used to be and protected the riders from injuries to a certain degree, it was still one of the most dangerous sports. Even with enhanced safety, occasionally a young father or beloved son was killed by an enraged bull tossing the rider into the air like a rag doll and stomping or goring him.

"Andrew, I don't want to sound like your mom, but make sure you stay safe out there. Although you want to prove yourself, we need you at the ranch, and even more so as a dear friend."

Andrew swallowed and nodded. No words were needed between him and Cody because both of them knew what it felt like to risk their life in the arena. They both knew the bitter taste of failure and the thrill of winning. They had experienced the pain of breaking bones and the financial pressure when they didn't win enough prize money or grab one of those precious sponsorship contracts. Yet they were both incapable of letting go of the passion that each rodeo triggered in their body and their soul. They both hated it from time to time, even though it made them feel complete as human beings when they heard the roar of the audience, tasted the dust of the arena's sand, smelled the sweat of the livestock, and felt their own fear. They faced that fear bravely with every ride they took, challenging the much stronger four-legged beasts.

Ruth had prepared a hearty breakfast and even baked fresh biscuits in the Dutch oven over the campfire. When Winona and Takoda joined them for breakfast, Cody felt sorry for his friend. The left side of his face was badly bruised, and his broken nose swollen. It was obvious that it was hard for him to breathe.

When Cody mentioned that he should see a doctor, Takoda waved off his suggestion. "I don't want to miss your run for nothing, young friend. Besides, I'm already in less pain than I was last night. Nothing that a few ibuprofen and my niece's wonderful willow bark tea couldn't fix."

Winona shook her head while she stayed busy refilling plates with scrambled eggs, bacon, biscuits, and gravy. "I tell you, he's as stubborn as a miner's mule."

Cody chuckled. "In that case, I think you take very much after your uncle."

Gary, who'd just stepped out of the camper, roared with laughter upon hearing that remark.

Winona threatened Cody with her cooking spoon, but a broad smile lit her entire face.

"Are you ready for the championship round, boys?" Gary asked.

Andrew and Cody nodded in unison.

"The other participants are mighty strong competition, and it won't be easy to achieve a top-twelve position, but we'll both be giving our best. The rest is in God's hands," Andrew said.

"Amen to that," Cody added. "Well, I better go over and feed and water Lightning." He rubbed his hands on his denims and walked over to the horse trailer.

THE STALLION WHINNIED softly when Cody came closer and lowered his head for his favorite ear scratching. A voice behind them startled Cody.

"Mister Cody Ferguson?" Cody turned around and looked straight into the face of a young cowboy in his mid-twenties.

"That's me. What can I do for you?"

"Sorry to approach you so bluntly, sir. My name is Joseph Garcia, but everybody calls me Joe. I am a bareback bronc rider. At least I try to be. I'm sure you haven't heard of me, but I have heard a lot about you."

Cody studied the young man's sunburned features. He wondered what Mr. Garcia wanted and intended to cut the conversation short because he needed to concentrate on the day's competition. But the next words out of the unknown saddle bronc rider's mouth caused Cody to freeze.

"I'm from Arizona—Payson to be more specific. I have a close friend there, and he has written a letter to you. My friend begged me to deliver it to you personally."

Now who could that be? Cody wondered. He couldn't recall having any friends left in Payson. Maybe something was wrong with his mother. God, he hoped he wouldn't get any more bad news that soon before the most important ride of his comeback. Thinking of it, this could indeed be an important document from the nursing institution where his mother had been moved after Alzheimer's made her unable continue living alone. Reluctantly, Cody took the envelope from the young man's hand. He wanted to push the letter into his shirt pocket, but Mr. Garcia stopped him.

"I beg your pardon, sir, but I think you should read it before you ride into that arena. I do believe this might be good news for you. If you will excuse me now, I must get ready helping some friends over yonder. I am honored to have met you, and I wish you good luck for today's roping competition. You and your stallion are a mighty fine team, Mister Ferguson."

Before Cody could say anything, young Garcia turned around and disappeared among the crowd. Confused, he stared at the letter in his hand. Reading bad news would likely distract him when he needed to concentrate the most, but finally, curiosity got the better of him, and he walked over to a bench under a tree to open the letter.

It was a handwritten document. At first, he couldn't believe his eyes. Cody didn't know whether he should tear the piece of paper to shreds, or if he should laugh or cry. It seemed like destiny played another nasty trick on him by forcing the past into his present life.

Cody took a deep breath, and after reading the signature and doubting his own sanity, he finally read the letter slowly from the beginning.

Dear Cody,

I'm sure you must be wondering how I knew that you would be in Cheyenne once again after all the years gone by. As a matter of fact, I have watched you and Gary gaining position after position climbing up the ranks as successful team ropers, achieving point after point. It was only a matter of time when you would re-enter the Cheyenne competition.

I can only imagine how shocked and most likely how angry you must be to hear from me. It took me a long time to work up the courage to reach out to you. I'm not asking for forgiveness because there's no way a man can forgive his friend for breaking his trust so cruelly. There hasn't been a day that I haven't questioned myself and wondered how in the world things had gotten so far out of control.

I don't know what I hate myself for the most—giving in to meaningless lust when I should have remained strong, or leaving my best friend behind, lying helpless in the hospital. I was a dang coward, and I'll never forgive myself for it.

I cannot undo what happened in Cheyenne two years ago, but there's still hope that I can do something for you now. When I returned to Payson, some people told me you left for good and that you blame yourself for being responsible for your father's death. Although I'm likely the last person you want to hear from about these events, I can assure you that your father's heart attack wasn't your fault. I found my mother's diary in which she mentions that your father had two massive strokes before that fatal one. Apparently, the doctors told him that his heart was severely damaged, and that he didn't have much longer to live. I didn't know about it, but my parents did, and they had to swear on the family's Bible that they would never tell you. Your dad didn't want to stand in your way of becoming a successful rodeo champion.

He might not have told you often enough, but he was very proud of you, Cody. Unlike yours, my parents have no reason to be proud of me. I had turned into a rotten character. At first, I blamed Lynn for losing your wonderful friendship, which was part of my life for so many years. But I fooled myself because if I had been the friend I claimed to be, none of this would have happened.

I cannot undo the past, but I tried very hard to learn from it. I have given up rodeo, women, and booze and went back to night school a few months after Cheyenne. Whether you believe it or not, I'm a registered nurse now. I studied that profession, intending to do something for the greatest friend I ever had. After getting my geriatric nursing degree, I applied for a position in the very nursing home where your mom lives. I'm her main caretaker, and I'm honored to be able to do that much for your family.

I wish you the best of success for the rodeo and for your private life. I have no right to ask for anything. Although I can't heal that wound in my heart that my own betrayal caused, I can at least take the guilt about your father's death off your shoulders.

May God bless you and keep you safe in the arena. I know you will succeed because you deserve it.

Since I don't dare sign this letter calling myself your old friend, I'll sign it with humble respect.

Tanner

Cody stared at the piece of paper in his hand in disbelief. Hearing from Tanner today was what he least expected. He had every reason to be mad at his former best friend and to tear the letter to pieces. It would be the most natural reaction after hearing from that rogue after all this time passed, and after he betrayed their friendship in the sleaziest way possible. But to Cody's surprise, there was no rage rushing through his body. He felt deeply confused when he realized he was actually thrilled to hear from Tanner. What was it that he mentioned about his father's death? He claimed that it wasn't Cody's fault?

He quickly read that paragraph again and couldn't believe it. After all these many months of guilt weighing heavily on his shoulders, he might finally be freed of that burden. If his father really had a damaged heart and two strokes before the last fatal one, it was likely he would have died anyway despite their argument. Maybe it had just been bad timing. Maybe Cody jumped to the wrong conclusions, confusing his own failure with the tragic circumstances of his father's death. It was possible, wasn't it?

Despite the hate he'd felt for Tanner, he was grateful for the letter the man sent. Only now did he know the truth about his father's illness. With a little help from his friends, he would be able to let go of the guilt that kept his soul prisoner for so long. It seemed to him that the second chapter of a painful past closed like a locked door, which he had no intention of ever opening again. Maybe his soul would finally be able to heal.

Out of all the people in Payson, it was good that it was Tanner who took care of Cody's mom now. *What a weird twist of fate*, he thought. "He better treat my mother well, or I'll come after him," he whispered.

"Come after who?" Winona's voice asked from behind him. He spun as he hadn't been aware that she was walking toward him.

Lightning welcomed her and searched the pockets of her denim jacket for a treat. She laughed and gave him one of his beloved apples. He chewed it noisily with juice dripping from his mouth.

Winona patted his neck, but then she turned and studied Cody's thoughtful face. "Are you nervous about today's competition?"

Instead of answering, he motioned her to sit down and handed her the letter. With a frown, she took it and started to read.

It took her a few moments to understand who the writer was, but once it dawned on her, she stared at him with a startled expression. "Wow, the past really seems to be catching up with you this weekend. So, what are you going to do?"

"What do you mean, what am I going to do? Nothing of course. I know that my mother is in good hands in that nursing home, and he better treat her nice, or I'll shoot his sorry ass. My father's gone, but I admit I am relieved to know the truth about his fragile health now. Looks like I can quit blaming myself for his death. If his heart was severely damaged, anybody or anything could have triggered off that one last attack. I might be able to let go of that guilt, finally, after two years. I'm even thankful that Tanner passed that information to me. I just wonder why my mother never told me about it. She should have, at least before Alzheimer's turned her into a zombie."

"That's not what I meant."

A confused expression clouded his face. "I don't get it."

"What about Tanner? What are you going to do about him? Will you forgive him? After all, he was your best friend for many years before that incident in Cheyenne."

Cody scoffed. It was a bitter sound. "The heck he was. He stabbed me in the back when he had the chance. I would have given my last nickel for this man and was by his side whenever he needed me. How did he thank me for all the support I gave him in each rodeo competition? Give me one reason why I should forgive him."

Winona studied his face with her calm eyes that radiated so much warmth. "Growing up on a ranch, I assume you know the Bible mighty well. Do you remember the story about that crowd who wanted to stone a woman to death because she had sinned with the man? The woman who sold her body as a whore?"

"Of course I do. It's the story of Mary Magdalene and how Jesus saved her."

"Amen to that. Do you recall what Jesus told the angry mob? 'He who is without sin among you, let him be the first to throw a stone at her.' Have you been without sin your entire life, Cody? Have I or Takoda been without sin all our born days? I doubt it. To decide whether you will be able to forgive him someday, you have to answer three questions. The first one is, what weighs heavier—many years of a great, precious friendship or the few days he betrayed your trust? The second question is, if he changed his ways—and according to the letter he did—would he deserve a second chance? And the last question is, wouldn't it poison your own life and future if you keep that betrayal alive like a festering wound on your soul?" With those words, she got up, stroked his right cheek tenderly, and left him alone with his thoughts.

"You're a wise woman, Winona Standstrong," he whispered and stood up to saddle Lightning and to get ready for the competition. Before he rode over to the arena, he folded the letter carefully and placed it in his pocket. The bitterness he had always felt whenever he thought of Tanner was gone. After all, he himself had fallen for Lynn just like Tanner had. The only thing Cody was aware of was the excitement sizzling inside of him and the stage fright while he waited for his turn in the roping competition.

McCraw was already sitting in the saddle, waiting for him. They nodded at each other. "Let's simply try our best, my friend."

Cody nodded and glanced over to the ranks close by and saw Gary, Ruth, Winona, and Takoda waving at him. Andrew stood close to the chute and gave him the thumbs up sign. Takoda raised both fists in the air, cheering at him like the warrior he was.

He smiled back at them and nodded. He felt relieved and free. "The sky is the limit, my spirit horse," he whispered and caressed Lightning's neck. The stallion answered with a soft whinny as if he understood Cody's words. But then, who knew? Maybe he really did.

THIRTY-FOUR
Winning

CODY CONCENTRATED, CLOSING out the roar of the crowd. He flashed for a moment on his nightmares, but his emotions were completely different from the panic he felt in his dreams. At this moment in the arena, Cody breathed slowly and evenly. He wasn't worried that Lightning would buck or fail to follow his commands. He trusted the stallion the same way the magnificent animal had learned to trust him. They were equal partners and completed each other in the arena and in their lives. Winona had been right when she said they had the ability to heal each other.

The steer finally stood straight in the chute. A quick glance over to John ensured that he was ready. Cody glanced at the rodeo hand and nodded. The chute opened with a loud clang, and the roar of the audience sent the steer running toward the center of the arena.

The noise of the arena vanished. Cody felt as if swallowed into a tunnel. *Keep the line straight behind the steer, don't move over too far. Direct him over to John.* Cody swung his rope. For a split second, he feared he would miss the steer's head, but then he forced his self-doubts out of his head and simply functioned. He took a fast dally around the saddle horn, and Lightning pulled the steer to the left and kept the rope tight. The stallion knew exactly what to do, and Cody couldn't have asked for a better partner in the arena. Within seconds, John threw his rope and caught the right rear leg.

The crowd cheered.

"Nine point five seconds. There is a five second penalty for having caught only one leg, so it is a fourteen point five for Ferguson and McCraw," the announcer said.

Cody didn't understand the voice rumbling through the speakers at first. It seemed as if he and Lightning were the only two creatures in this world. He felt the stallion's breathing beneath his thighs, and for a moment the image of a young warrior riding through the land of his ancestor's flickered through Cody's consciousness.

He turned Lightning toward the audience, and the roar of the crowd suddenly rushed back into his consciousness like the thunder of a waterfall rumbling over a high cliff. Judging from the way the audience applauded and stamped their feet, Cody guessed they must have performed quite well.

When the speaker announced their time, Cody knew that this was likely not fast enough to make the top twelve for the finals on Sunday, but one never knew, and he was proud of his performance nevertheless if one conserved the fact that this was only the second run in a competition with John as a heeler. Cody threw his fist triumphantly into the air, and a loud "yeehaw" escaped his lips. His roar of victory released all the pressure and focus he had bottled up before the round.

John smiled at him and slapped Cody on the shoulder. "Well done, my friend. Well done."

Cody looked over to his friends and waved at them with his hat. What he had always thought of as his personal curse of Cheyenne seemed to be broken, and he was back as one of the most promising ropers of the year. He led Lightning out of the arena and to his horse trailer, where he unsaddled him.

Gary arrived first and slapped him enthusiastically on the back. "I am so proud of you, son. You couldn't have done any better. You absolutely nailed it today. We'll have a barbecue to celebrate."

John turned to Cody. "Listen, Cody, we will likely not make the finals tomorrow, but I want you to consider teaming up with me as a professional team roper for the coming season. Roger called me this morning. Doctors told him that he needs further surgeries and looks like at least two years of rehab. I doubt that he will be back in the arena any time soon. Maybe never again. Think about it. You and Lightning did an amazing job despite being thrown into the cold water like this. You are more than welcome in team McCraw, unless Gary objects." John turned toward Gary.

Cody's friend grinned. "Well, I reckon I have to spend a bit more time with Miss Ruth over there in the near future, so I am all for it. However, that is a decision Cody has to make."

Winona and Takoda walked toward them and both hugged Cody.

"Well, I better hurry up and help Ruth to prepare that barbeque," Winona said.

Everybody was in a cheerful mood. After a while, the men got the final results of the day, and they missed the twelfth rank by less than two seconds. Neither John nor Cody was upset about not having reached the final run on Sunday because they had achieved more than anticipated in their first two runs together as a new team.

Cody, Gary, and Takoda stayed back to watch Andrew's bull-riding competition. Winona and Ruth started preparing their barbecue dinner. Both women didn't want to watch the bull riders. This discipline was too dangerous for their taste, and they were too worried for Andrew's safety.

Andrew achieved a good overall result. Just like Cody, he intended to climb the ranks the following year. So far, he was satisfied with this year's position in the rankings. Andrew was still young, and next year would offer him another opportunity. The feller was ambitious and planned to travel with Cody and John the next rodeo season. It was a matter of supporting each other, and Andrew admired Cody for his spirit, talent, and his remarkable comeback. The young man saw Cody as a role model, just as Cody had once chosen Gary Bradshaw as his mentor.

THIRTY-FIVE
The Tale about the Gold

THREE DAYS AFTER ARRIVING back home on the G.B. Ranch, Gary invited Cody on a camping trip to the western border of his ranch. Cody assumed it had to do with maintaining the fences and checking the pastures and livestock, but Gary shook his head. He motioned Cody over to the fireplace after they finished dinner.

"We'll take the horse trailer along and pull it with my pickup. Takoda will accompany us. We'll visit the ghost town of Bannack. It takes about an hour to get there, then we'll ride the horses from there and camp overnight at Grasshopper Creek. It's beautiful country out there. When we were in Cheyenne, I promised you to tell you the truth about that tale of hidden gold, and as you know, I always keep my word. I believe it's only fair for you to know why Takoda and his niece, and in the end, even you, got in such serious trouble with Foster and that other rogue, Morales."

Cody gazed at his friend and mentor but remained silent, waiting for further explanation.

"I don't want to talk about it right now, but you will get all the answers you seek mighty soon. Try to pack a few things, and I'll have Ruth prepare provisions for us. Takoda will arrive here early in the morning. I plan to head out at nine a.m. at the latest. I arranged for Andrew and the other boys to take over your chores. I haven't told anybody about the real purpose of this trip, and I want you to keep it to yourself as well. You better get to packing your bedroll and whatever you need. I'll see you in the morning."

Gary got up and returned his coffee cup to the kitchen, where he briefly hugged Ruth, who was washing the dishes.

Cody wished them both a good night and walked back to his cabin, lost in thought. Of course, he wondered what this trip was all about, and if there was any truth in the talk about the lost treasure collected by a gang of outlaws in the late 1880s.

After gathering some camping gear and warm clothes to change into during the trip, Cody showered and went to bed. Ever since Cheyenne, he'd felt calmer and hadn't been worrying as much about the future. He took it a day at a time. He had a good job, great friends, and was looking forward to getting to know Winona more intimately.

He glanced at the letter on his nightstand. It was dog-eared and crumpled, and he knew it word for word. He had read it countless times since receiving it. Sometimes, he wished he could talk to Tanner, and other times he was glad he didn't have to face him.

Cody thought about Winona's words often, and he had to admit there was a hint of truth in them. *He who is without sin among you, let him be the first to throw a stone at her.* Maybe someday he would be capable of forgiving Tanner. With that thought, he rolled onto his good side and fell asleep.

CODY STROLLED TO the ranch house just as the sun rose over the edge of the hills, casting a golden veil over the building. After a hearty breakfast with the ranch hands, he picked up his gear from the cabin and loaded it into Gary's pickup. Gary and Takoda joined him, and after the three of them loaded three horses, saddles, and some provisions from the kitchen, they drove off toward Bannack.

During the drive to the ghost town, Gary started to talk. "I don't know how much you know about the gold rush history in Montana. Most people think that the main gold strikes were in California or Alaska, but that's not true. Montana had a series of rich gold strikes between 1840 and the late 1880s. One of the mining communities was named Bannack, which is about twenty-five miles southeast of Dillon." He pointed to some hills. "See those hills? A lot of claims were staked right there. The two criminals who gave us all that trouble must have heard about the legend of Mister Henry Plummer and his gang of road agents. Plummer was a funny character because he got himself elected as sheriff in Bannack at the same time he ran a gang of outlaws. They robbed and plundered numerous gold shipments mainly coming from the Bozeman Trail. There were times when up to a hundred men rode for his brand."

Cody couldn't believe his ears. "So, you're telling me that this Plummer fellow was sheriff in a gold mining community and robbing other communities at the same time?"

"Yep. That was exactly the case. The people in Bannack were said to be very friendly and caring toward each other, but whoever got on Plummer's wrong side was a dead man. He was greedy and brutal. People didn't dare stand up to him. Some feared his badge, and others were scared of the men who rode in his outlaw gang."

"What happened to him? Did he give up on being an outlaw for the sake of wanting to be a lawman?" Cody wanted to know.

"Eventually, people were so sick and tired of the gang terrorizing them, other lawmen finally caught up with them. Some they chased out of the county, but they lynched most of them. Plummer was one of the gang members sentenced to execution. He and numerous gang members ended up at the gallows, dancing in the air."

"That means that Foster and this Morales feller must have assumed that gang hid a load of gold somewhere in the state of Montana. A lot of people believe in such legends, but what I don't understand is why they kidnapped and beat up Takoda. What does he have to do with that legend?"

Gary looked over at Takoda, who indicated he should continue. "The two guys thought that Takoda knows the location where the gold is hidden. That's why they kidnapped Winona, and later her uncle, to try to force our friend to reveal the secret."

Cody stared at his Lakota friend, his eyes huge with surprise. "So, do you really know where those outlaws hid the stolen gold?"

Takoda shook his head. "Plummer's loot is an old legend, and to my knowledge, nobody has found it. Hell, nobody knows if it really exists."

"Then, I don't understand why they thought that you in particular would know anything about it. If there's no proof that this is a true story, why in the world should you as a Lakota Indian know anything about the white man's hidden treasure? It just doesn't make sense."

Gary stopped the pickup, and Takoda remained silent.

Cody looked around and saw a ghost town.

"This is the town named Bannack, where Plummer was sheriff between 1863 and 1864," Gary said. "We'll take the horses from here. I want to show you something."

Cody got out of the truck and looked around. Takoda hadn't answered his question, but he intended to repeat it later. Cody loved pioneer ghost towns. They silently told the story of how the country had been settled and left him thoughtful. The wind blowing through the deserted streets spoke to Cody in the voices of long deceased pioneers whispering their hopes and dreams.

He saw a few old buildings, their roofs crumbling and their wooden walls weathered. A few decaying carriages stood near the buildings, some of them with broken wheels and sagging buckboards.

An eerie silence hung over the former town. The buildings and abandoned mining equipment stared back at Cody like silent witnesses of an era long gone by. He pictured people in old-fashioned clothing walking in the streets, children playing, and women chatting with each other.

He turned to help Gary and Takoda saddle the horses and pack some food and water flasks into the saddlebags. When they were ready to ride, Gary mounted his gelding and led the way onto a trail headed away from Bannack.

After two hours' ride, he stopped at a creek. "This is the Grasshopper Creek area. We will camp here for the night. Once we have our camp set up and a campfire going, we will make some dinner. Then, I'll tell you the rest of the story."

Cody nodded and jumped out of his saddle, hobbling his horse. He and Takoda collected plenty of firewood because they knew the night would be cold. Gary set up a canvas ramada to protect them from the frigid wind and placed their bed rolls close to the fire. Takoda helped Cody feed the horses some hay and a few oats they brought along. He sat down by the fire, watching Gary turn sizzling strips of beef and spring onions. He placed Indian fry bread in a flat pan right atop of the embers.

The smell from the cookfire made their mouths water. Cody filled the coffee pot with fresh creek water and looked forward to a hot, strong brew. The three men ate in silence as they enjoyed nature around them and the great-tasting food.

Takoda scraped his fork over his plate to clean it. "You know, Gary, I think Ruth has taught you a lot in that kitchen lately."

Gary guffawed. "You might be right about that, Takoda, but your kin in Arizona taught me how to make fry bread."

Cody joined their laughter, then got up and walked to the creek to wash his plate. When he came back, Gary poured them all a cup of hot coffee and passed around a jar of sugar.

Over the rim of his cup, Cody studied his friend Gary. He waited for him to continue the story, still waiting for the answers he was looking for.

Gary cleared his throat and poked at the embers. For a moment, he watched the sparks disappearing into the night sky like tiny fireflies. "You must have wondered how I was able to buy a ranch of this size."

Cody looked him straight in the eye. "I admit, I asked myself how you could afford such a spread and a comfortable home. I've known you as a man of unassuming heritage and was quite shocked when I saw your place, which reminds me more of a log cabin mansion than anything else. I asked myself if you married some rich old lady who won the lottery when I first stepped into your house."

Gary and Takoda laughed in unison. "To be honest, it wasn't an old lady, but I owe a lot to my Lakota friend here. When I bought the ranch, it was dilapidated. The original house was falling apart, and so were the two bunkhouses. The land was good, and it had potential, but the place itself was terribly run down. I bought the property anyway and tried to bring it back to its former glory. But it required a great deal of money, of course. Takoda worked for me from the first month. We clicked well and became dear friends within the first year. One day, he told me that he could help me to turn the ranch into one of the best properties in the entire county."

Gary poured himself another cup of coffee and stared into the flames for a moment. Then, he continued, regarding Takoda with the same affection a brother would look at his twin. "At first, I thought he was pulling my leg when he said he could get the money for me to build a better house and a bigger cattle operation. After all, the only thing I knew about him was that he was a Lakota from the reservation. He insisted on bringing me here to this very creek. Somehow, he convinced me to buy an old mining claim that was for sale. After doing so, I questioned my sanity, to be frank. I had never been a treasure hunter, and I wondered why for land's sake I spent a couple of thousand bucks on a mining claim from yesteryear."

Takoda laughed and said, "I could tell that you were certain that you would regret doing so."

Gary chuckled.

Cody looked from one to the other, his eyebrows drawn together.

Gary signaled Takoda to continue the story.

THIRTY-SIX
Takoda's Secret

"AS A TRADITIONAL Lakota, I live my life following the old rules of our spiritual beliefs," Takoda said while he lit a cigarette. He blew the smoke into the air, and his gaze followed it. "For us, Mother Earth is sacred, and prospecting the mines or rivers is a sin, as it hurts Mother Earth, leaving her with open wounds. We believe that following the yellow metal call brings bad luck on us. Eventually it did, if you recall the fate of the white settlers who desecrated our sacred Black Hills."

Cody recalled the many battles and phony peace treaties he read about and how resolutely the Lakota and other plains tribes protected that part of their land.

"One week, I spent a few days out here exploring. At that time, I was already helping Gary repair the ranch house. He treated me kindly, but I was no fool. I knew he would never have enough money to bring back the place to its former glory. I wanted to continue working for this fine man," he said, pointing at Gary.

"I decided to do a vision quest right here at Grasshopper Creek and ask *Tatanka*, our great spirit, to show me how I could help my new friend. The second night, the weather turned bad, and I had to seek shelter in one of the abandoned mines. A violent hailstorm swept across this part of the country. Temperatures got so cold within that I had to move my bed roll and campfire farther into the mining shaft. While I kept the fire going, I looked around, hoping that no wild animal would claim the mine as his new home. I was surprised to see that part of the rock sparkled yellowish, reflecting the light of the flames. I scraped out part of that rock with the tip of my Bowie knife, and to my surprise, it was a gold nugget."

"You got to be kidding me," Cody said.

Gary shook his head. "He is telling you the truth. Takoda came back to the ranch the following day and showed me the nugget. A friend of mine is a retired mining engineer. He confirmed that it is high grade gold of rare quality, but we didn't tell him where we found it. I claimed I bought it at an auction. I didn't want to wake sleeping dogs, if you know what I mean. The next thing I know, Takoda convinced me to buy the claim."

"You see, according to my traditional, spiritual belief, I wasn't allowed to develop the mine myself and violate Mother Earth. I couldn't think of a better person to share the great news with. I was sure that Gary would retain his good character, unlike others who are corrupted by a feverish greed for gold. But I had one condition."

Takoda took a sip of coffee while Cody tapped his foot impatiently, wanting to hear the rest of this incredible story. "I knew Winona had a chance to buy a fifty percent share of an art gallery. I asked Gary to invest in that gallery instead of sharing the gold with me. Plus, he had to help some of our tribal members in my name whenever the going got too tough for some of our elders without family to take care of them."

Cody looked at his friend Gary, who studied the coffee mug in his hands. *That explains a lot,* he thought. *No wonder he can afford to build a log cabin mansion or sponsor me for the rodeo.* But Cody felt no jealousy. He was happy for Gary because Cody knew how hard the man had worked since his childhood. Gary had started hard ranch work as a first grader. So, after a humble and hardworking life, Gary Bradshaw finally hit the jackpot.

"Do you still work the mine?" Cody asked.

Gary shrugged his shoulders. "There's more gold in there. Not as much as there used to be, but still enough to make a good living. I have all that I need, and considering my age, I would say the size of my ranch operation is big enough. But to answer your other question, neither Takoda nor I have any clue where the gold of those outlaws might be hidden, if that treasure exists at all. I bought the mine officially with all legal documents. It's located less than two miles from here and still holds enough gold. You could say it's the base of my wealth. I know I can trust you, and now I ask you to be discreet with that information. There are a lot of people like Foster out there, and nowadays people have no scruples about cutting your throat for much less."

Cody sat up straight. "I understand, and I hope you know that you can trust me. I have no ambition to risk the life of my close friends for the sake of money. I admit there were times when I would have probably given my left hand to become rich, but those days are gone. Now I understand much better what really counts in life."

THIRTY-SEVEN
Future Plans

TAKODA LOOKED AT Cody, his face rather serious. "What about Winona? I love my niece very much. She's the only family I have. She's like a daughter to me. I've seen the way she looks at you, and I can't remember her ever being that interested in any man after her disastrous marriage. I know that you have a liking for her, but I can't help but wonder if you're serious about my girl. She's been through a lot, and if you're not considering a serious relationship, I would prefer that you let her know now before you break her heart. Don't get me wrong, I really like you, Cody, but I know you were both hurt in the past. If you're not ready to commit to another woman, be honest and let her know."

Cody's face turned red. He wasn't prepared for that conversation with Winona's uncle.

Gary remained silent and stared into the fire.

Cody felt uncertain, and he missed his father, who could have given him the advice of a mature man to help him through this situation.

Gary nodded at him, and Cody realized that the father figure he sought sat right across from him.

"Speak your heart, son. You can't go wrong," Gary said softly.

Cody pulled back his shoulders and looked Takoda right in the face. "You're right, Uncle Takoda. I was scared to start a new relationship. I have old scars on my heart, but my tragedies have taught me how to separate the good people from the bad ones. When Winona was kidnapped, I was scared to death that something might happen to her. That was the first time I realized I would be foolish to deny my feelings for her any longer. Your niece is a headstrong person, but she has some of your wisdom, and that of her ancestors, too. She has a different point of view on certain things I turned a blind eye to, and I'm grateful for her advice and the insight she gives me."

Takoda studied Cody's eyes, trying to figure out if he spoke the truth. He prompted Cody to continue.

"The feelings I have for Winona go far beyond sexual desire. I love everything about her, and I think she's one of the most beautiful people I've ever met, inside and outside. With your permission, I would like to ask her to marry me, so I hope that answers your question if I'm ready for a serious commitment. The one thing that bothers me, though, is that I can't offer her much. I lost my father's ranch, and I am still ashamed about it. But I have a good job, and I am willing to work hard. Winona is so talented, and I am not in a position to support her artwork financially the way I'd like to do. Not yet, but maybe someday I'll be able to."

Gary put his mug aside and leaned forward, elbows on his knees. "Listen, son, I want to suggest something to you. I'm getting too old to run the ranch alone. I'd like to enjoy my retirement and, you know, have time to smell the roses. You proved to be a reliable and qualified head wrangler. I would like to offer you the opportunity to manage my G.B. Ranch. Of course, that would increase your income tremendously, including a share of profit when we cash in selling cattle. I would give you part of my property up on the hill behind the pastures, so you could build yourself your own house for yourself and Winona."

Cody stared at Gary. His jaw dropped, and he didn't know what to say. "Are you serious? You really want to put the management of your ranch into my hands? Holy cow, I don't know what to say. That's a very generous offer, and I would love to accept it. However, building a house of my own—I'll have to wait until I can save up some money."

Gary shook his head. "As I told you, there's still some gold in that mine. We're going to work in that shaft tomorrow while Takoda takes care of our camp. I am sure we'll bring back enough nuggets, so you'll be able to order the first load of lumber to get started on it. But before you do that, you better ask that girl to marry you. I have no doubt that she'll say yes."

Cody sat on the log, tears in his eyes. *Am I really this lucky after all the hardships I faced?* He swallowed hard and tried to speak, but no word came to his lips. He got up, walked around the fire, and hugged his fatherly friend to whom he owed so much he couldn't even put it into words. But words weren't needed because the two men understood each other without them.

"Welcome to the family, son. You're the boy I never had, but I promise you that as long as I'm alive, I'll be like a father to you," Gary whispered.

THIRTY-EIGHT
Proposing

WHEN THE THREE men returned to the ranch two days later, they carried a pouch filled with nuggets worth thousands of dollars. Gary announced Cody's new position to the ranch hands, and everybody congratulated Cody and wished him well. The entire team liked Cody Ferguson, and all were proud of his achievements. Ruth was very fond of Cody, and Gary, of course, treated him like a son.

The following day, Cody drove into the town of Dillon. He parked his pickup and walked straight to the gallery, where Winona was re-arranging a shelf with beautiful pottery.

She smiled warmly at him when he stepped through the door announced by the chime of the doorbell above.

"Howdy, Mister Ferguson. How are you today? What brings you into town?"

Cody looked down at his dusty boots and cleared his throat. *Oh, God, how do I start? What am I supposed to say?* he asked himself nervously.

Winona waited for an answer, a puzzled look on her face. When he still didn't speak, she invited him to join her for a cup of coffee in the back room of the gallery.

He followed her and looked around. "Where is the statue of Lightning?" he asked her.

"I sold it. The buyer wanted to have that horse specifically. I tried to talk him into getting another statue, but he wouldn't have it. It had to be Lightning and nothing else." She noticed his disappointed face and frowned. "Did you want to buy it?" she asked softly.

"Well, I really thought about it. You know that legend of the spirit horse that you told me about during my first visit here often crossed my mind, and I think you might be right. I do believe that Lightning is indeed my personal spirit horse."

"So, you came here to buy that statue today? If I had known, I would have reserved it for you."

Cody smiled. "Actually, I came because of something else," he said, his voice barely above a whisper.

Winona had to strain to understand what he was saying. "If it wasn't about buying the statue, what is it that I can do for you?"

"Winona, this is very hard for me. I'm what you would call out of practice when it comes to talking about my feelings. I suppressed them for such a long time that I fear facing them. However, I believe that if I keep to myself what I know and what I feel much longer, I might lose the most precious thing in my life." His voice rose in pitch.

She sat on a stool next to the workbench and waited for him to continue, her gaze resting on him.

"I thought I wouldn't be able to ever fall in love again. I was sure I would remain alone for the rest of my life. For a long time, I feared that I had lost the ability to open my heart and love someone. But then you walked into my life, and I realized that I hadn't lost the ability to love a woman, but I had never experienced real love before. I always thought that the man must be the strong one in a relationship and provide a woman with everything she needs. Now I know that both complete each other if they were meant to be together."

Cody remained silent for a moment, and Winona didn't interrupt him. She waited patiently.

"What I'm trying to say is that I need you around me to feel complete as a man and as a human being. You taught me how to let go of the past and to believe in a future for myself. You never judged me but accepted my weaknesses and my flaws. You always treated me with respect and supported me from the first day we met. I think you're a very precious human being, and to be honest, when you were kidnapped, I thought I would lose my mind if something happened to you. I need you in my life, and I want to ask you if you would do me the honor of marrying me."

Cody didn't dare look her in the face. His hands shook like leaves in the breeze, he was so scared she might say no. Considering her past and their cultural differences, he wouldn't have been surprised if she did turn him down. He was so lost in his reflections, he almost missed her answer.

"Yes, Cody. I'll marry you."

He stared at her, not believing his ears. "Yes? I mean... you really mean... yes?"

She laughed at him. "Yes, sir, but under one condition. We will marry twice, once in a Christian ceremony, and once in a Lakota ritual presided over by my uncle."

Cody nodded eagerly. "Of course, we can do that. Whatever you wish, darling. Oh, would I have to get a buckskin outfit for that?"

She howled with laughter, and that very moment she was the most beautiful human being he had ever seen.

THE NEWS OF Winona and Cody's impending marriage spread like a brush fire in Dillon and on the G.B. Ranch. Everybody was thrilled for the young couple and looked forward to the wedding. One evening, Winona found Cody sitting in front of the fireplace of his little cabin. He held the letter in his hand, a thoughtful expression clouding his handsome face, but when she hugged him, he quickly tucked the piece of paper into the breast pocket of his checked flannel shirt.

"You still think of him, don't you?" she whispered.

Cody didn't believe in hiding the way he felt. He wanted their relationship to be based on unlimited trust right from the beginning. He nodded. "You know, for almost three years, I hated him as much as I hated Lynn. The difference was that I kept that hate alive in my heart for the sake of suppressing how much I missed my best friend. We had some great years together, and some the adventures we faced were hair-raising." Cody chuckled, recalling one or another situation where he and Tanner barely kept out of serious trouble. He shook his head, pushing the memories about his best friend out of his mind.

Cody hugged Winona and kissed her tenderly. "Enough with the gloomy thoughts. I can hardly wait to call you Missus Winona

Standstrong Ferguson, nicknamed Little Sitting Bull," he added with chuckle.

He kissed her again, this time more passionately. He could barely control his desire for her and didn't want to scare her by being too demanding, but today, Winona surprised him as she climbed the steep stairs to his sleeping loft. He followed her and watched her undress in the silvery light of the moon shining through the little round window. He drank in the beauty of her naked body. Her hair covered her delicate curves like an erotic black veil. He breathed in the warm musky scent of her skin. How did he deserve the love of such a marvelous human being?

He took his shirt off, and she stepped toward him, opened his belt, and caressed his stomach muscles. She studied his naked torso where the moonlight illuminated the scars. She kissed them gently, and a moan escaped his lips.

"You're a very handsome man, Cody Ferguson. I'm proud to call you my future husband," she whispered.

It was the first time he'd received a compliment like that, and it warmed his heart while enflaming his desire for this stunningly beautiful woman.

They made love all night, exploring each other's bodies inch by inch, not willing to give in to fatigue. When they finally fell asleep in each other's arms, Cody drifted off with a smile on his face. Holding Winona's warm body in his arms, he slept dreamlessly. The nightmares and ghosts of yesterday remained silent. He was home.

Two weeks later, the church wedding took place. Except it wasn't in a church—it was held in Gary's barn. Ranch hands helped set up a dance in the same barn after the ceremony. Ruth and some town ladies were in the kitchen two days in a row preparing a buffet of vast variety. Some members of the Lakota tribe celebrated the young couple with a traditional wedding dance adorned in their native finery. Cody was deeply honored when the dancers pulled him into their circle.

Takoda led the ceremony according to modern Lakota traditions. He explained to Cody that in the old days the fathers negotiated the wedding and exchanged gifts. "There is no way that Winona wouldn't have a say in who she marries, but in the old days it was exactly that way. The girl had no say, but she could, of course, invite a warrior who attracted her interest to court her."

"How did they offer that invitation?" Cody wanted to know.

Takoda pointed at a blanket hanging over the fence of a paddock. "They stood in front of their teepee, wrapped in a blanket, and waited until the warrior they desired came by. Then, they opened the blanket, and if he stepped into the circle of her open arms, he accepted her invitation to court her."

Cody was just about to ask another question, when he saw Winona walking toward them. He stared at her, his eyes huge with admiration. Her long hair fell loose and covered part of her cream-colored buckskin dress. Delicate beadwork adorned the frock in geometrical patterns of red, blue, and white. Long fringes dangled around her moccasin boots. Every time she took a step, the smooth, tawny skin of her legs flashed between the moccasins and the edge of her dress, teasing his desire for her. She was a gorgeous sight, and he could hardly believe that this beautiful woman would be his wife in less than two hours.

Winona and Cody stood in front of a pastor waiting to get married according to the white man's law. Cody turned to see Ruth and Gary smiling back at him. Cody was the happiest man in the state of Montana that very moment.

A sudden thought dimmed his smile. He recalled his cheap wedding with Lynn somewhere in Nevada between two rodeo locations. None of his family or friends attended. There was no romance, no dance. A dinner in a fast-food restaurant and sex were their only celebrations.

Cody remembered the campfire talks with Tanner when they promised to be each other's best man. They made bets on who would get married first. Cody wasn't prepared for the feeling of loneliness for Tanner that swept over him in that moment. He stood there, his beautiful bride by his side before the town's minister. Cody was about to start a new and more meaningful chapter in his life.

Winona studied his face. She touched his cheek tenderly and smiled. He looked into those dark almond-shaped eyes and could have drowned in the depths of them.

She whispered so softly that he was the only one able to hear it. "I thought about asking Gary or my uncle to be your best man, but it would have been wrong. Gary is more like a father for you, and Takoda is the closest to my own father. There's still one open wound that keeps your heart bleeding and stands in the way of our happiness."

Cody frowned. He didn't know what she was referring to. Yet he couldn't deny feeling a certain sadness despite the happiness of the day.

Winona whispered, "I love you." She pointed to the other side of the barn at the edge of the crowd.

Cody followed her gaze, and at first, he could hardly recognize the people near the back. One man stood alone with the afternoon sun shining behind him. Cody had to blink a couple of times to adjust his eyes to the glare of the sun. He couldn't recall having seen the person before in Montana. He was tall and wore a black cowboy hat pulled low over his face. The people waited for the priest to start, yet Winona hadn't turned toward him yet.

THIRTY-NINE
Forgiveness

ODY STOOD ALONE before the minister, gazing down the aisle. *What could she be up to?* For an instant, panic overtook him as he imagined Winona refusing to marry him in front of all their guests.

Then, he saw how she gestured for the stranger to step closer. The man's reluctant steps brought him closer to the make-shift altar. As he crept into the midst of the congregation, he slowly removed his cowboy hat and ran his hand through his dark brown hair. He stopped in the middle of the barn, his face showing a pained expression, and his eyes were huge with fear.

"Oh, my, God," Cody exclaimed.

Winona flitted about nervously because she knew she had taken an enormous risk calling the person who stood in the center aisle. The groom and the stranger stared at each other, a hush going through the audience.

Gary turned pale like a ghost and made to take a step forward, but Ruth held him back and shook her head.

"This is between the two of them, and nobody can help Cody now. That's something he has to face all alone," Ruth whispered.

Cody teetered down the aisle toward the unexpected visitor. Winona's stomach lurched in anticipation of what would happen next. She hoped her judgment hadn't been misguided, and that Cody would be able to let go of the last element of his heartbreaking past.

Cody heard his own heart beating louder than a drum as he took one step after another. His pulse raced as his mind sought to reconcile the identity of the man before him. He'd pictured this moment for more than two years, envisioning how he would punch his former best friend right in the face. For countless wakeful nights, he had given in to the raging flame of intense hate. He stopped a few steps short of the unexpected guest, who lifted his head to face Cody.

Tears streamed freely down Tanner's face. "I know I have no right to be here, and I'll leave in a few minutes. Will you hear me out? I don't expect forgiveness because I can't even forgive myself. I have regretted what I did every day since that very day in Cheyenne. I still don't understand what got into me and how I could betray you like that. I cannot undo the past, but I came to wish you all the very best for a bright future. From the bottom of my heart, I'm truly happy that you have found true love. If there's one man who deserves it, then it's you. My wedding gift for the two of you is on the table with all the others over at Gary's house. I would be very honored if you accept it. May God bless you, Cody. I wish you and your beautiful bride all the best in this world."

Tanner looked at the hat in his hand, turning it nervously. Then, he looked Cody in the eye, nodded, and turned around. He walked down the aisle while Cody stood there, not able to utter a single word.

That guy has some nerve to show up at my wedding. I can't believe this. Seems to be the same unbelievable dare devil as the old days, Cody thought. But strangely, Cody had to suppress a chuckle rather than a shout. He watched his former best friend walking toward the exit and out of his life for the second time. The congregation was silent and confused, not knowing who the stranger was or what had taken place between Cody and the other man.

"Tanner?" Cody called after the departing guest.

Tanner stopped dead in his tracks. He didn't dare to turn around. His shoulders dropped, and it seemed as if he awaited a rash of insults. After a few moments, he turned to look at Cody.

Cody raised his chin. "Do you remember when we camped at Ellison Creek waterfall?"

"How could I forget?" Tanner answered softly.

"You promised me to be my best man back then," Cody said.

Tanner swallowed hard. "I know what I promised, and of the promises I broke. You don't need to remind me of that, Cody. My nightmares do that every single night."

"Maybe you were my best man in some way."

Tanner frowned, confused about Cody's words. "I don't get it. What do you mean?"

"If not for you, I wouldn't have found the most precious human being that ever crossed my path, my bride Winona. As weird as it may sound, I think you did me a favor by opening my eyes about the true character of my first wife."

Tanner remained silent, not knowing what to say.

"Today, I'm getting married to somebody who truly loves me. The priest is here, and all our friends. I know it will be a beautiful ceremony. However, one thing is missing."

Winona covered her mouth with her hands, and tears filled her gorgeous eyes.

Cody looked back at her and said, "You have given me more chances to heal than I deserve. You were right, my love. Like everybody else, I'm not without flaws myself." He turned back to Tanner, and a boyish smile suddenly lit his entire face. "As I said, one thing is missing. I don't have a best man yet."

Tanner stared at Cody. His jaw dropped in disbelief. "You can't be serious," he whispered, but everyone heard him.

"Listen, Cowboy, I have a drop-dead gorgeous bride waiting for me up there, and I don't want to waste any more time making her my wife. We have amazing food prepared for us all, and believe me, the cook will kick our butts to Denver and back if we don't get to that buffet on time. So, you better remove that hat of yours and join me up there. This is my first real wedding, and I could use some support, Hoss."

The two men walked toward the bride and the priest. Tanner took his position next to Gary, who finally took his hand and shook it.

"This is a once in a lifetime chance, boy. Don't mess it up this time. Cody is one of the most beautiful souls I have ever had the honor to know. If you betray his trust one more time, I'll shoot your sorry ass with my shotgun, I swear," Gary growled.

"Yes, sir. I understand. I know you're a sure shot, Mister Bradshaw. I won't risk it."

FORTY
A New Life

THE MORNING AFTER the wedding, Cody and Winona sat across from each other, unpacking their wedding gifts. A huge brown envelope from Gary contained two legal documents. One established Cody as new owner of ten acres of Gary's property. Attached to the document was a photo of a beautiful log cabin. The second document was a two-page employment contract as ranch manager containing a hefty monthly paycheck and a generous bonus agreement based on the annual cattle profits.

Cody wiped his eyes with his sleeve. He didn't want his newly wedded wife to see his tears, but the generosity of Gary Bradshaw deeply touched him.

Takoda presented the couple with two matching buckskin shirts. They were adorned with traditional elk teeth and beadwork.

Cody marveled at the valuable gift. "What an honor to wear something from such a rich tradition," he exclaimed.

"There's one more gift," Winona said and pointed to a big box wrapped in plain brown paper.

Cody read the card, and to his astonishment, it was the wedding gift that Tanner mentioned in the barn.

Remember when we dreamed about starting our own horse breeding ranch? I know you have a bright future ahead, and I'm sure nobody deserves it more than you. In my heart, you will always be my elder brother, and in my life, you will always be my role model for dignity, ambition, and honor. You have many qualities that I lack, and you're a very special human being. I was blessed to call you best friend for the best years of my life.

P.S. Why don't you start breeding some fine roping horses and name your new home Spirit Horse Ranch?

Tanner

The box was heavy, and he unwrapped it carefully. To his astonishment, the bronze statue of Lightning, which Winona created many weeks ago, was inside the box, reflecting the light in the cabin with its soft coppery gleam. "I'll be darned. That's the statue you created. But how in the world did he get it? Didn't you say you sold it?"

Winona tilted her head as she regarded him. "When I saw that you kept his letter and read it quite often, I understood that you missed Tanner, despite what he did. It didn't take me long to get his contact information in the nursing home where he takes care of your mom. I explained to him who I was. At first, he was scared to come to the wedding, but shortly after I contacted him, he came to meet me in my gallery. I would have loved to tell you about it, but I didn't want to force a decision on you. At that time, I wasn't certain if you would be able to forgive him. Tanner told me that whether or not he came to the wedding, or whether he would be in touch with you again, he still wished to give you a unique gift for the day you got married. I told him how you and Lightning had found and healed each other. When he saw the statue, he cried, and he touched the scars that I engraved. He told me that he hates himself because he had created the same scars on your heart like that jerk who hurt Lightning. He was touched, but not surprised that it was a horse that mended your broken body and heart. He bought the statue. Forgive me, my love but that will be the only secret I ever keep from you."

Cody hugged his wife and kissed her softly. "You have acted much wiser than I have, and you were right. Forgiving Tanner feels good, and it was as much a part of the healing process as Lightning was. I had to let go of all the things that happened in the past."

He turned around and stepped out on the porch just in time to see Tanner toss his overnight bag on the passenger seat of his rental car.

Cody walked over to him. "I like that idea of calling our new place Spirit Horse Ranch."

Tanner smiled shyly back at Cody.

"Thanks for your gift. I really love that statue."

"Your wife has an amazing artistic talent. I'm sure we will see more of her work in some of the major galleries in years to come."

Cody nodded. Then, his face turned serious. "I know that coming here wasn't easy for you and took backbone."

Tanner tilted his head and gave Cody a half-smile. "I know that forgiving me in front of all those people and inviting me to be your best man took more than backbone."

"Hey, before you leave, would you like to meet the real spirit horse?" Tanner nodded.

The two men walked to the pasture, where Lightning grazed in the morning sun. Cody whistled, and the stallion immediately trotted toward the two visitors.

"Wow, he's magnificent," Tanner said. When Lightning turned toward Cody, who tempted him with an apple in his outstretched hand, Tanner saw the old scars. A painful expression clouded his face. "Jesus, that stallion must have taken a terrible amount of beating."

"Sure has, but you know sometimes we have to go through a lot of pain to become the best possible version of ourselves."

Tanner looked down at the ground.

"I want to thank you for what you do for my mother. That means a lot to me, and I want you to know that you're always welcome here. I don't want to lie—it will take time for me to relax with you, but I think that old friends deserve a second chance. That stallion over there gave me a chance when he had no reason to believe in another human being. I intend to do the same, Tanner. Maybe we can travel to some of the rodeos together in the upcoming season. I could use some help trying to achieve better times in my second year as team roper."

Tanner swallowed and shook Cody's hand. Further words weren't needed. He walked to his car while Cody remained at the stallion's pasture.

Before starting the engine, Tanner looked at his friend one more time. There they stood, listening to each other in silent conversation in perfect harmony. A warrior and his spirit horse.

ACKNOWLEDGMENTS

I give special thanks to Dennis Doty, Nick Pernokas, my friend and talented Texas saddle maker, who helped me with countless questions about rodeo competitions and rules, and of course, to Pam Van Allen, my editor and "wordsmith."

ABOUT THE AUTHOR

Drawing energy from strong pioneer women of our past, author Manuela Schneider is driven to create captivating sagas that ultimately leave readers wondering, Will the story continue? To date, Schneider has written fifteen novels that feature powerful female characters immersed in a battle against hardship, riddles, and deception while searching for true love and a better life.

Her first composition as a co-songwriter of 2021's "Miner's Candle" has achieved recognition and won numerous awards in Arizona, Texas, New Mexico and even Europe. The song is played in seven countries worldwide. The award-winning western music video "Miner's Candle" based on the song was her first project as a filmmaker.

Currently she is working on three historical fiction manuscripts and has four new books in the publishing process. Her second short movie has won numerous awards already including the Cannes world Film Festival in France.

When not penning riveting stories of Western boomtowns, pioneer life, cowboy heroes, and treacherous outlaws, Schneider can be found traveling all over the world and writing classical country songs. More information can be found at https://www.manuelaschneider.com